I0574167

The Mafia's Consigliere

Juan Manuel Sánchez

The Mafia's Consigliere

First Edition: 2023

ISBN: 9781524318543
ISBN eBook: 9781524328511

© of the text:
  Juan Manuel Sánchez

© Layout, design and production of this edition: 2023 EBL

All rights reserved. No part of this publication may be reproduced, distributed, or transmitted in any form or by any means, including photocopying, recording, or other electronic or mechanical methods, without the prior written permission of the Publisher.

To my brother José Modesto,
the tortoise has come out of his lair.

To the three women in my life, my mother Valeriana,
my wife María del Mar and María del Mar junior.

Table of Contents

Chapter I
Omertá – The Law of Silence

"Most men would rather seem than be."

Aeschylus of Eleusis

Los Angeles, California, (USA).

It was a hot morning on a busy day.

"Objection, your honor, this is irrelevant, and unrelated to the case," the lawyer exclaimed forcefully.

"Objection sustained. Do not answer the prosecutor's question," said the judge firmly.

The defense lawyer in this trial for drug trafficking and murder was the Hispanic-American lawyer Valentino Walker Breska, born in Madrid, Spain, to an American father and Spanish mother, known to all as 'Breska'.

Breska rose to fame in the Californian city by successfully defending a mob-associated narco accused of murder, obtaining a not guilty verdict from the jury.

The lawyer had moved from his hometown to Los Angeles some twenty years previously, when he was hired by a prestigious law firm, after studying law at the Complutense University of Madrid. After working for the firm for a couple of years, he set up his own law practice with the help of his parents' money and some income from clients.

Breska lived in a large mansion with his family in the exclusive neighborhood of Beverly Hills. His family consisted of his beautiful wife, Emma Miller, and their three wonderful children, Evelin, Marc and Stalin, who were twenty-four, twenty-two and nineteen respectively.

"Breska & Associates", whose main professional activity was focused on criminal matters and industrial and intellectual property law, was based in Los Angeles. It was comprised of fifty lawyers, who provided services to Hollywood's leading film producers, directors, actors and screenwriters. The firm had revenues of approximately two billion dollars a year, a very large portfolio of clients, great media contacts and, of course, the best contacts in town at the political, legislative and judicial levels.

Breska and his family had enormous personal wealth, totaling close to four billion dollars. Thus, the lawyer and his family led a life of high standing in this Californian city, getting whatever they wanted whenever they wanted it.

His children studied at Caltech, a local university that was considered to be one of the best in the world. His wife drove her Ferrari Testarossa around the best stores in Melrose, Beverly Hills and the Hollywood area, making substantial purchases whenever she wanted.

Their home was a six-story mansion that covered thirty thousand square feet of land, had two enormous swimming pools, and was home to some incredible works of art including paintings and sculptures by the likes of Goya and Picasso. Unusually, much of the mansion's ceiling was covered in stalactites.

The Breska family was assisted by two butlers, three maids, two bodyguards and three guards. The house was equipped with a state-of-the-art security system, which was automatically activated every time a member of the family unit entered or left the mansion, who otherwise had to notify the guards when they wished to leave or enter. The mansion also had three Doberman guard dogs. It had two beautiful garages, where the lawyer kept a Lamborghini Huracán and a Porsche Cayenne Coupé.

It was 1 pm., and Breska was with his oldest child, Evelin, taking a relaxing swim in the pool next to the dining room. He had just returned from the Los Angeles Court where he had been defending his client, Patricio Sedeño in a case involving drug trafficking and murder. He was considering the fact that he had a 2 pm meeting at the Diplomat Prime restaurant in Hollywood with New York Senator Warrent. He had known Warrent for a number of years both professionally and on the golf course.

Breska was fifty years old and although he was not tall at five foot seven, his physical stature ensured he still emanated power. He was well-known for the depth of his criminal law knowledge, his oratory and negotiation skills, as well as his general good disposition. In short, he was the white shark of the law in Los Angeles.

Climbing out of the pool, he dried off and moved diligently and swiftly to the bedroom to get dressed. From there, he called out to Evelin, telling her to signal to her mother, who was on the top floor of the mansion, that he would be home around 7:00 pm., after the meeting with the senator and that he was leaving in a hurry.

He pulled out the remote control and pointed it at the garage where the Lamborghini was locked up. Once in the car he pressed the mechanical start button, stepped hard on the accelerator and shot off down the main avenue of Beverly Hills, dodging all the vehicles in his path, zigzagging, at a speed of one hundred and twenty miles per hour, until he reached the restaurant.

He was both a little late, and a little sweaty; his tuxedo had suffered as he drove through heavy traffic in eighty-five-degree heat. As he walked through the foyer of the restaurant he noticed Senator Warrent, already seated at their table. He was drinking champagne. Breska

hastily fixed his tuxedo and walked towards the senator.

Once in front of Warrent, he saw an older man with short gray and blue eyes. He was both well preserved and of slim build.

"Good afternoon, Senator, I apologize for the delay. Like you I am not generally late."

The senator did not utter a word, he was eating the shrimp and fruit cocktail appetizer he had been given and did not bat an eye. Finally, he finished chewing and turned coldly to Breska.

"Hello, lawyer, you are twenty minutes late for your appointment. What happened? Since we have known each other you have never been late. Has something extraordinary happened to you today or is it a simple delay on your part that means I have to scold you like a child?"

Breska did not hesitate or create a story. Indeed, he was a straightforward man so he got straight to the point, "Warrent, I got a little careless taking a dip in the pool with my child, Evelin, I have no excuse. The relaxation of the bath and the stress of the trial got the better of me. I apologize."

The senator dropped his frosty act and invited Breska to sit down so the two men could begin their meeting. Breska ordered a plate of beef tenderloin with garnish and a glass of the senator's French champagne.

The lawyer noticed that there were two very smartly dressed men in suits, ties and Panama hats two tables away from them, but he assumed they were society diners in the restaurant on that warm California afternoon.

The meal between Breska and the senator was almost over when he addressed Warrent in a concerned tone, "My film production company clients need a license for the opening of commercial premises on the land they own, pending re-zoning by the City Council. It's in Hollywood Studios. They need to start filming with Universal Pictures this coming month. We are gambling on a five hundred-thousand-dollar commission for each of us and a five billion dollar plus film project. You, Sir, hold the key to the deal with your control of the senate, your contacts with the other trusted senators, the members of the New York City Council and the Mayor of New York City."

Warrent gave the lawyer an attentive and direct look, then said, "Breska, I will need two of the senators from the Chinatown area to vote in favor of the license for your film production company clients, and they belong to a gang of ruthless and unscrupulous criminals. Otherwise, it is not going to be possible. This will cost you one million dollars and an endless party for several senators and my company in the club "Las Mariposas".

Breska held out his right hand, wielded between tenacity and nervousness, and gave it unhesitatingly to Warrent, who accepted it, conditional upon payment of the amount stipulated within forty-eight hours in New York City.

After their meal, the lawyer and the senator bid each other an affectionate farewell and each went their own way. Breska came out of the meeting confident that his clients would be granted the necessary license for the favorable rezoning of the land on which the premises, owned by the film producers, were located. The film could be made by Universal Pictures in Hollywood in approximately one month's time and everyone would get their share of the cake.

The lawyer went to get his Lamborghini in a leisurely manner, pressing the automatic button and instantly starting the car, this time more smoothly than the last.

He was driving normally, within the speed limit. He stopped at a red traffic light, thinking about the outcome of the meeting with the senator and how happy his clients were going to be. He noticed that the car behind his had the lights on full, and was so close it was almost grazing his license plate.

The driver of this mystery car had the accelerator almost full throttle, holding it with the brake at the same time, even slightly impacting the rear of the lawyer's car, both accelerating and braking at the same time. Inside his vehicle, Breska lost his temper. As the lights changed the lawyer accelerated again, reaching ninety miles an hour. The car behind kept pace and even deliberately gave small blows with the clear intention of driving it off the road.

It was already dark and there was hardly any traffic since they were on the outskirts of Beverly Hills. Breska thought for a few seconds and stopped the car slowly. He didn't want to risk an accident. The mysterious car pulled up right behind him, still completely glued to his license plate.

The lawyer, now in shock, looked through the rearview mirror of his and saw two men sitting in the car, both were wearing Panama hats, which reminded him of those at the senator's lunch. One of the men got out of the car silently, almost as if he planned to ambush Breska and wanted to be sure that no one passing by would see anything. Walking with slow steps he reached Breska's car, approaching the window on the driver's side. He tapped on the window until the lawyer opened it, putting the two of them face to face.

The man headbutted him before abruptly pointing at the lawyer; "Mr. Breska, I have a message for you from the Lamborda family," he said, dropping a sealed white envelope between his trembling legs.

Then he returned to his own car and the men disappeared like two birds of prey in time, immaculate, in that damned mysterious car, screeching the wheels at full speed and without Breska being able to see the license plate number.

His heart was paralyzed by all that had just happened. He could not even breathe or think, he was in mental paralysis due to the enormous shock, the world was coming upon him at every moment, he suffered a truly untenable situation under the full moon that early evening.

Would this new threatening situation be good or bad luck for Breska?

He sighed a thousand times and took a deep breath before opening the sealed white envelope. He read: *"Attorney Breska, we know of your ability to handle legal matters, we have been after you for some time, we have been tracking you here in Los Angeles for many months, we are expecting you tomorrow at Café Carrera at 10.00, don't be late. Capisci!"*

Breska was even more shocked. The sweat on his now sore forehead was evidence that he had not imagined the whole situation. He had, in fact, been headbutted and had just received a strange summons. He was thinking at four thousand revolutions per second and wondering what could those people want from him? In all his years in Los Angeles nothing like that had happened to him. Sure he'd had problems with clients and people related to the professional world, but nothing out of the ordinary, certainly never anything violent. But in any case, this had just happened to him, it was like being asleep at night dreaming of demons infiltrating your body.

"Ah," it dawned on him as he mused meditatively, his mind wandering back over the lunch with the senator. "Why didn't I see it before?" The lawyer was now thinking very intuitively, but he still couldn't come to any concrete conclusions.

With these thoughts in his head, the lawyer returned to his mansion in Beverly Hills, turning it all over in his mind like a pressure cooker to try to remember details of those men and that message, to tie up the ends of all this macabre story that had fallen on him like a storm in the tropics.

By the time he got home it was 11 pm, already late for the lawyer, as he remembered that he had told Evelin to tell her mother that he would be back around 7 pm. He wasn't sure what excuse to give his consort for his excessive delay in arriving at the mansion, especially since he had a bruise on his head that gave him away.

He was used to not notifying his family if he was going to be a few hours late but four hours would normally mean a call to let someone know he would be late. His wife was waiting for him downstairs, right next to the garage entrance.

She greeted him in annoyance, "Where have you been, Breska? With whom...? What time do you call this...?"

The lawyer did not know how to respond so he let his answers fade one after another in his mind, until he hit on a good one, "Emma, honey, I was delayed, Senator Warrent was scheduled to give me a free lecture on politics and history about the new people in Chinatown, and he really went on and on. I'm sorry I didn't warn you, really, honey, give me a kiss."

His wife looked at him in annoyance; her husband's desolate eyes betrayed him as he withdrew his cheek after the peck of a kiss she delivered. She wished him a goodnight and left him to rest before his mysterious meeting the following day at 10:00 am.

But the lawyer did not sleep, he was writhing between the sheets, tossing and turning in bed, thinking about that scene and why it happened to him and only to him. He took a Valium to see if it would help him sleep, but it did nothing. His eyes were like saucers as he thought about those guys who looked so cruel and imposing, he had many questions about the safety of his family. What would become of them from now on, he wondered worriedly. Finally he dozed off just before his alarm sounded on the table beside his head.

It was 7:00 am. and Emma was still sleeping very soundly, as if everything was absolutely calm. Breska, however, was still thinking about the meeting and trying to analyze it. He was going into Zen mode, finally feeling some tranquility as the initial restlessness and nervousness gave way to acceptance and peace of mind. He would enter the meeting itself without being in it; his stomach and body tension would dilute until almost achieving total relaxation. He got up, showered and dressed in a shiny suit that he wore to work for big occasions, with the bravado and unusual intention of impressing those guys.

He walked towards the garage where he kept his Porsche, looked in the glove compartment to check for his Colt handgun, for which he had adequate ammunition already stuffed into his suit jacket.

He called Mr. Gisbert, one of his bodyguards who would accompany him when things got ugly. Gisbert felt as if he was family. They got into the Porsche and headed towards Beverly Hills Avenue towards the Café Carrera. They arrived just a little ahead of time, at 9:50 am.

Breska and Gisbert looked closely at four high-end cars parked outside the door. On the driver's side, all of them were occupied by burly men, two of them smoking cigars and the other two wearing Panama-type hats, like those at Senator Warrent's meeting. In addition, on the terrace of the café there were about five other guys, all smartly dressed surrounding the entrance to the café. It was like some kind of World War II bunker right outside the front door.

The hostile looks of those men betrayed an aggressiveness he hadn't expected. Between ideas and cracked thoughts, the lawyer and Gisbert walked to the main entrance of the café, where they were dispossessed of their firearms. The bodyguard remained at the door with the rest of the men; only Breska entered. Once inside, he looked around, and not finding anyone likely, he asked the waiter who motioned him to go to the back. At the back of the café a smartly dressed man was waiting for him. He was wearing a trench coat and the now entirely expected Panama hat.

Breska, walked over and introduced himself, "I am Breska, I'm meeting someone here... I don't know if it's you..." his voice was very low and faint.

The man in the brown Panama hat spoke firmly, "I am Bernardino Mancini, the capo of the Lamborda family. Mr. Breska, we have been following you for quite some time here in Beverly Hills. We know how you go, what you do, who you associate with, who you live with, what time you get up, how many dogs you have, how many lawyers work for you, your influential friends, your wife and children's names, how many millions of dollars you make, the movements of your accounts, the bankers you know, the cars you drive, so let me tell you one thing, Mr. Breska," Breska's face was frozen in a mask of agony and fear. The kingpin continued, "We highly value your ability as a lawyer. We see your qualities and know you will excel in our world. Your great knowledge of criminal law, your orations in court, your mediation skills and your general honesty mean you are the person we are looking for to represent us in our, shall we say, shady operations."

Breska, having regained himself, interrupted him, and said very carefully, "Excuse me, Mr. Mancini, I have my life here in

Los Angeles, my family and I have lived here for years, we are very comfortable in this place. I am only here because of the way you summoned me. I am here against my better judgment, I might add. This is an outrage, Sir."

The capo of the Lamborda family stood and stared down at Breska. He looked directly into his eyes and said, "In two days you will take your family and go on vacation to San José in Costa Rica. Everything will be prepared by us, some friends and clients are waiting for you there to do some work. I expect you to say yes to this. I expect you to join us. It won't be easy but I assure you that you will be rewarded. You will grow to like working with us. You will lack for nothing. No one will be able to lay a finger on you, they will be annihilated if they do. We will double what you earn now. You will swear to uphold the Omertà, our Law of Silence in order to join us. This will happen before the trip to Costa Rica, in an undisclosed location in front of other members. From that oath you will be our consigliere, the one of the Lamborda family. You will have only one client and that will be us, you will have more work than ever before. In fact, tomorrow they are expecting you in New York tomorrow at 4 pm. You must go to China Town to the Omertà event, capisci!"

When the boss finished speaking, Breska was staring vacantly. He was in turmoil. Everything he knew had just turned upside down. He wondered what options he had. Could he shoot everyone? Could he denounce them to the FBI and live? The reality of his new situation was beginning to sink in. Was this really his life now? How would he tell his family, the lawyer wondered. He pondered the answer. Would he explain to Emma and the children that he had a new important client he would have to serve? This was nothing new in his line of work. Or would he tell the truth? He was in a difficult situation to be sure. He decided to tell them as truthfully as possible, but with reservations, of course. It was the Mafia that had come to see him, and this did not happen every day in the life of a lawyer. The question was how he was going to tell this story to his beloved family.

Breska and Gisbert were leaving that surreal meeting with their guns back in their possession, with strong thoughts of unloading more than one bullet into the bodies of those dangerous men, when the lawyer looked disconsolately towards his long-serving bodyguard, who said, "What, Breska... You're going with them, you can't say no to the Mafia, don't be silly, go and you won't have any problems. Don't worry about me, I'll get a job here in Los Angeles."

That touched his heart, they had been together for many years and both of them were saddened by this enforced change. They arrived at the mansion in the Porsche. Idling, they drove into the garage, slowly stopping and locking the car. Breska went inside looking for Emma. He found her smoking a cigarette in the foyer of the upstairs penthouse bedroom, the highest area of the mansion. There she was. She saw him arrive and immediately noticed the look on his face.

"What's the matter, Breska, I see you and I don't know you, what's going on?"

Contrary to what one might expect in a matter of this magnitude, her husband went straight to the heart of the matter, "Emma, my love, the mafia came to see me. They have hired me as a lawyer to handle their cases, they will pay me double what we earn here, they will give us protection and security. They assure me that no one can touch us. Our children can go to the best universities in New York, you can buy as many dresses as you wish, you will go to the best stores, you will have the most precious friends, all in politics and justice. In fact, they are sending us on a tremendous vacation to San José, Costa Rica. We leave tomorrow for New York.

Emma did not hide either her certain joy or her bewilderment, she was a person of challenges and, contrary to what her husband had expected, she was excited for this new adventure. She was an enterprising and adventurous person. Here she did not analyze or ask questions. She moved right into practicalities. She pointed to Breska and said, in a leisurely manner, "I'll tell the kids about the vacation in San José by way of New York. They'll be happy."

And so it was.

What madness! Breska was still immersed in his thoughts, trying to get his head around the surreal new world, trying to analyze recent events. He concluded that what he had assumed would be difficult, conveying the news to his family, turned out to be the easiest thing in the end. He was incredulous.

The Breska family packed their bags with great haste and grace, leaving the mansion for Los Angeles airport bound for New York, taking American Airlines flight number 7721 the next morning. A moving company could handle everything else.

> "Ambition breaks the bonds of blood and
> forgets the obligations of gratitude."
>
> Salustio

Chapter II
Bonds of Blood

"One must be in harmony with the
strength and not in opposition to it."

Bruce Lee

WHEN THEY ARRIVED IN NEW YORK, two men were waiting for
him. Both wore Panama hats. One had bushy eyebrows and the
other had a mane of extremely thick hair. The family was ushered
to their Lexus SUV and driven to a house outside the city in a
private estate. It was a closed place, with a lot of land, a private
driveway and obvious cameras. Breska's family was taken to the
most secluded part of the estate, the guest area.

From there, Breska was put in a car and taken to an unknown
location in Chinatown. In the car in which he was traveling there
were three men, who spoke very little. They told him that the
capo and capo dei capi (Boss of Bosses or Godfather), as well as
other members of the mafia, were waiting for him.

They arrived at their location. It was a kind of hideout in a
dark and gloomy cave, where some very steep stairs protruded,
Breska managed to go down the steps, very slowly, sometimes

being helped by the men who accompanied him, until they reached a kind of room, illuminated only by a dim light.

Around a large, round table sat a number of men including the capo and other people Breska did not know. They all sat down when ordered by the Godfather. The ceremony began: "Precisely on this holy evening, in the silence of the night under the light of the stars and the splendor of the moon, I form the chain. In the name of the Lamborda family, with words of humility, I sign the holy partnership."

It was the Mafia boss—specifically the head of the Lamborda criminal organization—who spoke those words into the darkness. Around him, arranged in a circle, several members of the organized crime gang followed in respectful silence, these words marked the entrance of a new member into the highest category of affiliation of La Lamborda, a kind of elite whose members have access to the most hermetic secrets of that organization.

"The Sicilian code of honor that prohibits reporting on criminal activities considered matters that concern the persons involved. This practice is widespread in cases of serious crimes or in Mafia cases where a witness or one of the incriminated persons prefers to remain silent for fear of reprisals or to protect other culprits. In Mafia culture, breaking the oath of Omertà is punishable by death" (excerpt taken from the Omertà code of the Calabrian Mafia organization).

Now the capo turned to Breska, "Welcome, Counselor, thank you for being here. You know what you have come for, we were all waiting for this moment."

As the capo stared at Breska, Breska responded, "It is an honor for me to be here."

The capo began the ritual, questioning the lawyer, "Do you swear the secret code of Omertà before all of us, as a member of this organization, by declaring yourself as consigliere and will you respect the code of honor of silence which is punishable by death?"

Breska responded, already less nervous than he had been in Los Angeles, "Yes, I swear and accept the office of consigliere respecting the code of honor."

The capo then took a pin he had on the table, stuck it in the lawyer's index finger, causing him to bleed, and while spilling the blood, he pointed at him, "If you do not respect our code of honor you will be buried in ashes like this pin that now burns with our Supreme God."

Breska nodded.

The mafia group attending the event consisted of:

Capo, Bernardino Mancini, Godfather of the Mafia.

Consigliere, Attorney Breska.

Clan Captains: Maranzzano Rizzo and Lucky Russo.

Men of Honor or soldiers: Pimponassa Blanco, Gamberra Conte and Gianluca Mesina.

After the Omertà oath, everyone kissed Breska's hand and right cheek, congratulating him on joining them. Immediately, they gave him the plane tickets to San José, Costa Rica, as well as clear instructions as to his pending business in the city. It would not be a typical vacation for the brand new consigliere.

Surprisingly for the lawyer, the drug lord handed him a million dollars in a large black bag, as if it were a garbage bag, thus fulfilling the agreement made at the lunch with Senator Warrent. The revelry at the "Las Mariposas" club was forgotten.

There was no time for more. The lawyer was starting his new life as a Mafia lawyer, as a consigliere, and he couldn't quite believe it.

But Breska kept analyzing and thinking about why he found himself in this situation and asked himself many questions: why did the Mafia have to cross his path? Was it because he found himself in the wrong place at the wrong time? Was it because the lawyer really wanted this kind of life and was willing to meddle in it, without really knowing where he was going to get? Was he a masochist? His mind kept spinning, he found himself more disillusioned than on other trips with his law firm clients.

Here he was, about to travel to San José with his family worrying about his new life. Breska was a mentally strong guy and so he was able to put aside his worries and focus quickly on the moment at hand. He had suffered a lot in life before settling in Los Angeles and wanted to make the most of it until the last moment.

Breska and his family arrived at the busy and ostentatious Riu Guanacaste hotel, in the city of San José, Costa Rica, for their 'vacation', all brimming with joy, except for the lawyer, who was looking confused. They checked in and were given their resort bracelets and cell phone apps, allowing them access to the unlimited food and drink on offer at the hotel.

AUGUST 6, 2021.

The Breska family had spent two frantic days, full of unforeseen events. Most Spanish lawyers take their vacations in August since very little happens in the world of the law in August. And so, Breska found himself and his family surrounded by tourists from Spain, Canada, England and the USA. All had beers in hand, many were drinking in the swimming pool, eating sausages, pâté, chorizo, smoked meats, local nuts and dried fruits as lunchtime approached.

One of Breska's clients, a handsome Englishman with airs of grandeur and arrogance, a resident of Chinatown, New York, absented himself for a moment from the festivities with the excuse of needing to call a "trusted" friend, and that he could not delay too long. Breska stood, surprised that anyone would leave such a party. The handsome Englishman left even his half-full beer as he went off to make his call. The lawyer could not believe what he was seeing. The Englishman left, striding away from the pool. In an instant, he lost sight of him as he entered the hotel. The party continued.

Sometime later, people began to leave the pool to head to the dining room for lunch. Breska and his people took over one side of the dining room and the tourists were all on the other side. There was no sign of the Englishman. Breska went in search of him. He told his colleagues to eat without him. He pressed, with some trepidation, the elevator button, watching as it rose to the third floor where he knew the Englishman, Mr. Howard, was staying.

The hotel had seven floors, the elevator was on the sixth floor and was descending. Breska had to go and check on the Brit who had left a half-full beer to go and make a call. Meanwhile, on the fifth floor, a beautiful blond woman dressed in white exited the elevator.

Sweat was beading on the lawyer's forehead. He wiped it off with his grimy hands. It really was sweltering but last the elevator arrived.

"Damn it," said Breska as he entered and with some trepidation, pressed number three, knowing this was where the Englishman was located.

Once the door opened, he left and looked for the arrows indicating the number of the British man's room. Not finding them, he went around and around, until he finally saw the number of the room by the staircase to the right. He speeded up. Room 309 was right there. He wondered, briefly, "where is this Englishman?" He reached the door and almost slipped. He knocked on the door of the room with his right hand in a very abrupt manner. Silence. Behind the door there was no sound at all. He noticed that the lock on the door had been forced, that there were clear signs of it being broken. Breska, in his nervousness, had not noticed the precarious state of the door. He tried to push it open, using blows to the broken lock. He hit it several times until finally it opened.

He crept into the room, seeing nothing from the entrance, which was very strange. The entrance to the suite was small, and the lawyer was determined to find the Englishman. He went first to the main room, his eyes like saucers. Here he found the television and the bed, but no Englishman. He crept into the kitchenette, and finding nothing, crept out again, feeling more and more certain that something was wrong and that he needed to proceed with extreme caution. He was in a narrow passageway so held his breath as he walked towards the bathroom. Here he found Howard lying in the bathtub, his head at a very strange angle and covered in blood. Breska realized he had been shot.

The lawyer was used to dealing with criminal clients and people involved in the world of drugs, firearms and crime, nevertheless, he was truly shocked by the scene. Next to the corpse was a note that read:

"Lawyer, our mutual client has escaped to La Palma, Canary Islands (Spain), and you must immediately leave your vacation and follow the instructions we will give you in the next few days. Capisci!"

The lawyer left room number 309 with the note in the pocket of his summer shorts. He left in a hurry and with an uncontrollable resentment as he saw the hotel's cleaning staff working their way along the corridor. Sighing, he felt both discouraged but also ready for the work he was expected to perform as the exclusive lawyer of one of the most bloodthirsty mafia groups in New York City.

Breska went straight to the dining room to try to eat lunch, but he had no appetite. His wife and children were there, as well as his friends and other clients, who received him with odd looks. Slowly, the lawyer told his wife that he wanted to talk to her alone for a moment to explain an unforeseen situation, that an anomalous and urgent matter had arisen and needed to be dealt with as soon as possible. Already at a considerable distance from the other diners, the lawyer explained to his wife the contents of the note very calmly and patiently, in his own way. She was not unused to this type of news since her husband worked in shady affairs of the Mafia. Emma was beginning to miss her life of luxury in Los Angeles. One by one they said goodbye to their friends, colleagues and clients at the Riu Guanacaste hotel in San José. Everyone was shocked at the speed with which they left and let them know it. They went straight to the airport to catch flight number 2349 to Madrid, from where they would fly to La Palma, Canary Islands and the lawyer would await his next instructions.

The life of the Breska family was beginning to take a 180-degree turn. Sitting at the airport, the lawyer thought back to his initiation into the mob. Some time before, the lawyer had become an exclusive member of the New York City mob under circumstances that were anomalous and atypical for a lawyer with his experience and clients. The Mafia had intimidated him into working with them, which was odd since generally a consigliere of the Mafia clan is a member of the family or a person intimately linked to it through kinship or close friendship. The family was the Mafia group Lamborda, from New York's Chinatown. This neighborhood was located to the southeast of Manhattan. This particular Chinatown is very authentic and is populated with Chinese and Italian immigrant families. Despite the apparent filth, the bad smells and the dodgy street vendors who want to take you to a back street to sell you any counterfeit you can imagine, Chinatown is charismatic and has a vibrant atmosphere. Canal Street is the real hotbed and heart of Chinatown where you can find many stores selling imitation clothing brands, luggage, shoes, jewelry, perfumes, electronics, souvenirs and even furniture or food. Do not pay too much attention to the price indicated, if you are one of those who like to bargain, you will have found your paradise, as the sellers are waiting for you . Here, in this stunning neighborhood Breska set up his office, only fifty square meters in size, where he could meet and discuss with the members of the Lamborda Mafia group to cover up all the shady and illegal affairs in which they were involved.

The most curious thing about the lawyer's office was that the office was located on the top floor of a washing machine store, coincidentally named after the same family, Lamborda. It was located on Mott Street, adjacent to Canal Street. On the first floor was the actual washing machine store, run by the capo, captains and soldiers of the mafia group.

One of the dirty tasks, the biggest of them all, which was entrusted to the lawyer, required him to study, prepare and gather the necessary documentation in order to obtain the license for the opening of the largest casino Chinatown, even turning enemies into friends, applying Machiavelli's doctrine, by order of the capo and the Godfather, where the end always justified the means.

So Breska sat at the airport thinking about this and about the events in room 309. He was also keeping a watchful eye on the departure time of flight number 2349 to Madrid. The flight was finally announced over the billboards and loudspeakers at the San José airport, so Breska and his family looked a little more cheerful as they moved toward the front of the line to board the plane, along with a large crowd of tourists returning from their vacations.

Passports in hand and heads held high, the members of Breska's family paraded one by one until they took their seats on the flight, of course wearing their protective facemasks. As they settled into their seats, suddenly there was a loud cracking sound next to the pilot's door of the plane. Captains Maranzzano Rizzo and Lucky Russo, exited the tiny toilet in the plane and addressed the lawyer without hesitation, gesturing with their fingers to come to the far end of the jet. The lawyer stood up from his seat, under the gaze of the men of honor. He headed towards the end of the plane where they were waiting for him as a stewardess signaled for the flight to take off. There was a deafening noise in the cockpit part of the plane.

Just as Breska reached Lucky, he slipped a letter into the pocket of the jacket of the elegant suit he was wearing, giving him an affectionate kiss on the right cheek of his face and wished him a pleasant journey.

Breska immediately began to read the letter where no one could be watching him, which read: *"At the Hilton Hotel in La Palma call 65699947477. Capisci!"*

After landing in Madrid, Breska and his family continued their journey to the island of La Palma, unpredictably, like the race of a tortoise in front of a hare in the forest.

> "Misfortune puts friends to the test
> and uncovers the enemies."
>
> Epictetus

Chapter III
The Escape

"Nothing happens by chance, deep
down things have their secret plan,
even if we do not understand it."

Carlos Ruiz Zafón

SENATOR WARRENT WAS TRYING TO GATHER HIS trusted senators before the Senate Chamber in New York City, in order to obtain the license for the filming in Hollywood studios, the deadline for its beginning would be in approximately one month and with the company Universal Pictures. In this way, he could fulfill the commitment agreed upon with the lawyer at the Los Angeles luncheon.

The time for the vote was approaching, the senator and his trusted group were preparing for the emotional act, everything was happening in a sudden and crazy way in the business agreed with Breska, it was like being on the beach about to enjoy a good swim when you are swept away by a giant wave; unexpectedly, you feel rolled and buffeted and out of your depth. The worst thing was that the senator was unaware of the course of certain events.

It was the sum of a good handful of votes of some senators, all necessary to carry out the mission entrusted to them, including Warrent.

10 am. AUGUST 5, 2021.

The senate was to meet in the month of August in the form of a recess, as an extra day within the vacation for the vote on the film license. The senator had his entire group of senators on hand to push the button for a favorable vote on the film production company's license.

The President of the New York City Senate asked all senators to cast their votes with the telematic button system, through a push button located in their comfortable seats in the chamber, each vote was personal and non-transferable.

Warrent was very relaxed and willing to carry out his vote, he looked at his trusted senators, where he did not perceive anything strange, everything was in accordance with the circumstances agreed upon at the Los Angeles lunch.

The senators in Warrent's group were smiling widely, like a circus of permanent clowns, all laughter was in full swing, and the senator was even more confident. He handled himself in the strictest sensibility of a senator who has everything under control and magnified it in his mind with a view to a positive result.

"The vote begins," said the President of the Senate Chamber. "Senators, press your buttons for the vote on obtaining a license from the film production company Universal Pictures for the filming at its Hollywood studios."

Almost all the senators nodded and pressed their electronic buttons. The President of the Senate, with an attitude colder than ice, proceeded to give the result of the vote, "We did not obtain the quorum necessary for the requested license." There was no sound in the chamber. "We will now move on to the second round of voting," said the President again with a serious look on his face, taking his steps in accordance with Senate protocol.

Warrent was beginning to smell a kind of inner chink, he was beginning to doubt the first result of the vote, wondering how was it possible that the favorable votes of the senators he trusted had not been obtained if everything was under control? It could not be, he thought, but his persistent and ambitious character made him assume a favorable outcome for the second vote.

The senator looked again, this time in a more fixed and direct way, at each and every one of his trusted senators, without perceiving any distinctive trait of bewilderment and discouragement, looking at them with intense emotion and discovering a new smile for each one of them for the second vote.

But while Warrent's over-thinking caused him to concoct an outcome that was not a total victory, a total defeat in the vote did not cross his mind, he was not in his right mind.

The Speaker of the New York City Senate chamber was back on the floor for the second vote, "You may now vote for the second round of voting, this time being the final result."

Warrent leaned back in his seat, like a vulture scanning the horizon for its prey, as if he was sniffing out the buzzing atmosphere of his senators.

All voted together and when the vote was over the President gave the result. Warrent was preparing for the final victory in the battle of the silent chamber. At last this calculating and distant President took the floor,

"Result of the vote, thirty-one votes in favor, thirty-two votes against, out of the total of sixty-three votes of the chamber, the vote does not go ahead."

Some sibylline whistles could be heard, Warrent could barely believe his ears, "It's not possible, it's not possible!" he repeated to himself over and over again, "Fuck!" In his mind he would never have considered such a defeat, he was not prepared for it. The victory of the vote should have been guaranteed and no other possible outcome was foreseen.

Now, however, the faces of some of his most trusted senators betrayed them, there was a tragic air of betrayal and conjecture, like a very bitter sip of a good wine on the upper lip of a robust mouth.

Warrent, for his part, got up very discouraged and disarmed from his chair to address his senators, catching none of them, as they all tried to escape his wrath, running to their fast sports cars, scraping their wheels on the asphalt as they hurriedly the private parking lot.

And what was the situation for Senator Warrent now? He could no longer honor the commitment to Breska, the granting of the license in favor of the lawyer's clients, the film producers for the filming with Universal Pictures in Hollywood studios, and he did not know what to say or how to act, he was very nervous, restless, rather desperate.

The most worrying thing was that within the group of these clients of the lawyer and friends of the senator there were people who had no respect for life or for anyone, they were only interested in business and those that succeeded, not those that failed. In these cases they applied the Mafia Law, within codes of conduct, that probably only these men understood.

In this sense, one of these codes of honor stated verbatim: "One must not steal from another man of honor or in general from anyone...".

For these mob people, this was applicable to the millimeter, in this case to Senator Warrent since they would understand that he had lost respect for them by not getting the license for the film and not being able to carry out the more than five-billion-dollar business.

Breska had already stated the terms to the senator at the Beverly Hills luncheon. According to that deal, they would collect a commission of one million dollars to be divided between them at a party at the Las Mariposas club, with delivery of the aforementioned amount within forty-eight hours in New York City.

Warrent couldn't get over his astonishment, he couldn't work out what could have gone wrong. What the senator did not know was that Breska now worked for one of the largest criminal groups in the city of New York, and they had the aim of obtaining a license for the opening of the largest casino in Chinatown. Of course, it was the Lamborda mafia group.

The lawyer had done his part with the best of his skills to control the municipal council, which operates under the New York City Council to determine the control of the use of the city's land. He had already worked to get permission for the installation of the Grand Casino of New York in Chinatown, as the mafia had instructed him.

The commercial premises owned by Breska's clients were in Chinatown and could be used for full-fledged gambling casinos, which would need to be authorized by the Lottery division of the State Gaming Commission, and here the group of senators attached to Warrent would have a lot to say. The senator was flushed and perplexed. Could Breska have allied with the rest of the senators to prevent the vote on the license for the screening of the movie from going through? Could it have been the Mafia? The senator did not know what to do or where to go, but one thing he knew for sure, that his life was in grave danger.

Then, a ray of light came devilishly out of the darkness of Warrent's dulled thought, like a wilted flower in the field in spring, to go home and prepare for a trip "in extremis", of great urgency, to get lost in time and space. He sought out a computer engineer friend, who issued him a new identity, provided him with the latest generation of mobile applications, with security codes, QR scanner and a new passport so he could disappear entirely. His new name was Liam Strudel, he was no longer Senator Warrent.

Mr. Strudel was hurrying across Cody Cross Avenue in Manhattan where he lived with his wife Jolanta Wright and fourteen-year-old daughter Olivia, neither of whom were home when he arrived at the door. He left with the bare minimum in his suitcase. He was going to take the first yellow cab that approached him, he made a clear gesture to stop with his right hand raised on the left side of the road with the intention of getting into it. The senator got into the cab quickly, where he found a Pakistani cab driver, with long hair pulled into a ponytail, who helped him with his suitcase while he asked him in an attentive and kind way, "Where are you going?"

Liam replied in a hurried manner, "To the airport, put the bag in the car, it is an urgent trip, I have a very important matter at hand and I can't be late. Full speed please, I'm not fussy about the route, but take me quickly to the airport, I will be good to you."

"Let's go, sir, you have found the right person," said the cab driver with confidence.

During the trip, the Pakistani was carefully observing, through the rearview mirror of the car, a silent man with an astonishing face. Behind them were three other vehicles traveling at a normal speed and a fourth car, traveling in the right lane, farther away and at an excessive speed, which was rapidly approaching Liam's cab. Nevertheless, they arrived safe and sound at JFK International Airport. The senator sighed in terror, like a hyena being chased by a lion on the savannah. He paid the polite Pakistani and thanked him for services rendered. He gave him a big tip, a hundred dollars, for his careful help in reaching his destination safely and fast.

"Goodbye, sir, thank you and good luck."

Given the state of blockage in Liam's mind, he didn't even answer the cab driver. Once he got out of the car, he ran, as if he was an Olympic athlete, until he reached the information board displaying the international departures. He did not see the flight to Madrid, it did not appear for the moment. He began to think about why he got there and why he was so anxious and stressed. He was looking hard but still couldn't find it, he just couldn't see the flight to the capital of Spain.

He sat in the long, uncomfortable seats in the airport lounge, watching as three guys, all wearing Panama hats, watched him with piercing stares from four rows down from where Liam was sitting. He didn't know them. The senator kept replaying the senate vote in his mind and thought about what those guys might do. Their gazes were obviously directed at him. Would they be closing in on him? The island of La Palma, Canary Islands, Spain, awaited him. Why?

Thinking about that vote of his group of senators and trying to find arguments for the failure of the vote, he became very nervous, he felt he had to keep watching those strange guys, while getting impatient about the lack of information about his flight to Madrid and the negative sense of the things that were about to happen to him following the vote earlier.

Suddenly, the departure of the flight to Madrid was announced over the loudspeaker of the terminal, Liam carefully approached the boarding gate of the flight, like a couple in love on their first date.

With his brand-new identity and brand-new passport in hand he approached the boarding gate where a beautiful woman, a flight attendant, asked to see his passport. Liam was not used to going through these requirements before taking a plane.

Finally another stewardess smiled at him and gave him passage. He walked hurriedly to the long aisle that led him to the plane bound for Madrid. He took his seat and contemplated his long journey to the island of La Palma.

There was no sign of the three men in Panama hats who had been sitting in the New York airport seats four rows down from the senator. Could they have found themselves on an entirely different flight? Could Liam's new information have thrown them off the Senator's scent? Could the three guys who he assumed were on his trail have found themselves traveling to somewhere 10,000 miles from Madrid? Surely anything was possible.

Liam was traveling on an American Airlines Airbus bound for Madrid with the express purpose of continuing on to La Palma, in the Canary Islands. He arrived in the capital of Spain flushed and worried, still none-the-wiser as to why the vote didn't go as expected and what this meant for his future. What he did know was that he should hide in the most hidden place on the island of La Palma, so that those unscrupulous guys with no sense for life would not find him. If they did, he knew the outcome could be fatal.

Upon his arrival at the Madrid airport, the now ex-senator made his way to an information board to check on his flight to La Palma. He picked up a newspaper from a small stand and read a most unpleasant headline: "The Mafia is at work again in New York City murdering a New York politician, with no known perpetrator of the crime."

Liam shuddered, his heartbeat increased and he could not control it, he was sweating profusely. He tried to calm himself down, but he could not, he was exhausted and couldn't catch his breath. He sat down on a bench at the airport, and breathed deeply, again and again, until he managed to calm down. At last he calmed down, his heart rate returned to normal, but he wondered with great sorrow which politician had been killed by the mafia. One of the senators in the vote, maybe even one of his friends?

The senator was carrying a backpack weighing fifty kilos and could not get it off his shoulders. Between his bitterness and sorrow, his body started to shake as he waited there in the uncomfortable seat of the Madrid airport, for the flight to the island of La Palma.

The senator realized he had to look for new places to hide from these very dangerous people. He rushed to catch his flight, which he had seen on the information boards was about to depart. He had left everything behind in New York – his entire life and his family. No one knew anything of his whereabouts or his new identity. All because of a very serious and dangerous moment, his life was now at serious risk. He had accidentally gotten involved with the Mafia who had a strict code of honor and did not react well if business did not go as they expected.

Flight 2980 on which Senator Liam was traveling arrived on the island of La Palma on August 8, 2021, with no significant news. La Palma was a strategic and perfect hiding place for anyone trying to hide, especially criminals, who needed to lay low for whatever reason.

The first reason it was so perfect for hiding was that it was an area of great superficial extension and with immense groves and forests, as well as truly paradisiacal places far away from daily life. The second was that La Palma brought together beauty and mystery in equal parts. In the Caldera de Taburiente National Park, besides enjoying its exuberant natural attractions, one could also appreciate the sacred presence of the rock known as Roque Idafe, considered the axis of the world by the Auaritas, as the aborigines of La Palma are known. And in the Roque de los Muchachos there are cave paintings and carvings that are considered sacred.

West of La Palma, supposedly, was the island of San Borondón, one of the small islands that together with the seven large known islands were also part of the Canary archipelago: La Graciosa, Alegranza, Isla de Lobos, Montaña Clara, Roque del Este, Roque del Oeste and San Borondón. The mysterious "lost" island of San Borondón has long appeared in the folklore of explorers. Legend has it that during the Spanish conquest of the Canary Islands in the fifteenth century, a mysterious island was sometimes seen to the west of La Palma. As sailors tried to reach it, the island simply disappeared. Swirls of thick fog, sudden storms and fierce winds would impede access to the island and make it seemingly disappear. It is said that Christopher Columbus believed in its existence, since supposedly the island was briefly inhabited by monks, including St. Brendan, from whom the island received its primitive name, later changed to Borondón.

Close to this secluded spot on the island of La Palma, far from any bustle, from the noisiest surroundings, where the Mafia group would not think he could be found, Senator Liam intended to settle. He maintained several contacts with people he trusted in the New York neighborhood of Chinatown, and through real estate agencies on the island of La Palma, he rented a well-furnished house located far from any urban center, deep in the forest, in the most hidden and strange place on the island.

The real estate agent offered him a wooden house in a remote part of the of the island, in a paradisiacal place, located in the forest, where only experienced climbers and big game hunters came with any guarantees of safety, it was a place with gorgeous sunsets, with exotic birds, and deep silences throughout the day and night.

The house was owned by an English family who were very settled on the island. They had this property for rent and could even be persuaded to sell if Liam so desired. Soon they reached an agreement. There was no money problem.

Once he installed his belongings in the hut, he called his wife on a burner mobile number to communicate his whereabouts.

"Hi, honey, I'm really sorry, I'm very, very sorry, I don't know how to explain this to you," Liam said to his wife, "Love, I'm on the island of La Palma, Canary Islands, Spain."

Everything stopped, the conversation went silent until finally Jolanta came back to life, "Warrent, you've lost your mind! Where the fuck did you say you were?"

"I'm in La Palma, Canary Islands, Spain," said Liam in a dry and direct tone, like when a boxer knocks out an opponent in the ring in a heavyweight bout.

His wife thought that the senator had suffered an emotional shock or some kind of mental disorder, which would have altered his neurons considerably. Jolanta was very surprised and believed that something very serious must have happened to him to be so far away. She weighed his answer and asked him, "What's wrong with you, Warrent? I've never seen you so strange as you are now, you disappear from the house and then only call from a burner phone from the other side of the world! What the hell is going on... What about your daughter, Warrent?" Jolanta's lamentation turned into weeping, the kind that has no return or retreat, until her husband, the senator with a new identity, cautious and discouraged, answered her,

"Some mob men are after me from New York, now my name is Liam Strudel. It's a matter of a mistake in a vote that went against them, it's about a movie deal and they think I'm the one to blame for not getting them the license to make it in Hollywood studios, it's a deal of over a million dollars and these people don't mess around, they're coming to settle the score, they're coming to get their money, it's a mistake and to protect you I've come here, honey, for a while until everything is settled, I was going to explain everything to you..."

Jolanta almost collapsed, "What about the mob? My God, Warrent, it can't be true, what are we going to do now, what the fuck did you say your name was, how can this be possible?"

Once they hung up, Warrent, now Liam, was stunned and saddened by his wife's reaction and didn't know what would he do from now on He called Jolanta again, his beautiful blond wife, who picked up the phone and started speaking immediately, giving him no chance to say a word, "You know what kind of trouble you have gotten yourself into, whatever the fuck you say your name is now, Warrent, what your daughter and I need is for you to stay out of trouble and leave us alone. Whatever they tell us or when we get news of your shady and filthy business I will report you to the FBI and the DEA. The first and only thing that matters is the safety of your daughter and me. He who does it pays, neither your daughter nor I are responsible for your dirty deeds, good luck to you Warrent."

The senator asked his wife forcefully, "Are you threatening me, Jolanta?"

"I don't even know what to call you anymore, Warrent. Don't ever talk to me again, you fucking idiot."

Jolanta was incredulous, she could not begin to understand how the events had unfolded with her husband, the Mafia, the political trouble he could have gotten into. All she could see was that she and her daughter were targets now.

Night fell in the small hut. There was not a soul in this secret place, only Liam and his new German shepherd dogs guarding his hut. He had bought them from a friend of the hut's owner.

The house was equipped with all the latest electronic devices and security cameras, as well as bulletproof glass in the large window, which looked out over the beautiful forest. Liam started to look at the few documents he had brought with him from his New York home, the only ones he had had time to collect given the situation. In them he found nothing of what he had expected and again the tremors of death crept in: should he call his wife so that she could send him the secret classified documents so that he could study the case he now had to face?

She obviously could not begin to imagine what was coming Liam's way. Because he had come with almost nothing but the clothes on his back, and in the face of an extreme urgency he felt helpless, hidden and locked away and at risk of losing his life. He labeled himself a frustrated thinker, but the best thing was that no one knew where he was, and this gave him some peace of mind.

He put on Beethoven's "Heroic Symphony", a piece that mirrored his feeling of melancholy and the fullest loneliness. He felt as if he had been relegated to the loneliest being of all humans by the foul play used with improper and dangerous people. It wasn't his fault that the extremely noxious and grotesque Mafia was looking for him. After lamenting his poor luck for a while, he fell asleep next to his beautiful German shepherds in that wooden house deep in the forest.

The plane with Breska's family, some friends and relatives, landed at the airport of La Palma from Madrid, with no problems the day after the arrival of the senator on the island. He was ready to carry out the plan outlined by his Mafia clients. As planned, they would stay at the Hilton Hotel in La Palma, room 109 for Mr. and Mrs. Breska, and next door for their friends and relatives.

Suddenly, and with almost no warning to his relatives or the others, Breska approached a beautiful, black-haired woman at the hotel reception.

He said, "Excuse me. My name is Breska, are there any messages for me?"

"One moment, please, Mr. Breska, I'll see if there is anything," she said and almost immediately handed him a tiny blue envelope she found hidden under the counter.

"Thank you very much, ma'am." With those words, the lawyer turned and walked slowly towards the stairs, ready to return to his room. He stopped, and looked around very carefully in case anyone was spying on him. Once he was sure he was alone he opened the blue envelope, which contained a letter that read: *"When you are at the Hilton Hotel in La Palma, lawyer, call the number 65699947477 following the instructions given to you. Capisci!"*

Immediately, the lawyer went downstairs and called the number from his prepaid card phone. A voice he didn't recognize answered, "Hello, Mr. Breska. Follow my instructions; take notes if you need to. Quickly now. The sun will rise tomorrow at about 8 am.. You must go to the city of La Palma to hire the best detective agency on the island. We need for your sake and that of the family to find our mutual client who has hidden himself here, as you well know. You have all the data in room number 110 of the hotel, ask for Irina, she will help you. Capisci!"

There was no waiting around for Breska; he decided to search avidly for the best detective agency on the island, which according to his contact in the Mafia should be real sleuths of the investigation. He proposed an exhaustive investigation through his contacts in New York, people of his trusted environment and his new Mafia world. He felt as if he was doing the unspeakable in order to locate the most competent and effective agency of private investigators in the area. For his own sake, that of his family and closest circle, he should hire the best detectives, no argument, he knew that no mistakes could be made in this business he had gotten into, despite being very new to their world. The consigliere had been in the Mafia group for too short a time to have been given such an important assignment. He did not feel equipped to make decisions for them, but he had been chosen for his professional merits and his personal qualities, as a real devil of the law, having good relationships and contacts in the city of New York. The capo had full confidence in Breska. The lawyer pondered and thought more than a philosopher, asking himself: why have they entrusted me with this arduous task? It should be Bernardino and his gangsters in charge of this mission, not me, the lawyer thought insistently.

Breska was already getting used to the idea of what it meant to work with the Mafia, and it was not going to be as he had imagined. The lawyer's family, on the other hand, did not understand the travel arrangements or the instructions from his 'clients', they had no idea that these were not just any clients of the Los Angeles law firm. The consigliere's family spent their time playing and having fun on each trip, never getting to know about the lawyer's real life with these people. The family's children were going online to pursue their college studies, being much more concerned with partying, enjoying the beaches and nightlife.

Breska did a lot of research and thought hard about who would be his next tireless companions on the island. The next morning he went downtown to meet with a Mr. Bryan Spencer, who had been highly recommended to him by his Mafia colleagues.

It was 8:30 am. and the sun was casting gorgeous orange hues over the beautiful island. Bryan Spencer, an American detective who had emigrated from the U.S. to the island for personal reasons, was connected with racketeering, bribery, white-collar criminals, professional swindlers, murderers, drug dealers and organized crime gangs. He almost seemed to move like an alligator after fresh prey. He was a man who fit the profile the lawyer was looking for. The sign at the entrance to his agency read: Bryan @ Associates, Private Detectives.

The consigliere entered the office trying to be as unobtrusive as possible. He was still somewhat cautious, not being entirely sure who or what he would find in these parts. He saw an endless number of people in the waiting room. It looked like some kind of prison riot in Colombia. He pushed and shoved his way through the crowd until he reached a kind of reception area. There he found a thick, black-haired woman with overlapping teeth, talking passionately with a blond woman, dressed in white. Something must have been going on, since they kept shouting at each other but due to the noise in the agency and the sheer number of people in the place, Breska could not deduce what they were discussing. The lawyer went to the first one he met, almost tripped over her giving her an involuntary nudge, it was the beautiful blond woman dressed in white. Her green eyes captivated the lawyer.

"Excuse me, Miss, my name is Breska, I'm here to speak to Mr. Spencer."

"Mr. Spencer is very busy this morning, he is not going to be able to assist you at this time, what is the matter and how can I help?"

Breska gave her no choice, he told her firmly, "It is a matter that does not wait, I come recommended, Mr. Spencer knows what it is about, it has already been discussed with him on the phone a few minutes ago."

"Are you the man who comes without an appointment on behalf of Alejandro Escudero, the broker of the English real estate agency on the island?"

"That's right," Breska replied.

Now she addressed the lawyer in a more polite tone, "Mr. Breska, please go to the back room, that one in the inner corridor, and Bryan will be with you shortly."

The consigliere went to the aforementioned interior corridor, finding in the back room a dark-haired gentleman, with a very dark complexion, an athletic, stocky body, who was talking to a client who was sitting in the armchair in front of him. Upon arrival, before entering the room, he knocked and said, "My name is Breska. I come from Alejandro, the broker of the real estate agency."

The broker at the agency was the Mafia's contact on the island for real estate investment matters.

Bryan answered quickly, "I'll be right with you, Mr. Breska, I need five minutes to finish up here. Please sit down on the bench outside."

The lawyer sat patiently on a bench, leaning against the side of the room of that stunning office, waiting for the end of the detective's conversation with his client. Breska was impressed by the agency's office.

After Detective Spencer's meeting with his client was over, he ushered the consigliere in. The lawyer looked around the office before sitting down in an armchair in front of the desk. He was surrounded by framed pictures of fingerprints, detective eyeglasses, hats, scarves, tailored suits and crocodile shaped shoes. There were also pictures of the police unit, the city courts, and right on Detective Spencer's desk was a very thick file filled with thousands of folios, which read, 'Case Mr. Warrent'.

Bryan began to speak with great calmness and certainty, "Mr. Breska, I know perfectly well why you have come here, although I see many people in this agency, your case is the first on the list since you appeared here from New York. From this moment on, all these agency clients will take a back seat and I will be your detective from morning till night, twenty-four hours a day, from sunrise till nightfall. I will be your shadow and hound dog from the moment you get up until the moment you go to bed. But we are not alone, please come with me."

They both left the detective's office quickly, as an arrow leaves the bow when it is displaced by the string. They came to a sort of cubicle that was hidden inside the main room, where they found two men who were talking about their lives. Both showed tremendous respect for the presence of Detective Spencer and the lawyer.

One said jokingly, "We've been waiting impatiently for you, Detective Spencer. Hello, Lawyer. My name is Antonio Lozano and this is Lucas Carrión, my partner in the investigations of the agency's clients, happy to assist you and serve you for whatever you need.

"Thank you," the lawyer replied firmly.

Suddenly, Detective Spencer took control of the situation, saying, "Gentlemen, from this very moment you answer only to Mr. Breska, I want to see you in full action, boys, pay close attention to what I am going to tell you. I expect you to be so glued to Mr. Breska and his entourage that you will not sleep, you will eat only when your body starts to throb. You will eat, sleep and breathe Breska and his environment until we are done and if you do not, you will regret having been born, having met me and I will use all available weapons against you to make you disappear from this world, I assure you."

The detectives had heard Bryan give them orders on many occasions but never had they had heard him like this. They were very concerned and both wondered silently what case they had ahead to threaten them with so much trouble. Both detectives were incredulous and amazed at their boss.

And the strange thing was that Bryan had told them nothing about this affair, about Mr. Breska, about what kind of assignment it was, they were ignorant in their own house and cursed Bryan over and over again. What was he getting them into?

Breska, for his part, showed a proud and friendly face in direct contrast to their boss. The pair were now beginning to wonder what kind of trouble they could get into, as well as how much they could make for such an important case.

But "Bryan @ Associates, Private Detectives", first and foremost, was a family of sorts. After many years of tracking together, after several investigations into men bent on silently cheating their wives, fraudulent accident and health insurance victims, parents concerned with their children's future and their relationship with the world of alcohol and drugs, the detectives had followed more than one businessman revealing accounting data and bankruptcy, one or several partners for misappropriation of their company's money, etc. They had also followed people related to the world of crime, drug trafficking and extortion. But they had never had an assignment of this nature, Antonio and Lucas were in time to refuse to contract it.

Then, an unpredictable thing happened in front of the astonished men, Detective Spencer slammed his hand down on the table, and said,

"What the fuck is wrong with you, you idiots, you bastards? You don't say anything, you fearful, low-down, son-of-a-bitches!"

Detective Lucas told Bryan that they needed to adjourn to the next room without Breska's presence in order to talk about what was happening. He frowned. Quickly, the three left and Lucas closed the door with a slam.

Detective Spencer began the story, bringing out his capacity and ability to handle himself in these delicate and dangerous environments,

"You will be very surprised with what I have just told you, boys, keep in mind that I have not had time or occasion to tell you anything about this matter, there has been no material juncture, I was called by some guys from Chinatown to take care of this matter without any complaints and I could not refuse. Besides, I have several favors and compliments pending with them that I must repay now and I can't argue. Dear boys, this is a job for the New York Mafia, for the family Lamborda who want to commission us through their consigliere, Mr. Breska, the man here with us today, who will follow the instructions of the criminal organization. The assignment is to search for and locate Senator Warrent in order to put him at the disposal of the Lamborda group. We know he is most likely hidden in a house in the forest of La Laguna, on this island. Do not take anything for granted, gentlemen, he can be found in any place, domicile, house, dwelling, local, room, hiding place, hideout, hideout, cave or whatever God wants to call such a place."

The Spanish detectives Antonio Lozano and Lucas Carrión were now even more perplexed following the speech of their boss, they liked this kind of challenge, ignoring any threat to their own safety. They really had no fucking idea who they would be working for. It was the Mafia, nothing less than the Mafia, people without scruples, who valued no life, who were without love for the human being and with the only purpose of getting what they wanted. If they did not get what they wanted then the Law of the Mafia or Code of Silence was implemented, allowing them to crush whatever stood in their way.

"Well, boys, we work for the Mafia now," said Detective Spencer, "What do you have to say, we have been hired by the Mafia, who came to see me, we start now."

Lucas and Antonio nodded. They offered their boss, who had had them under his control for more than a decade, no objections. How had the detective agency been commissioned by a member of the Mafia, in fact, the lawyer for the criminal group? There were many doubts and anything could happen.

> "In life everything comes, everything
> happens and everything change."

> Anonymous

Chapter IV
The Assignment

"Wise men learn a great deal from their enemies."

Aristophanes of Athens

ANOTHER DAY DAWNED IN THE SENATOR'S LOG CABIN. A plastic surgeon friend of his had operated on him from head to toe, and he didn't even recognize himself when he looked at himself in the bathroom mirror. As he combed his hair, he remembered that damned vote that had turned his life upside down. He still couldn't figure out who had been behind it all.

Apparently, two of his most trusted senators had ultimately changed votes and he hadn't been the least bit aware of it. He'd thought he'd had everything under control, so why had this happened? How was he going to get to the bottom of this mess?

Feeling contemplative he took his dogs for a short walk in the lush forest. His mind was set on the idea that he should contact his wife Jolanta again. He trusted that she could find him all the necessary documents to unmask the senators of the failed vote.

The forest was silent except for the sound of birds. The senator was in another world, absolutely far from any civilization.

Walking through the forest he heard a noise. He wasn't alarmed exactly but he had left his Winchester rifle in the hut. He stopped for a few seconds, listening for the movement of the plants and the tall trees in the grove. No one was expected there since access was nigh on impossible for any ordinary citizen, only the occasional mountaineer, risky hiker and hunter came this far. He continued very slowly, his legs trembling. Suddenly, a very large wild boar crossed his path, stopped and stared at him. His German shepherds barked wildly until it slipped back into the bushes.

He returned to the hut planning to call Jolanta. He dialed Jolanta's number from his prepaid card cell phone. The senator had two numbers and he always called from his prepaid cell, which made it more difficult for him to be traced by the mafia and, ultimately, by whoever was looking for him. He was sure that this card was almost impossible to trace by police services and hackers. No matter where he was, Liam could recharge the card from the log cabin just by accessing the phone company's website. And he had Wi-Fi under a false name.

But the senator was wrong. The Mafia and the police already had very advanced technological means to interfere in cell phones with prepaid cards, although a judicial authorization was needed to tap communications as it was a constitutional right in the Spanish State. Not that the Mafia cared.

It rang once, twice and finally Jolanta picked up the phone.

"Hello?"

"It's me, honey, I need to talk to you, it's a matter of life or death." Liam spoke to her in a conciliatory tone.

"What number are you calling me from, Warrent?" His wife kept calling him by his real name.

"That's not important now, honey, are you willing to help me?" asked the senator impatiently.

"Warrent, fuck you. I told you if you bothered us again I'd give all your data to the FBI and the DEA, is that clear, asshole?" Jolanta wasn't messing around, she was so angry with her husband that she gave him no choice. She hung up on him. The senator had no desire to call her anymore. Liam was in a distressing situation, he had no documents or evidence to defend himself against the mob guys, he had left everything at home in New York.

He thought for a moment like a real senator and not like an idiot, "fuck, what an asshole I am", he reflected. "If the evidence is in emails, then it's in the cloud, I can access that here."

The senator was very hopeful about this possibility. He opened his computer and entered his access codes. They were not there, neither were the documents that could help him to tear apart those who could persecute him, there should be endless evidence in his favor, but he did not find them much to his misfortune. Now the senator knew he really had to prepare himself for the worst.

Bryan and his cronies ended the meeting in the room next to where Breska was impatiently waiting. The detectives returned to him in the spirit of formalizing the contract for professional services. They found him deep in thought, settled in an arm-chair in the chief detective's office, whispering to himself about whether he had found competent detectives and what the future would hold for them from that moment on. He turned to Detective Spencer and asked, "Gentlemen, can I have full confidence in you?"

Detective Spencer responded briskly, "Everything has already been discussed with my colleagues and we have all agreed to do the job, now we need to discuss our fee."

Breska, who was beginning to understand the ins and outs of what it meant to work for the Mafia, insisted emphatically, "Do you really know where you are going and what is going to happen to you from now on?"

Bryan took command, turned to his colleagues with a frown on his face, "Don't worry, lawyer, my partners and I know how to work in this kind of situation, they know it's time to leave or stay and accept the consequences. I've already explained it to both of you, right, guys?"

"Yes, sir," they both replied cordially.

"Well, the price for the research to be paid by my clients is two hundred thousand dollars, which will be about one hundred and seventy-five thousand euros, this is the limit to which I am authorized to pay," said Breska.

Bryan, who was leading the charge with his fellow detectives, nodded, knowing that what he said would not be disputed or modified by the investigators.

"Prepare the research assignment sheet, Bryan," said Breska.

Bryan went to retrieve some files from a closet, and extracted a template document, reading at the top "Bryan @ Associates, Private Detectives", which he showed to the lawyer.

Breska observed the document carefully, saw that it reflected the generic conditions of service, highlighting specifically the fees to be paid by Breska's clients. The amount of one hundred and seventy five thousand Euros was to be split into two payments, ninety thousand Euros at the moment of the acceptance of the assignment, in cash, and the rest, once the assignment had been concluded. It was emphasized in the contract that the deadline for the completion of the task was set at one month from signing, extendable in case the investigation had not been completed. It stated that within this period the senator should be located and placed in the hands of the Mafia through the Capo Bernardino Mancini or one of his captains or soldiers of honor.

What would happen if the detectives did not find the senator within that time frame? They would find themselves in the crosshairs of the Mafia, where there was no reasoning to be done, just the application of the penalty of Mafia Law. In one way or another, they too had joined the Mafia circle, with potentially harmful consequences for their lives.

Breska and Detective Spencer signed the paper on both sides and duplicate copies, stamping their signatures on the unusual contract to give it legal form. Bryan, Lucas and Antonio had gone over to the criminal side in a roundabout way, although Bryan had already done some favors for several guys in Chinatown. They would get down to business.

The Mafia almost never took legal contracts into account, they preferred to adopt brutality and violence when things didn't go as they expected. The detectives were truly unaware of Mafia acts, they had only seen them in mafia movies, but never in reality.

And what was the Mafia Law? The Law of Silence or Omertà is the Sicilian code of honor that forbids reporting on criminal activities. In Mafia culture breaking the oath of Omertà is punishable by death. This was Mafia law.

For lawyer Breska it was not so difficult to not reveal confidential criminal information about his Mafia clients. Thanks to his status as a lawyer, the state could not force him to testify about illegal activities of his clients, with few exceptions. This was provided for in the code of ethics of the legal profession and its professional statute. Breska was untouchable, he enjoyed immunity as protector of his clients before the state apparatus, in short, before the law.

In the Mafia world it is well known that, after a failed suicide attempt, Buscetta, a member of the Mafia in Italy, collaborated with the judge and explained to him the organization, functions, actions and "modus operandi" of the Mafia. It was Buscetta's statement that revealed to the world the existence of a strongly hierarchical and organized criminal organization called "Cosa Nostra".

The "Cosa Nostra» (in common parlance generically called Sicilian Mafia or simply Mafia) is an expression used to indicate a criminal organization of the mafia-terrorist type present in Italy, particularly in Sicily and in many parts of the world. This term is now used to refer exclusively to the Mafia of Sicilian origin (also to indicate its international ramifications, especially in the United States of America, where it is identified as the American "Cosa Nostra", although today both have international diffusion), to distinguish it from other Mafia associations and organizations. The contrasting interventions of the Italian State became more decisive from the 1980s onwards, through the research of the so-called "anti-mafia pool", created by judge Rocco Chinnici and later led by Antonino Caponnetto. Judges Giuseppe di Lello, Leonardo Guarnotta, Giovanni Falcone and Paolo Borsellino were also part of the group (definition of the "Cosa Nostra" taken from the free encyclopedia, Wikipedia).

Lawyer Breska, the consigliere for the Mafia, returned satisfied by his day's work to the Hilton Hotel, to room 109, where his relatives were staying. As he approached his room, a beautiful blond woman, dressed in white, beckoned to him to go to the room next door to receive his next instructions. And who was this beautiful blond lady, Breska wondered excitedly? He realized had just seen another beautiful blond woman as he walked up the stairs.

He knocked on the door. No one answered. He knocked again and this time the door opened and a very attractive woman appeared, she was blond with blue eyes, slender curves and a model's body, beautiful, tall, with perfect breasts. She was with Irina, the first woman the lawyer contacted through the Mafia.

"Mr. Breska, we have a message for you," the women told him, "it's from Capo Bernardino, and it reads as follows, "Lawyer, you must go as quickly as possible to the detectives and find the senator, this is the data we have, Capisci!"

The Lamborda Mafia clan set about trying to locate Senator Warrent. From the most intrepid honor soldier to the clan's captains and at the headquarters of their laundry office in Chinatown, the Mafia group began to organize a forced trip, following the instructions of Capo Bernardino Mancini, who had the last word.

To do so, they contacted New York's JFK. They went to the trusted customs agent, Mr. Jordan, so that everything would be ready when the mobsters passed through customs control. The U.S. Customs and Border Protection was headed by a New York Mafia associate of the Lamborda clan. To become an associate of the criminal organization, Jordan had to turn a blind eye on many occasions when members of the Mafia clan passed their goods, luggage and firearms. The Mafia paid a fee to him in exchange for favorable treatment for services rendered by the clan in support of the customs agent's family and friends.

The capo of the Mafia family had supplied the clan with all kinds of weaponry through his arms trafficking contacts in the United States and Spain. And the question was: how could they get through all that arsenal? The answer was relatively simple, since once a person became part of the Mafia clan, everything was focused on achieving a common goal, in this case, to assassinate Senator Warrent.

The Lamborda Mafia group began their move from Chinatown to the Spanish state, loaded with an unparalleled and brutal arsenal of weapons, they were duly prepared to meet the objective.

Once they went up the airport escalators to the boarding area, about sixty feet away, they spotted Jordan, to whom they waved with clear gestures and raised hands. He showed them the way to a room isolated from the other passengers. The traveling Mafia clan was composed of Captains Maranzzano Rizzo and Lucky Russo, as well as the honor men or soldiers Pimponassa Blanco, Gamberra Conte and Gianluca Mesina, the latter being the group's hitman.

Bernardino, the Mafia kingpin had previously reached out to his battle-hardened contacts at Fort Hamilton military base, located in Brooklyn, whose mission was to provide the New York metropolitan area with support for the installation of the U.S. Army National Guard and the U.S. military reserve.

The Boeing C-17 military aircraft, led by Mafia associate Sergeant Thomas Cook, was preparing to take off for Afghanistan with instructions from the U.S. Department of Defense in compliance with the NATO and United Nations plan for peacekeeping and international protection of those affected in Afghanistan. The container was stacked with a large number of assault rifles, carbines, M16 rifles with bounded sight, silencers and grenade launchers.

Everything had been forged a few weeks prior at the club "Las Mariposas", owned by a fictitious company of a Mafia front man, a company set up by Breska, with money from the Mafia converted into bearer shares in various tax havens. In the club were the capo, the Captains Maranzzano and Lucky, as well as the men of honor Pimponassa, Gamberra and Gianluca. Also present were Sergeant Thomas Cook and Customs Agent Jordan. It was a hair-raising meeting, called by Capo Bernardino and duly authorized by the Mafia commission and directed by the capo dei capi or Boss of Bosses, the Godfather of the Mafia, who was above the capo in the hierarchy of the Mafia organization, considered the head of the two most important families in New York.

The Godfather, as he was called by the other members of the clan, had the last word in making decisions concerning the killing of a powerful and very relevant man in New York society, such as Senator Warrent.

The club was created by the boss Bernardino, like the one in the TV series "The Sopranos". It was composed of very beautiful women, who worked for the Mafia clan and would perform for clients, associates and other members of the Mafia. The Mafia had a secret and hidden room inside the club, which contained a large round table, many velvet armchairs and sofas, several English-style wooden chairs and a safe where the Mafia put the money coming from the club.

They were all summoned by Bernardino. They were having a great time, they had the best Moët & Chandon rose champagne, which cost around one thousand dollars a bottle, Macallan Scotch whisky, aged in Spanish and American oak barrels, and cocaine for the guests. Several ladies from the club performed striptease for the well-to-do and wealthy mobsters. It was all laughter and revelry in abundance from the Mafia clan's attendees.

The decision about Warrent's murder was made in advance by the Godfather, who passed it onto Bernardino who then gave express instructions for the other members of the club to enjoy everything without any consideration whatsoever. But, of course, the members of the Mafia had to carry out the plan without excuses, taking whatever they found along the way, without haste or remorse.

Jordan accompanied the Mafia to the existing hideout at the airport, away from all the passengers and the anti-mafia police at the customs checkpoint, as well as the FBI and the DEA. Once there, inside the secret room, Jordan addressed Captain Lucky Russo in a friendly tone, "The expected arms shipment is in the hands of Sergeant Thomas Cook, who is leading the Boeing C-17 military aircraft bound for Afghanistan. It will arrive in Madrid at the scheduled time and once it is in the military base of Aranjuez it will be transferred to Afghanistan, once the military arsenal has been transported to the island of La Palma."

Lucky was satisfied with the information received at the airport. There was no doubt that Jordan owed big favors to the Mafia, when they viciously dealt with a violent neighbor of the agent who would not let him live in peace and who constantly threatened him. Lucky beat up Jordan's neighbor so badly that he had to be rushed to the hospital.

Lucky said, "Jordan, make sure that the whole war plan goes smoothly, and know that we are very proud of you."

The agent responded honorably to the mobster: "It will be a pleasure; I have fun with you."

Lucky answered the agent with a smile, "You think this is fun?" and a huge laugh rang out and echoed throughout the room. "He said he's having fun, guys," Lucky pointed out to the rest of the clan members.

"He said he was having fun, ha, ha, ha."

The gangsters said goodbye to the Customs Agent and set off on their way to Madrid. They went up the escalator, passports in hand, to the boarding gate of a civilian flight bound for Spain. The American Airlines flight bound for Madrid, was about to take off loaded with gangsters, chartered by Captains Maranzzano and Lucky. Soldiers Pimponassa, Gamberra and Gianluca were aboard. A blond stewardess dressed in white, with blue eyes and a slender body, authorized them to enter the plane. Everyone in their path was laughing with this beautiful lady.

Breska was at the Hilton Hotel with Irina; they were seated on the sofas in the majestic hotel's lobby. She handed him all the documents and more precise information about the location of Senator Warrent's whereabouts.

Irina addressed the lawyer in a cautious tone, "Mr. Breska, this is the data I have received from Chinatown! Capisci!"

Irina retired from the sofa in the hotel hall very happy. The consigliere, already a little moved by the performance of his Mafia clients, was on his way to take a rented car at the door of the hotel to the office of private detectives Bryan Spencer, Antonio Lozano and Lucas Carrión.

The detectives were anxiously waiting for him, they had never had a similar case in their entire professional life. Arriving at his destination, Breska immediately took another rental car, signing the delivery receipt to the car rental company as the legal representative of a fictitious company, created by him in the tax haven of Panama with the help of his colleagues there.

He arrived at "Bryan @ Associates, Private Detectives", where he met the three detectives, who were waiting for him at the door of the agency eager to start work. As he arrived, they hurriedly got into the car, almost without giving him time to close the right rear door of the vehicle, Bryan gave him two taps to close it. Breska took them to a hidden place on the outskirts of the city of La Palma, where a helicopter was waiting for them with its propellers already in motion. They boarded the helicopter, and took their seats, while the helicopter took off in a surprisingly swift manner.

After two hours of flight, they arrived at a paradisiacal place, they were lost in the immense forest of the Laguna. They were surrounded only by beautiful fruit trees, with very steep ravines, where only the most expert game hunters, daring mountaineers, highly skilled climbers and people knowledgeable about the area could reach. It was tremendously difficult to reach this site, located in the most hidden place of the island, full of absolute silence of nature.

At last they arrived at an esplanade, next to two abandoned houses. They landed and then drove to a hidden wooden house down a long and very creepy road, right down the middle of a steep slope next to a steep ravine. It was the house rented by the mob for the detectives and the lawyer. The house was owned by another Englishman, who knew the ins and outs of the Chinatown Mafia clan and who maintained contacts with Senator Warrent. After another four hours of driving in a large off-road vehicle, they arrived at the wooden house. It was fully equipped with state-of-the-art audio and video recording systems. It was brown with orange tones, hidden to the south of the forest.

Detectives Bryan, Antonio and Lucas were prepared with tools and innovative devices to carry out the investigation, among which were hats, caps, sunglasses and audio and video recording glasses with tiny cameras invisible to human eyes, pencils and tiny audio and video recording pens, tracking tags to be attached to the investigated vehicles through the telematic system via internet, with connection to tablets, cell phones and laptops, watches and state-of-the-art video and audio recording and photographic cameras, and all the agency's files of the "Warrent" case.

The consigliere was equipped with a huge carry-on suitcase, three James Bond-style leather briefcases with the documents Irina had delivered to the hotel and two laptops. They settled into the wooden house, dividing the beds and bunks between themselves. Breska stayed in one room and the detectives crowded into two other rooms.

Night fell and everyone went to sleep, tense and uneasy. Once in bed, Breska phoned Irina from his prepaid cell phone, informing her that they were already in the house and would be staying there to carry out their mission.

The sun's rays shone brightly on another new day in the wooden house of Senator Liam Strudel. The senator's German Shepherds were making their way to his room hoping to be taken out for a walk and to relieve themselves. He was still sleeping, plagued by a bad dream. He woke up, "Fuck, these dogs," he exclaimed. It was September 15, 2021. The senator was still very worried and nervous. He was saddened and broken by his situation. He couldn't stop thinking about that damned vote. Why was it so disastrous and why was everything prepared for a different result than the one he had foreseen? He still couldn't get over his astonishment. He could not find any explanation for what had happened, asking his inner self insistently: had it been one of his trusted senators who had betrayed him or was someone else involved? He turned over and over in his mind and could not find an explanation. He came to doubt even Jolanta. He didn't even think about Breska.

Liam was unaware that Breska worked for the mob. He had no idea that he had been given the million dollars for the act of Omertà for the fulfillment of the order to obtain the license for the opening of the largest gambling casino in the Chinatown neighborhood, or that there was no turning back for the lawyer.

The senator thought firmly that two of his trusted senators must belong to the criminal group and must have betrayed him, since he trusted the lawyer completely, he had no suspicions about him. That is why he thought of everyone except Breska, he already distrusted even his own wife after the last call he had with Jolanta. What motive would the two senators have for not voting in favor of the license for the filming by the film producers who were clients of the lawyer? What was certain was that someone had betrayed him and swore revenge in spades, since the money had not been delivered by Breska. He wondered why the mob murdered the politician in New York City. Had it been any of the senators on the ballot or even a friend of his?

The senator could only hide. He became uncontrollably bitter and could not bear the thought that the Mafia was after him and that his life and that of his family was at risk. He began to search the internet anxiously to see what he could find. And he came across the first big surprise. There was no trace in the New York press of the murder of the politician, nor any other reference data, he still did not know against whom the Mafia had committed the alleged crime.

The senator took his dogs out for a short walk through the forest, when instantly pronounced earth tremors began to be felt. The leaves of the bushes and tall trees in the area moved forcefully, as well as the earth beneath his feet, he could hardly stand. A thunderous noise began and he felt as if the ground would swallow him up. His German Shepherds were barking frantically, they were panting compulsively and were scared out of their minds. One of them lunged at him and almost bit him in the face. But suddenly, everything stopped. The earth stopped shaking. The state of nature returned to normal and it was all just a good scare.

Liam returned to his wooden house sweating and shaking all over. There he left the dogs in the driveway and quickly turned on the television to listen to the local news. The local Laguna TV station reported a mild earthquake of magnitude six on the Richter scale. There had been no property or human damage. Liam was still perplexed by everything that was happening to him.

Breska opened the windows of the wooden house where they were staying. It was getting dark. Bryan, Lucas, Antonio and Breska were playing a game of poker with an eye toward starting the investigation into Liam, to them Warrent, the next day. The game was ruthless, as was usual among the Mafia; huge amounts of money were being bet without any regard. The room was filled with smoke thanks to the cigars the detectives smoked continuously. Breska did not have that vice but did not mind the others smoking. The final bet was that whoever won the game would fuck a stunning girl they had contacted on the Internet. Everyone was beside themselves, except Breska, who was impatiently waiting for the next day's sunrise. Detective Bryan turned attentively to the lawyer, "Why don't you want a little whiskey?"

The lawyer answered firmly, "I don't want alcohol, Bryan, it sometimes causes me problems."

Bryan, who was a heavy drinker, not taking no for an answer when he was in the middle of a good glass of whiskey, addressed Breska again in a jocular tone, "Come on, man, if it's just a drink, it'll do you good."

Breska, who was already starting to become furious, said to the detective in an intemperate tone, "You can drink, but leave me alone. Are you so stupid that I have to repeat myself? I already told you I don't want to. Do I look like I'm joking, asshole?

"Don't get mad, Breska, it was just a joke. No reason to get angry, take it easy, man, I was just having a good time! Can't you take a joke, lawyer?" exclaimed the detective.

The lawyer got really serious, looked him in the eye and said, "Bryan, I'm not in the mood for any bullshit, there's a man hiding in the woods and we have to find him. We don't have time to play stupid games and fuck people from the internet. May I remind you that tomorrow we have to leave very early to find our guy and you seem to think you are on vacation. Fuck, that's enough, dammit."

He got silence for an answer from the detective. His face changed radically. He became very serious and worried. Lucas and Antonio were playing the final of the poker game. Bryan and Breska had dropped out by this point and the two were left to go head-to-head. Lucas had a full house and Antonio had a straight flush. There was a thousand dollars on the table for the winner and the opportunity to sleep with the prostitute.

Lucas said to Antonio, "Letters on the table, what do you have my friend?"

"First get your cards out, boy," said Antonio, looking at him with a frown on his face.

Lucas placed his cards face up on the round table, exhibiting his full house with the certainty that he was a winner.

Then Antonio placed his hands on top of the table, and he said with an air of superiority, "I have a straight flush," and showed his cards to the detective. "I'm sorry, boy, these are the things in life, sometimes you win and sometimes you lose," he said with no resentment on his face. Then he picked up the thousand dollars and said, "I'm going to call that prostitute friend tonight."

Night fell in the lost forest. The detectives and the lawyer went to their beds without wanting to see what was coming for Antonio. A lot of commotion was heard in the room.

Another day dawned in the forest of the Laguna. Bryan, Lucas and Antonio, the latter looking hungover and disheveled, began to prepare the gadgets to carry out the investigation into the location of the senator. It was a matter of life and death to locate him. There were no excuses. In this, the Mafia was not forgiving although they didn't know that for sure. They thought it was like a fairy tale or a simple poker game but nothing could be further from the truth. Breska was studying the senator's papers. Suddenly, and abruptly, the ground began to move just below his hiking boots and the papers flew off the desk.

The trees and bushes around the house made furrows in the ground. There were big gusts of wind and it felt like a wild movement of the earth, the entire wooden house felt as if it were being torn from the ground and the windows shattered. The consigliere crawled into the dining room, and tried with great difficulty to turn on the television. At that moment, everything stopped. It became quiet again in the Laguna. That thing with an unknown name lasted a scant five minutes. Breska turned on the television. Local Laguna television announced a mild earthquake, magnitude six on the Richter scale. There had been no damage to property or human life.

Their house, though, had suffered some damage. Windows had broken and there were new plumbing problems. Someone reliable would have to be called in for repairs. Bryan, Antonio and Lucas emerged, stunned from the room next to the living room. The three of them in unison said, "God, what the hell happened, damn it? Breska, where are you? Are you alright?"

The detectives went quickly to the dining room, where they found him seated and crestfallen.

"Why didn't you answer, Breska, we thought something had happened to you."

The lawyer did not waste time on emotional judgments before his fellow fatigued companions, "Thank goodness we're all well, that's the most important thing now, damnit. A few minor repairs and we will be fine. The television said it was a small earthquake of magnitude six on the Richter scale."

"Let's call the repairman to fix this mess." The detectives, now much calmer, nodded to the lawyer.

They decided they should now wait for the damage to be repaired before setting out on their mission. They were approximately two hundred and fifty miles from the town of Cabeza de Vaca.

Why did these earth movements occur and what could be their origin?

> "Man is not so much concerned with real problems
> as with his imagined anxieties about real problems."
>
> Epictetus

Chapter V
Natural Site

"If you don't climb the mountain, you'll
never be able to enjoy the landscape."

Pablo Neruda

THE BOEING C-17 MILITARY AIRCRAFT commanded by
Sergeant Thomas Cook, bound for Afghanistan on an
international peacekeeping mission for the US Government, was
about to land at the Aranjuez military base prior to making the
transfer to Afghanistan, and leaving the arsenal on the island of
La Palma.

The contact of the Mafia in Spain together with their allies
for arms trafficking was waiting for them on the runway of the
airport of La Palma. This jet would not be recognized by the
airport control tower as it was going on a military peace mission
to Afghanistan. Landing on the runway, the Sergeant's allies and
the arms dealer, Mr. Ryan, had prepared the containers for the
inclusion of the cargo in a Spanish private plane.

The secret flight was organized by the Mafia to land on a
hidden runway in some unknown place in Laguna. The landing

had been forced, since the plane slid on a small dirt runway in the middle of the Laguna Forest. Arriving at the ground runway loaded with the weapons, the Allied chief and Ryan called the sergeant and radioed that everything was in order. The guns all arrived at their destination at the time Thomas Cook had scheduled.

The sergeant was very happy because the plans had gone as expected and the Mafia was celebrating. A convoy loaded with soldiers from the fort of La Palma began to move the cargo to a place near the immense forest. Everything was successfully put at the disposal of the gangsters. The Mafia had the weapons they required to assassinate Senator Warrent.

The American Airlines flight from New York to Madrid via La Palma was about to land. On the flight were Captains Maranzzano and Lucky, as well as soldiers Pimponassa, Gamberra and Gianluca.

A blond stewardess dressed in white, with green eyes, welcomed them at the landing gate. Now both mobsters and weapons were on the island of La Palma. The plan was to meet the lawyer halfway to give him precise instructions about the project. He was in the wooden house with the detectives, and from there the gangsters would continue on in another SUV to the house they had rented.

This house was located in the deep forest of the Laguna nature reserve, surrounded by many trees and barely visible to the naked eye. The estate was owned by yet another Englishman in the area, who often rented it to a Mafia associate for members of the Lamborda family.

Breska was driving in a 4x4 heading to a dirt road to meet the gangsters; he had left the detectives at the house. In a secret place surrounded by the lushest vegetation, full of super steep ramps, he would meet Lucky and Gianluca. They were tucked into another SUV, with the engine off and were waiting in anticipation. Worried about the execution of the Mafia plan, Breska approached Lucky and Gianluca's SUV. They were both relaxed and smoking Havana cigars. Breska walked to the driver's window and said, "How are you guys doing?"

"Stop with the nice-nice. We have come to give you the instructions that you will already have in your privileged mind," Lucky replied cheekily. Lucky then went to the trunk of the SUV and opened it. He took out some papers in a brown envelope and handed it to the consigliere, then said, "These are the instructions, lawyer."

They left the place very quickly after informing Breska that they would meet at the rented house. "We will be there to continue with the plan, counselor."

Breska was not in a hurry, he hurriedly picked up the papers and began to read: *"Consigliere, the senator is hiding somewhere in the forest, you must find him as soon as possible, lest he gets word out about our business and this reaches the ears of the FBI and the DEA. Lucky, Maranzzano and our hitman Gianluca already know how to carry out the ambush. The detectives will have to find him so that they can assassinate the senator. I don't want any mistakes, lawyer, I have full confidence in you and in what you are doing for the good of the organization. You will be rewarded, believe me, Capisci!* «

The consigliere had no choice but to accept the challenge, he remembered that enthusiastic deal he had made with the senator to get the license of the film production company and make a great movie. He was beginning to understand what it meant to work for the Mafia, and he was already forgetting his wonderful life in Los Angeles where everything had been perfect.

Why had he chosen to work for the mob, or had they threatened him to the point where really he had no choice? Would it have done any good to confront them by reporting them to the FBI and the DEA? He grabbed the key to his 4x4, started the engine and headed off to meet his fellow detectives at the log house.

It was night and the moon was waning over the lagoon. Not a soul could be heard in that secret place hidden among the trees full of bushes, shrubs, birds of prey and the occasional wild boar. It was extremely difficult to reach this very high mountain of the lagoon, where one could breathe fresh air and nature in abundance. The flow of the clean water of the river ended the silence of the splendid night. He arrived at the wooden house, found the house lights on. They should all be there preparing for the plan, thought Breska, but to his surprise the detectives were having a barbecue on the terrace of the house next to the ravine.

"You damned inept people!" He addressed the three of them so loudly that his voice must have carried for miles. "You bastards, you assholes! You bunch of sons of bitches!" The lawyer turned to Bryan, and said, "What do you want? Do you want to be killed? Have no doubt that they will kill you. Did you come here to work or to suck dick, you utter assholes?"

"Breska, don't worry, we have everything ready for tomorrow. We will be ready at 6 am. to make a move. The whole plan is drawn out on the corkboard next to the TV, we have done our homework, we were celebrating with some whiskey and grilled meat."

Breska went to check and he found, as Bryan promised, a well thought out plan on a corkboard. The responsibilities of each of the three detectives were well laid out. Such was the surprise for the lawyer that he told the men, "Boys, good job, but now pack up this crap, because tomorrow is going to be a very hard day."

They all went to bed without complaint.

It was September 19, 2021, and it was almost dawn in the Lagoon. Everyone was sleeping well except the lawyer, who had been awake most of the night worrying about the senator. He thought about how the search could go as he tossed and turned.

When the alarm clock went off at 6 am., everyone was on the move. The detectives had no hangover, quite the opposite of what Breska expected. They left for the mountains to carry out a detailed and millimetric study of the area, planning to return at noon.

Suddenly a loud noise was heard: Boom, boom, boom, boom, boom. The earth shook again.

"God, what the hell is it this time?"

Breska and Bryan quickly went out the door of the house, to the terrace area next to the ravine, where there was a great view. They could see most of the surrounding lush forest. Next, Antonio and Lucas came out behind the lawyer and the head detective to see what had happened. They all gathered on the terrace next to the ravine. From there, only the trees of the immense Laguna Forest could be seen. They all agreed on one thing: they had never heard anything like it in their lives. It almost felt like the end of the world, like the end of days. It seemed that life was coming to an end.

Breska went to turn on the television. He tried to turn it on, but it wouldn't work when he pressed the remote control. He tried again. He pressed the remote control many times, but it still didn't work. He plugged in his laptop, turned it on and found he had no internet connection. . His cell phone also had no data, so he had no way of finding out what had happened. He saw a call on his cell phone from a hidden number. It kept ringing, the lawyer's pulse was erratic, he finally picked it up,

"What the hell happened? Breska, holy shit!" Lucky's voice was immediately recognizable, he spoke very fast and kept cursing, "Shit, shit, shit, shit!"

Breska gently cut him off, "Have you seen anything on the news, Lucky?"

Lucky, almost without letting him speak, replied, "It was a volcano!"

"How... what was what?"

"Yes, you heard me, lawyer, a tremendous volcano has erupted not far from here. It was in Cabeza de Vaca, about one hundred and twenty from where we are."

"How did you find out what happened? We don't have Internet or television here!" said Breska.

"The boss called me and told me, asshole. You are an idiot. It seems unbelievable that you don't know that we know everything, that's how we are, lawyer, wake up if you want to survive in this jungle. A volcano has exploded in the area of Cabeza de Vaca, in La Palma, it started to release lava, my friend, we are fucked. It's called Cumbre Vieja, let's see if you understand that, lawyer," Lucky told him haughtily. Then he cut off the phone conversation.

Breska was finally able to turn on the TV and was astonished by what he saw. Everyone was speechless, they were perplexed, once Breska reported what happened to his colleagues. And the question was very obvious,

"What are we going to do now, Breska?" they asked.

"Guys, we work for the Mafia, there are no excuses of any kind here, there is a senator in hiding and we have to find him no matter what, even with a volcano erupting around us," answered the lawyer in a very cold and distant way.

On the other side of the forest were Captains Maranzzano and Lucky, as well as soldiers Pimponassa, Gamberra and Gianluca. They were in the wooden house eager to continue with the plan programmed by the underworld. For them, the senator had screwed them the possibility of having the license for the production of the movie with the film company Universal Pictures, a big film project worth more than five billion dollars. The mobsters were eager to kill the senator, they were looking forward to this adventure and to rise within the ranks of the Mafia.

The pair were playing pool; two balls remained on the table. The black ball was at Lucky's disposal. Maranzzano was about to shoot the green ball into the hole. The two balls were very close together, so he had a hard time hitting his ball. Maranzzano hit his shot and accidentally potted the black ball ending of the game. He had lost a bet of three thousand dollars! This money for the gangsters was like buying a packet of sunflower seeds, something totally irrelevant and of little importance among the gangsters given the immense amounts of money they handled. That didn't stop Maranzzano from flying into a rage when he lost the game, he didn't like to lose even playing marbles. He went to the terrace, which overlooked a steep ravine. He lit a cigar to relax. He took many puffs in a row, until he could barely breathe. Lucky burst out in jubilation at winning the game and laughed to himself before heading to the terrace where Maranzzano was.

"I need the money now. Pay up, I know you. Bets have to be paid and I'm not in the mood for jokes."

Maranzzano went into his room, took out a wad of bills and placed them on the table. "There you go, I'm a man of my word," he said grudgingly. Lucky took the bundle and saw that the three thousand dollars were there, as his partner had said.

Godfather Bernardino had given express and precise instructions for the assassination of the senator. It had been authorized by the Mafia commission, that was not just any old thing. Strangely, the mobsters in the wooden house had not been disturbed by any earth movement caused by the explosion of the volcano. They had played pool so happily and contentedly. And the worst thing was that they were not at all worried about the events, unlike the detectives and the lawyer.

The capo passed on the news as if he had gone to buy bread on any given day. He didn't even flinch, also because the Don was in no danger from the eruption of the volcano when he was in New York. What was a staggering reality was that the volcano had erupted, and lava was beginning to flow down the mountain. And the mobsters were not that far away. They didn't seem to care; it wasn't in their plans.

The local television news predicted an unbearable seismic situation and people's lives, as well as their homes, were beginning to be in serious danger. They would have to take shelter and possibly even evacuate. But the gangsters had to execute a plan and even the volcano couldn't get in their way. That was how they were when they were given orders. They knew that the mission was more important than their own lives. They lived under the Law of Omertà.

The press of La Palma described the volcano as an extremely difficult situation, there had been more than 25,000 small earthquakes on the island over eight days. The eruption initially had two fissures separated by almost 700 feet and eight mouths. Authorities such as the Civil Guard, which deployed more than 120 troops on the ground, estimated that the total number of evacuees could exceed 10,000 in anticipation of the lava flowing towards the coast. Several roads were also closed to traffic as a precaution.

Over the following sixteen hours, three lava flows occurred, reaching a height of twenty feet. More than 5,000 people were evacuated from the neighborhoods closest to the path of the lava flows, including hundreds of tourists. Late in the day, a ninth mouth was counted in the area of the Tacande neighborhood. The lava flows were not very fluid, which facilitated the evacuation;

however, in their advance towards the ocean at approximately 2000 foot per hour and at a temperature of 2000 °F, they had caused numerous material damages, such as the total destruction of buildings, communication routes and installations close to the area of the first eruption.

By 2 pm, the main flow had reached the town of Todoque, the most populated of the affected area with 1200 inhabitants and was moving at a speed of about 400 feet per hour. At that time the lava was advancing through two rivers: the one located to the southwest in Las Manchas had "minimal movement" of only about ten feet per hour, while the second, fed by the new mouth, was the one that reached Todoque.

During the afternoon, the volcano noted an increase in seismic tremors and, consequently, in the eruptive activity of the four active vents. Also, a ground deformation of ten inches was observed. The technical director of Pevolca spoke of a period of "mini-stability" and, although it was "quite explosive", the lava flows had slowed down and were advancing very slowly. He also confirmed that there were nine vents, with four active in a single fissure.

The director of the National Geographic Institute (IGN) in the Canary Islands pointed out that the eruption was entering a more explosive phase with large ash emissions and a decrease in seismicity. She also indicated that the flow continued to slow down to about twelve feet per hour. One of the two lava flows, the one that reached the neighborhood of Todoque, continued to widen its front and exceeded 1600 feet , while the northernmost tongue had stopped.

Two more vents were opened, creating two lava flows that moved down the slope at a speed of about 200-260 feet per hour. Shortly thereafter, the evacuation of the towns of Tajuya, Tacande de Abajo and the part of Tacande de Arriba, not previously evacuated, was decreed. In addition, the explosive activity and the emission of ashes intensified, causing the suspension of all commercial operations at the Airport of La Palma and La Gomera, due to the presence of these particles in the air and the low visibility produced.

The western part of the main volcanic cinder cone collapsed. In addition, a new mouth was opened, which caused a much more intense and fluid lava flow. This new lava flow was moving above the first one, which was still advancing very slowly (a few feet per hour), because, in the lower parts, the viscosity increased a lot due to the decrease in temperature of the lava. That is why the height of the lava flow increased. The casting branch in Todoque was barely advancing. The deformation of the terrain had not varied much in the previous three days. That meant that the material that was entering the magmatic reservoir was being compensated by the material that was coming out. Up to that day it had expelled slightly more than 920,000 square feet of magma. The column of smoke and volcanic ash rose to a height of four miles and the ash reached practically the entire island of La Palma and part of La Gomera. This circumstance kept the airport of La Palma inoperative. The shipping companies reinforced their lines to the island of La Palma; however, there were large queues of passengers and many pedestrian passengers in the port of Santa Cruz.

The last lava flow was reactivated reaching an average speed of about 330 feet per hour, passing the neighborhood of Todoque, running approximately 500 feet west of the center of this population center. Towards 8:30 pm it was located one mile from the coast.

"When you change the way you look at things,
the things you look at change as well."

Anonymous

Chapter VI
Lava

"Fear is the uncertainty in search of security."

J. Krishnamurti

LIAM PANICKED WHEN HE SAW THE NEWS on television. He saw the volcano erupt and started to tremble. He had never seen a volcano erupt in his life. He had lived through a storm caused by hurricane winds back in August 2021, produced by one of the most devastating hurricanes in the U.S., Hurricane Ida in New York. That had caused innumerable material damages and even deaths in New York City and New Orleans, but nothing like this natural catastrophe.

He began to wonder why he had chosen La Palma to hide out. Better, surely, to have gone to Jamaica, Nassau, the Bahamas or the Cayman Islands to enjoy a hurricane cocktail than go through this suffering? He didn't know if he should leave or remain hidden. Surely better to remain hidden. His head was awash with ideas and plans.

He took his pair of German Shepherds for a walk through the lush forest, this time taking the Winchester, which he loaded with ammunition. He also took a thirty-eight-caliber revolver, which he kept loaded with bullets on a kitchen table. He looked like Sylvester Stallone in the movie "Cornered". He began to travel through the forest with a compass that had been given to him by his father in a farmhouse in New Orleans. In addition, he had very good applications on his prepaid card cell phone about routes and trails in the area. He wanted to be sure to keep away from everyone.

As he went deeper and deeper into the forest, everything was full of bushes, weeds, plants, tall trees, salt marshes, wild olive trees and palm trees, which brushed his body as he passed by them. He also came across the occasional snake on the path.

He had had enough of walking and thinking. He was stymied but eventually decided that he could best protect himself by remaining hidden in the jungle.

As he walked back to the house, he heard a noise in the trees. Five hundred feet away, he saw the plants moving. He began to panic. He walked very slowly, step by step, almost without moving until he was hidden among the trees. He crouched down so that he could not be seen from far away. He rested his weapons on the ground and dropped his back against a large tree. He was alert and fully focused on what might happen.

Suddenly, an enormous wild boar appeared. It was running very fast towards the senator. It was already about one hundred and fifty feet away and did not stop running. It had smelled the human and now wanted to taste it. Liam aimed his rifle at the boar's head as it ran towards him. He had only a few yards left now. The rifle jammed. It was getting closer and closer. Finally he shot. There was a tremendous noise. The boar fell at the senator's feet. It was an accurate shot to the animal's head. His pair of German Shepherds abruptly pounced on the boar's body. He calmed them down with great effort.

"Now how do I turn this animal into food?" Liam asked himself very shakily. Mind you, if he could manage it he would have food for several days.

The volcano made Detectives Bryan, Lucas and Antonio doubt more than ever whether they would be able to accomplish their task. Breska had been very clear: they should do whatever it took to find the senator, no matter what, even with a volcano erupting around them. The lawyer knew there was no excuse for the mob, not even the risk of losing his life and the lives of his fellow detectives. The underworld put the senator's assassination before anything else. This was no card game.

Bryan turned to the lawyer, angrily stated, "We should get out of here, Breska, look what's going on, our life before anything else, no Mafia, no bullshit."

"What are you saying? Should I remind you what I told you the day we signed the contract at the agency? Working for the Mafia means following orders. Whoever disobeys them will end up dead," the lawyer answered very firmly.

Bryan didn't entirely agree, "The only thing that should take a man's life is death by natural causes, an accident, a terminal illness, but I refuse to be killed for no reason. We are in serious danger if we stay here, Counselor, I am going to think about packing my bags and leaving. I'm sure my colleagues are with me. That volcano will soon bury us and we will be fresh meat for the birds and snakes."

Lucas cursed, "I'm not going to stay here, lawyer, I'm not going to lose my life so easily, that volcano will be the death of us all. In three or four days we will burn in hell!"

"Fuck that shit!" Antonio joined in, "No Mafia, no bullshit, fuck them, our lives first and foremost!"

Breska felt cornered by the rudeness of his colleagues. He saw that they were not really aware of what it meant to work for the Mafia, they had no fucking idea. They were finished. The conversation was entering a hostile atmosphere, but the lawyer was an expert in mediation, he knew he could fix it.

"Guys, we still don't know when the volcano will reach us, we don't even know if it will come here, maybe the lava will be diverted to the ocean and won't reach where we are. How stupid you are! To anticipate something that has not yet happened is synonymous with ignorance, it seems unbelievable, guys. All I know is that I am here talking to you, what will happen in a while is unknown, we might die, sure. But remember, guys, working for the Mafia means obeying orders and not getting up thinking otherwise, if you do not abide by the rules of the clan, you are lost, really lost."

Bryan, Antonio and Lucas began to reflect and to reason coherently. They nodded as the lawyer spoke. Bryan was the boss of the investigators so his opinion was worth its weight in gold to Lucas and Antonio, he pointed out to them, "Breska is right, let's see how the volcano develops, we will have time to get out of here if necessary. Now we have to fulfill our task, we have no other choice."

"Make your choice," the lawyer said, "If you take that road, you will be burned."

The detectives remained silent. Breska was thinking of solutions when he saw the reaction of his colleagues, it seemed as if he was in a courtroom imposing his criteria on the judge, it was motivating. He knew he was good at this, he had a lot of experience. It was something innate in his being. Finally, there was a compromise in the decision to continue the investigation hired by the mafia, they had no other choice. Breska was satisfied. But only for a moment.

SEPTEMBER 23, 2021.

A few rays of sunlight made their way through the clouds. The volcano was advancing at breakneck speed, or so the detectives thought. It was 5 pm. and Breska's colleagues were about to carry out their plan, which they had carefully prepared.

The lawyer passed on the information contained in Irina's papers, one of the mafia's contacts on the island. Irina, together with the beautiful blond woman with blue eyes, was in charge of transmitting to Breska all the dirty laundry of the Mafia. They were sort of associates of the Mafia on the island. The Mafia sent girls to the club "Las Mariposas", in exchange for big favors with relevant businessmen and politicians. In the papers there were coordinates for the senator's location and the underworld did not usually fail. Warrent, as they called him, was approximately sixty miles away from the wooden house of Breska and the detectives. There was no time to lose. Tick tock, tick tock....

"The tortoise was in his lair", this was an expression used by the detectives when someone they were investigating was known to be in their home and therefore could be located. The detectives began to put all the recording devices and investigation tools inside the SUV, then Breska, Bryan, Antonio and Lucas got into the vehicle.

They were tense and nervous, except for the lawyer, who was used to dealing with everyone and everything. But the lawyer had forgotten one thing, he was working for the most devastating and bloody criminal organization in New York's Chinatown. They headed towards the steep mountains of the Laguna, deep into the immense forest. They were no longer concerned with the volcano, or so it seemed.

The detectives carried with them the latest generation of recording devices on the market, microchips, tiny hidden cameras that could hardly be seen, minute microphones, car tracking devices via email, glasses, caps, hats and disguises for the investigation, with the aim of not being recognized by anyone. They had the best computer and mobile programs of the moment for wiretapping recordings. Google Maps helped them a lot. They were very well prepared for the occasion. They had a thousand and one devices to track Warrent and now it was time to put their necks on the line.

The jeep drove slowly up the steep slopes of the forest. Visibility was extremely poor due to a dense fog. After a long time in the car they approached a very hidden area, where they couldn't imagine finding anyone but then, just in front of them they spotted a wooden house with a large window facing south into the forest. The lights were on.

They all wondered if anyone could be hiding out in this strange and secret place. Breska stopped the SUV and turned off the car's lights. They began to approach very slowly in neutral, as they had hit a steep drop-off, so as not to cause noise. They were already barely thirty feet from the house. They all began to sweat.

Breska parked right under a tree that camouflaged the car well. They almost ran into it given the penetrating darkness. Gesturing to each other to remain silent they left the SUV and began to remove their investigation equipment. The lawyer took out his Colt gun, which accompanied him every time he went to a dangerous case. Deep in his heart he felt sad for the senator's situation, but he had to fulfill the Mafia's demand, he already knew what could happen to him if he did not.

The detectives advised Breska to stay by the side of the car, close to the branches of the tree, and out of sight. As a lawyer, he had no role as an investigator, he was only to be present to see everything and to account for it later. Bryan, Lucas and Antonio split up. It did not look like there were any people in the house since there was no noise or obvious signs of life. They were all impressed by the magical and hidden place they had found. At the same time, they were beginning to suffer from anxiety and fear.

Bryan and Lucas checked around the back of the house while Antonio examined the front door with great care. He could see nothing inside through the huge glass windows. The three of them met at the front door. They decided in a split second that Bryan should enter the house. He was carrying his .38 revolver. Lucas and Antonio stayed close to the front door, behind their partner-in-chief.

Bryan used a master key to open the door very delicately, making sure that there was no one inside, it was just all that it seemed. He managed to open it after a few eternal seconds, pushing the door very slowly, like when one walks back home after a hard day's work.

He entered the main hall; the light was still on. Nothing was visible. He started walking to the kitchen, there was no one there either. The bedrooms and the living room were empty. Just then he ran into Antonio and Lucas, who had come in looking for their boss.

"Fuck, what a scare you gave us, Bryan!"

Their hearts felt as if they were beating at two hundred beats per minute. They all looked at each other in surprise and alarm. In Senator Warrent's wooden house, as they called it, there was not a soul.

Bingo! They found some personal belongings. They felt better knowing that they were in the right place. It made them excited. But where had the senator gone? Bryan, Antonio and Lucas decided to set up microphones in several places in the house: in the living room, the kitchen, the living room and the bedroom. They also placed the hidden recording cameras at the front door and in the main areas of the house. Once the work was done, Bryan went to see Breska to tell him what had happened.

The lawyer was very uneasy about the time that had elapsed since his colleagues left, but convinced himself that their taking so much time meant they had found something. So Breska waited impatiently.

Bryan approached the side of the tree cautiously to tell the lawyer, "Warrent is not in the house. The tortoise has left his lair so, we've set up hidden microphones and recording cameras to locate him. Don't worry, we'll soon have him by the balls."

The lawyer was mulling everything over. He said to the detective, "Let's get out of here immediately, Bryan, good job. Call the others quickly while I start the SUV and communicate what happened to the clan."

While Bryan went to find his colleagues, Breska called Captain Lucky Russo. The lawyer was very guarded when talking to the mobsters, and when he picked up the phone he told him in a very calm manner, "Lucky, the tortoise is located, he should not be far from home, we have found the site."

Lucky brought out his genius, "You must find him, that was the damn plan. What do you mean by, 'he isn't far away? I recommend you find him for your own good, you idiots!"

Breska, who knew how to deal with his clients in these situations, used his mediating skills and wise mind with the mobster, and said, "Lucky, let us do our job, we know where we are moving and what we have to do, I'll let you know as soon as we locate him, don't worry, we're close."

"For your sake, find him, otherwise I'll destroy your asses so hard that you won't even be able to sit down."

"Easy, boy, we'll find him."

Lucky had serious doubts about their ability.

Liam had been brooding ever since he heard news of the volcanic eruption. He had just wanted to protect himself during this time. The solitude in a lost forest gave him time to think, like a prisoner serving a life sentence. And like a prisoner he had constructed a 300 foot tunnel, just below his house, to hide from the mafia and the volcano, should either appear at his door. The tunnel was not visible above ground. He had created almost a second home away from any lurking danger. The senator was being very astute. Seeing this death up close had brought out the best in him. It was impressive what this man could do. There he was lying down with his pair of German Shepherds, enjoying the beautiful wild boar. He was very calm, knowing that no one would find him down there, not even the lava could get him. Thus far it seemed to be passing by but not coming too close.

But how had it been possible to build that long and unusual tunnel? When death is at one's heels, it is surprising what one can achieve. One's deepest and most hidden survival skills can come out...

Liam would generally only use the tunnel to transport food to his wooden house. But he had even prepared a sleeping area in case he had to remain down there for any length of time. There was no sunlight, only a few small lamps placed to give passage from one end of the tunnel to the other.

The gangsters got down to work with the news. Since the consigliere had passed on the information to Lucky, the underworld members were already preparing the weapons deposited in the house by the military convoy and by the gangsters, brought in the American plane commanded by Sergeant Thomas Cook. They loaded ammunition into assault rifles, carbines and M16 rifles with rifled sights. The gangsters had some silencers in their hands, and now they cleaned the grenade launchers and the weapons. Captains Lucky, Maranzzano and the hitman Gianluca were happy. So were soldiers Pimponassa and Gamberra. They were more prepared than a military squad in a war, or so it seemed. They were waiting to receive orders.

Capo Bernardino contacted Lucky to relay the following message to Gianluca, "You know I trust you, give that pig what he deserves. Have no mercy on him. He deserves to end up in a dumpster."

Lucky, while whispering in his ear, added, "Finish him off, don't give him any escape. Eliminate him."

The gangsters played poker to pass the time before the fun began. They eagerly awaited the *Lupara Bianca*, as the Mafia called such bloody acts. They entertained themselves by cooking classic Italian sausages and meatballs made of pork and tomato sauce because of course, mafiosi also love to cook and to eat good food.

They were waiting for the consigliere's call. The mobsters' SUV was loaded with some of the weapons brought by Sergeant Thomas Cook. The volcanic lava was advancing faster than expected and was spilling over the bushes and fields of banana plants, destroying anything in its path. It was getting closer and closer to the houses of the city of Laguna, where its citizens were beginning to abandon their lifelong homes and businesses. It was the greatest tragedy that a volcano had caused in a very long time.

The eruption had several vents within the main cone. The opening of a fifth mouth had increased the flow of magma to the surface, causing the lava to flow out, and soon it would reach the sea. However, this traumatic natural situation did not cross the minds of the gangsters, who had one goal and had to execute it, above everyone and everything, even with a tremendous volcano erupting near them. The wooden houses in which all were hiding out were not going to be exempt from the tremendous advance of the lava. It was like a gigantic wave caused by a tsunami and the Mafia's men had no immunity from its devastating power.

Warrent hurried through his subterranean passage with food for himself and his dogs. They were starving and couldn't hold out much longer. He reached his wooden house by a hidden ladder, which led through a small mound of stones. He slowly ascended and checked around him to ensure that there was no one around. He went to the door of the house, opened it, not noticing anything strange, everything was in order, as it had been when the cleaning staff had cleaned it prior to his arrival.

He saw a call from his daughter Olivia on his cell phone. He collapsed, not expecting to ever see that number on his phone at all. Blurred and nervous, he picked up the phone wanting to talk to her.

"Warrent, or whatever your name is, Dad, Mom is in bad shape because of you, you abandoned us without explanation and we are here in New York, not knowing what to do or where to go. You have betrayed us, you have betrayed the people who love you, Dad...."

Warrent, encouraged by the call, set out to be a compassionate and empathetic person, then told his daughter with a heavy heart, "Olivia, honey, I had to come here to avoid being found, I am not to blame for anything. They have set out to accuse me of a failed vote and I had nothing to do with it, it was the other two senators, not me. It is a mistake. My life and yours may be in danger. Do you understand now?"

Olivia, attentive to the conversation, stood her ground, calmly said, "Mom is willing to go to the FBI and the DEA with almost every piece of paper she has on the mob and your shenanigans unless you come to New York urgently, she's giving you the last warning, she doesn't even want to talk to you, Dad."

Warrent was firm in his innocence, he told her nervously,

"I haven't done anything, honey, it's a big mistake to be implicated in something I haven't done. I think they're trying to kill me." He could no longer find a way to address his daughter, his desperation was boiling over.

Olivia finally told him, "Dad, we are not going to help you, you deserve the worst, I don't love you anymore, you have let me down and you have put us in danger with your lies and deceit. Now Mom will go to the FBI to denounce your dealings with those people and your friend the lawyer." She hung up the phone without allowing her father to answer.

It was unthinkable that a fourteen-year-old girl would talk this way and be so sure of what she was saying, it was a case to analyze in college. Liam, as he was now called, didn't know where to put himself or what to do.

That conversation was recorded on both hidden cameras and microphones, which remained at the disposal of the detectives and, therefore, of the Mafia. What would the Mafia do now? So far, the FBI and the DEA had no knowledge of the senator's racketeering, extortion, drug trafficking, prostitution and illegal gambling activities with his trusted colleagues, the Mafia and other New York politicians. No one had dared to go to them. It could be the beginning for law enforcement to investigate the senator and his associates, including the mob. A sacrifice could be expected.

Jolanta went to the FBI office in New York. She was eager to tell of her husband's vicissitudes, in revenge for his deceitful rebuff and for having cut himself off from his family in such a sudden manner. She didn't believe her husband even in her sleep. She thought he was in the thick of it. She had proof of it, or at least she thought so. She was met by detectives Mr. Malone and Miss Brigitte of the mafia-related squad, who worked for the New York City anti-mafia and anti-corruption office.

Bryan, Antonio and Lucas were about to watch the hidden camera recordings and listen to recordings made in the senator's house. Would they find the evidence they were looking for, or would they stumble upon recordings of unprecedented and unexpected content?

"To ignore the unexpected (even if it were possible) would be to live without opportunity, without spontaneity, and without the rich moments of which life is made.

Stephen Covey

Chapter VII
Serendipity

"What one man can invent, another can discover."

Sherlock Holmes

THE DETECTIVES WERE IN THE DINING ROOM of the house rented by the Mafia. It was windy as hell outside. The news from the La Palma volcano was disappointing. The lava was advancing faster than expected and the detectives did not want to continue in that place so far away and isolated from civilization. The smoke and dust of the ashes already in the houses and businesses of La Palma. It was a novel and extreme situation for all the inhabitants of the city.

Breska was leaning on a railing on the terrace of the house, caught up in his thoughts. He waited impatiently for his colleagues to start up the recording equipment in the senator's house. Bryan was trying to put the recording in digital format. He finally got it right and immediately called the lawyer with a hopeful shout. Lucas and Antonio were very excited as the lawyer joined the meeting. They all looked at each other as seriously as if they were in a Western. Their piercing glances betrayed that something big was about to go down. Bryan played the recording and they heard nothing. He replayed it. That didn't work either.

Breska could wait no longer, he exclaimed in despair, "What have you assholes done, you can't hear shit!"

The lawyer did not swear often, he was very polite and correct in his language, but since he began working for the mafia his language had coarsened. He insisted again, sharply, "What did you guys record? You can't hear anything, you idiots. If this doesn't get fixed, we'll be murdered and thrown in a ditch."

"Wait, Breska, you're impatient, this has to work," Bryan told him.

He performed several checks with the applications on the laptop. He restarted the computer.

"Now, boys, you can see the recording! Computer shit!"

Now Breska was no longer protesting, he was concentrating. The audio recording from the microphones could not be heard clearly, it could be seen that with the seismic movements of the earthquakes days ago, some sound quality had been lost, but something could be heard.

However, the video recording was crystal clear. It showed Senator Warrent talking on his cell phone in his living room. Everyone was stunned. None of them recognized Warrent. The facelift had paid off. Breska pointed to the others in despair,

"That is not our man. He resembles him in height and physique, but from the face I know that is not the senator."

Bryan also did not recognize him from the information Breska had given him as part of the background on the Warrent case. He asked,

"And who can this man be? The only person who can be around here is the senator according to the information we have, guys."

Lucas was a detective in the purest traditional style, he pointed out, with pleasure, "That has to be the senator, it can't be anyone else, there's nothing here but forest, bushes and animals. From the information we have, I'm sure it's him."

"And who can it be if it is not the senator? It can't be anyone else," Antonio said emphatically.

The three detectives were trying to fix the audio so that the conversation Warrent was having could be heard. Bryan hit the nail on the head with the fixes. Finally, they could hear but not as well as hoped. From the result of the audio and video recording the investigators drew the following conclusions: that Warrent had spoken to someone, apparently a girl, where they could deduce that he left them and that they were in New York; that someone was willing to go to the FBI and the DEA to denounce him. They still couldn't confirm if it was their man or not. They had very little information to pass on to the Mafia. In addition, when they all left the senator's house quickly, they did not have time to take personal belongings to gather more data. In short, this was a disaster in the eyes of the Mafia.

Breska addressed Bryan boldly, "What a botched job you've done, detective, it couldn't be more mediocre."

The American responded vehemently, "Lawyer, for now, and I say for now, we have very little. In a few days we will have what we are looking for, don't worry, you are too impatient."

The lawyer did not have the same opinion as the detective, he told him with displeasure, "I thought you were more effective and faster, I tell you honestly. The Mafia will not accept this information, they will send you straight to hell."

"Really, Breska, don't worry, we'll find him. Rest assured," the detective told him emphatically.

The lawyer left the meeting and went to the terrace to reflect.

The Mafia was focused on nothing but finding the senator, and fast. The mob would not forgive him for the failure of the vote. The underworld was unable to obtain the license for the production of the film, they had lost a multi-million-dollar movie deal, no less than some five billion dollars thrown down the drain.

The Mafia was clear, they had lost their license because of the senator. For them he was an idiot. He had to be eliminated, even if it was a traumatic decision. The Mafia was not in the habit of assassinating politicians or policemen. The Godfather, as he was called by the members of the Mafia clan, the Boss of Bosses or capo dei capi, had already given the go-ahead to the Mafia commission, which had met expressly with the other bosses of the other families to make this decision, but not without the rage and anger of some of these Mafia bosses.

Almost everything hung on the detectives' information, although the mob, as expected, had already taken its own steps in ascertaining the senator's whereabouts. Through their associates in New York's Chinatown, they had information on Warrent. But this information was not entirely reliable because it came from another family in the city, the Lucini Mafia clan, which controlled almost all the drug trafficking and part of the gambling in New York.

The Lamborda clan was one of the most important families in this city. They had contacts everywhere including banks, state agencies, the FBI, DEA, CIA, the AFT and in the main state decision-making bodies. Any decision taken was instantly known by this mafia group. Being a mafia associate required an unequivocal commitment to unconditional membership in the underworld. Betrayal of this deal was paid for with death in most cases.

The Mafia functioned like a big company. The boss was like the executive of a corporation. They were governed by the principle of hierarchy. Ranking in the Mafia was a matter of honor and merit. Becoming a boss was identified with carrying out a few murders within the group. In general, one became a boss by having killed another boss or an essential member of the underworld. Everything was absolutely hermetic in this sense. There was no fissure, or so they believed.

The decision to assassinate Warrent was authorized by the Godfather and there was no turning back. It had been celebrated in grand style at the club "Las Mariposas", owned by a shell company created by the consigliere. The lawyer had to obey Godfather Bernardino's orders, even if he did not like them.

But information from the detectives was not forthcoming. The Mafia contact for this action would have to get to work so that the data on the senator's real location would arrive soon.

Bryan, Antonio and Lucas could not find the senator. Breska was getting impatient once again. It did not cross his mind to not find his old friend. He felt extremely sorry about the situation. But this was working for the Mafia. It was painful for him.

From the audio and video recording made at the senator's house the detectives had found no convincing evidence to take to the mob. They only had a sparse recording where someone, apparently a girl, had been talking to the senator, that the senator had left her and that she was with someone else in New York. They learned that she was willing to go to the FBI and the DEA to file a complaint, but they had no further information. They did not recognize the senator either. There were so many unknowns and unsolved mysteries.

That's why Breska was pretty pissed off with Detective Bryan. The lawyer pondered it all on the terrace of the house. It was hot and his brain was smoking. It didn't cross his mind not to find the senator. Added to this had been the eruption of the volcano, which was steadily descending down the mountainside. It felt as if they were in a race with the volcano. They simply couldn't leave without finishing their job. They were very clear about what could happen to them if they did not finish it.

Breska was more aware than the detectives. He wondered if they really understood. The lawyer approached the detectives, who were in the dining room.

"Bryan, you can't stand still, damn it! If Warrent doesn't show up within forty-eight hours, we're in trouble. This is serious. It's really fucked up."

Bryan brought out his detective streak to tell the lawyer, "Breska, we do have something and it's hard to believe you haven't noticed. From the recording we know that it is a girl who has almost certainly spoken to the senator. Doesn't Warrent have a daughter named Olivia who is in New York? If we get to the daughter we will have the solution, we will have bait for our fish. We should go back to the senator's house to check the connection to the recording cameras and find out for sure. Someone has to be at the senator's house if it's not Warrent. Is that okay with you guys?"

Lucas and Antonio agreed. The lawyer also agreed with Detective Bryan and, moreover, proposed, "I'll tell Lucky and Maranzzano that we're on the verge of unwrapping the candy bar, that we have the senator in our sights. With that, they'll sleep easy and give us a break. Do you guys agree?"

"Okay, Breska," all three replied.

Breska got the SUV so they could drive to what they thought of as the senator's house. Bryan, Lucas and Antonio got into the vehicle with some of their gadgets and gizmos. The lawyer started it up. As usual, every time they drove on these hair-raising roads, they were all very focused, looking at the difficult cliffs and endless slopes.

Breska insisted that he should talk to the mobsters to tell them that they had almost found the senator. He had to tell them in the most subtle way, as was required of a Mafia consigliere. That, to a large extent, was what the underworld had enlisted his services for.

Was that reciprocal or intimidating on the part of the mob to hire the lawyer? The lawyer was an expert in handling tense and confusing situations, he had enough mental maturity and ability to say things at the right time, with confidence and security.

Bryan, for his part, playing the role of head detective, gave them all an overwhelming assurance that they were going to find Senator Warrent's whereabouts. In addition, Lucas and Antonio had done their homework on finding all the information on the senator and his daughter Olivia in order to offer more leads. After all, nowadays, in addition to the latest digital technology investigation devices, they had a multitude of resources through the internet, social networks, WhatsApp messages, mobile applications and software. Research had come a long way and was improving with each passing day, as was medicine. Everyone was chatting in the dark of the night.

It looked like a haunted and dark forest. When the conversation seemed to be at its calmest, suddenly the car began to zigzag as Breska lost control. After a few seconds of alarm he managed to regain control and bring the SUV to a halt. Everyone was very frightened in the silence of the night.

They stared at each other, lost in thought, with nothing to say. Their faces were long and they were frowning. This was serious. Breska got out of the car to see if he could find out what had happened. The right front tire was flat but they weren't going fast enough to get a flat tire.

Bryan, Lucas and Antonio got out of the car. They could see almost nothing on that dark night. They were almost without light. Only the lights of the car, which were still on, illuminated them.

What could it have been, a mere puncture or something intentional? If so, by whom? Everyone looked at each other expectantly, very uneasy. They were already considering an attack by someone, perhaps someone had set a trap for them, they thought.

Putting suspicions aside, they set about fixing the wheel. It was simpler than it seemed. The car had some foam in the trunk that was poured on the puncture and they could drive again. But this was a temporary solution, a mechanic would have to check it and they were far away from anywhere. They continued with that fixed wheel but something about the car did not feel the same now. There were clicks on the side of the front right door. Bryan was minding his own business. All he had in mind was getting to Warrent's house again. He was obsessed with it.

There was no time to lose. Besides, as the inveterate detective that he was, he only thought about finding the senator, he took it for granted he would find him. It was a maxim of private investigation, to find the investigated.

"Nothing is more misleading than an obvious fact."

Sherlock Holmes

Chapter VIII
The Test

"To a great mind, nothing is small."

Sherlock Holmes

THE RELENTLESS SEARCH FOR WARRENT was becoming the daily chore of the three detectives. They were like Russian KGB spies. They had a mere thirty yards to go before they reached the wooden house. Again, they spotted the lights on in the house. They all flushed with the thrill of the chase.

"There we have it!" Bryan exclaimed happily.

"Don't get excited! We don't know if anyone will be there this time. You are naive. Until the tortoise is in its lair, we have nothing," said Breska calmly. "What a bunch of inept idiots you are. You're seeing the skin of the bear before you catch it,"

"He's there, it's there for sure," said Lucas.

"I can't believe you're such an asshole, Lucas, we haven't found anyone yet and you're already reaping the rewards. How deluded you are," said the lawyer grumpily.

Antonio was the most realistic of the three detectives, "He's right, we haven't come up with anything yet. Lucas, you're an asshole."

They finally arrived at the house. They had turned the car lights off just a few minutes before to avoid being seen. They left the SUV parked next to the same tree as before. From there they could not be seen. They got out of the car, all four of them. Breska told them he would wait by the side of the vehicle. The lawyer was very uneasy. Bryan, Lucas and Antonio were about to enter the house. Bryan through the front door and the other two through the back door. Bryan was armed. Detectives Antonio and Lucas were surprisingly unarmed. Bryan took a breath before entering. He checked that there was no noise inside the house. Still, he was sweaty and nervous. He picked up his skeleton key again to open the door. He began to open it very slowly, as slowly as an octogenarian in delicate health.

Lucas and Antonio went through the back door, which was close to a very steep ravine, they were at risk of falling. With another master key they opened the back door. All they could see was darkness.

Bryan opened the door observing a certain silence around him. He entered the house. The slowness of his legs was noticeable. He saw no one in the main living room. He went to the kitchen where he spotted food scraps lying on the floor. He kicked at them and continued to the bedroom. He found no one. Suddenly, he heard noises in the kitchen. He shuddered. Fear came over him, even with the gun in his hand. He was going there slower than a turtle. He just wanted to get out of there. Suddenly, Lucas and Antonio appeared.

Bryan said to them very angrily, "You fools, I could have killed you. Why didn't you let me know you were here ?"

"Boss, if we gave you a shout, someone would have discovered us," said Antonio in a self-absorbed manner. Lucas nodded emphatically.

"Let's see if you'll be more careful another time. I can't take you anywhere, you inept people," said Bryan, who was quite shaken.

They began to make a tour of the house. Again, they did not find the evidence they were looking for. Bryan, Lucas and Antonio were very disappointed. They were trying to locate the senator and couldn't find him. "What now?" they wondered. It was impossible that the senator was not in the house. Where could he be? "They must have killed him," they thought.

"If he has been killed, we can get rid of the dead body," said Bryan cheerfully.

Breska watched the time pass by the tree. When his colleagues did not return he decided to go and find them. He saw his colleagues waving their arms and gesticulating in the distance. He expected the worst. He arrived and banged loudly on a table at the entrance of the house.

"You idiots, we're screwed! What the hell did I hire you to work for the mafia for? You are worthless! You haven't found a single convincing piece of evidence for us to pass on, we're really screwed, I'm serious, you just like to barbecue and play cards. Wasting time is what you do. I'm going to make decisions ipso facto," said the lawyer in a very angry tone.

Bryan brought out his optimism again by addressing the consigliere in a friendly tone, "We will find the senator without any doubt, your problem is that you have no patience."

"Lack of patience I...? The impatient ones are them as things are, since at any moment they will eliminate us," the lawyer pointed out. "If you guys really are such a bunch of morons, our job and duty now will be to convince the Mafia that none of us should have our heads blown off. We've been at this for a long time and we haven't found anything worthwhile. But I'll take care of this, as always," the lawyer said, crestfallen. Breska was starting to get upset, his thoughts were turning to how he could resolve the issue with his exclusive client, the Mafia. There was a blood pact and the deal with the underworld could not be reneged on. The lawyer had planned to contact Captains Lucky and Maranzzano to pass on the news they had about the senator, but he did not know how to proceed now.

He didn't know whether to tell them directly what they had found. If he did that, he ran a serious risk that the mob would make some disparate determination for the detectives. And this could mean the beginning of the end for his colleagues. The mob would not go up against Breska. On the other hand, he thought of giving up a white lie to the Mafia, where he would try to delay the news he was getting from the investigation with the detectives. This was most unlikely, especially since the Mafia knew everything before any of them did.

Breska was at a crossroads. He didn't know what to do. He didn't have much time to think. He had to act quickly for his sake and that of his fellow detectives. The news from the volcano was truly disturbing. The lava was advancing, reaching homes and businesses in some areas of the island of La Palma. This was a tragedy for the island. Breska saw on Google Maps that from the area where the wooden house in the forest was located to the lava flow there was already only about twenty miles. An untenable situation was developing for Breska, his colleagues, the senator and the gangsters. They were all at risk of being caught by the erupting volcano, by the force of nature. Their lives were in more danger from the volcano than the Mafia.

Around the middle of October 2021, the lava emission from the volcano was increasing. Many roads were cut off and two lava flows were coming down at high speed. The arrival of this volcano to the lagoon and its forest was a matter of a few days. Everyone was there, each one doing what he could. The arrival of the lava flow would cause real problems to the mobsters, the detectives and the senator.

Liam's German Shepherds were hungry. So was the senator. It had been many hours since his last visit to the wooden house through the underground tunnel he had built. And he had to get out of his hiding place again. It was like a real kidnapping of sorts, which had taken place without the presence of the kidnapper on site. That's how Liam felt, as if his life and that of his family had been kidnapped. He had been cornered by the mob. This was happening to him, the one who had accidentally got into bed with the Mafia. Liam had been very touched by that phone call from Olivia. It was on his mind constantly. He felt as if smoke was coming out of his ears.

News from the lagoon confirmed the lava's advance towards the forest house and there was no sense of stopping. On the contrary, more and more lava was flowing along the flattened platforms at the foot of the slopes, very close to the senator's house. He got the information when he went through the tunnel that linked to the kitchen of his house, where there was still WIFI coverage. There he began to fill a plastic bag, where he was putting the food for his beloved dogs, the only ones he had left in the entire world for now, and perhaps forever.

Liam started talking loudly in the kitchen. He could almost be heard throughout the forest. He was always a great lover of music; he couldn't help it. He used rhetoric like the Romans on the podium, as if it were a deep Flamenco musical tone he raised his voice higher and higher,

"Why the hell am I here?" he hummed the lyrics to a made-up opera song. "I find myself trapped in a life without equal, my family has abandoned me, I can't live without them, more I can't do here, fucked up in a dungeon and with nothing and nobody, how unfair life is, the only thing I have left is loneliness," the senator sang solemnly. At times, it was like Mozart . He was bringing out the deepest part of his being with that song. He continued, "I'm locked up here, stuck in a dark and gloomy tunnel. Hiding from the mafia so they don't kill me, just tucked in a dungeon under the wooden house where I live, dragged through life..."

Liam was exhausted by the singing. The senator had no idea of the existence of the hidden video and audio recording cameras, or the microphones installed in the kitchen. In that place he was sure he would never be found by the members of the Mafia.

He left to go back to his secret place with the food for the dogs and to satisfy his own eager appetite. He had not expected that magical musical performance. He was very happy with what he had done, he never thought about what that classical music song could mean. He was dying to know. His intention was to relax as much as possible after that unpleasant phone conversation with his daughter Olivia.

But of course, everything had been recorded on the video and audio cameras and microphones installed in the house. Now the detectives had the evidence they were looking for. But they would find a different result than the one they were expressly looking for, it was called "serendipity", that is, finding by chance the evidence of the senator's whereabouts, not sought on purpose, and on top of that in the most unexpected and extravagant way that would ever exist. Liam did not know what was in store for him.

Capo Bernardino was supposed to meet with the Lucini family's capo to get information about the senator's whereabouts in New York City. It was all because of that talk the consigliere had with Captains Lucky and Maranzzano.

Breska had told his fellow mobsters that he needed information about the suspicious activities carried out by Warrent together with his trusted senators, the Mayor of New York City and the New York City Council, which approved land rezoning licenses in New York City.

The Lucini family was another very influential Mafia group in New York City. Their illegal activity was centered on drug trafficking as their main business. They were also involved in the gambling, prostitution, extortion and bribery of politicians in collaboration with the Lamborda family. The boss of the Lucini family was Mr. Zannini. A bloody man if ever there was one. He became the boss of that family when he murdered the previous boss of that clan.

The meeting of the capos was scheduled to take place at the Restaurant De Gretia in New York City. Zannini and Bernardino arrived at the meeting at the scheduled time in the company of their bodyguards. It was in a secret room of the restaurant, in the area reserved for mobsters. The bosses of the two most important families in New York City, holding almost total control of all the dirty and illegal businesses in New York, were going to meet. There were also other organized crime families in New York City, such as the Russian Mafia, the Japanese Yakuza and the Jamaican drug trafficking mafia. In total, there were five families that made up the so-called "Cosa Nostra" in New York City.

Bernardino invited Zannini to an exquisite meal at the restaurant. They were to collaborate to find the senator's whereabouts. They sat opposite each other at a round table, eating oysters, Italian cold meats, Sicilian wine, lobster, grilled octopus, Spanish Iberian ham and a leg of suckling lamb for each of them. To finish, a glass of brandy de Jerez and a Cohiba cigar.

During the meal, the Capo Bernardino spoke respectfully to Zannini, saying, "The senator is almost within range, he is on the Spanish island of La Palma. We know he is in a wooden house, in the forest. My men and some detectives have found him. The only thing missing is the final blow. I give you my word that within twenty-four hours he will be annihilated."

The boss Zannini put him on notice with great impetus, "Thank you for inviting me to this delicious meal, I really appreciate it. It cannot be easy for your men on the ground. I have read about the volcanic eruption. Here in New York our family is very upset that we didn't get the movie producers license through, there was a lot of money at stake, we had a lot of common interests with that movie. I am confident that tomorrow his head will be inside a freezer. We have all been fooled by this two-bit senator. We also have information on this bastard. The child of this fucker is well hidden. He is an inveterate womanizer; he loves to go out drinking with whores. Already in the club "Las Mariposas" he was doing his thing with the waitresses and the whores. At one point when he was in a private room with a whore, one of my soldiers saw him talking to someone from the FBI. He was sharing some information so they could hunt us down, so they could finish us off, these FBI bastards. It was Warrent who was betraying us, apparently he had allied himself with the FBI to get away from here and not be seen."

Bernardino was impatient, "I thank you for your words, as for this meal, it is what you deserve for our friendship. Now I ask you, my friend, are you aware that the Englishman Howard was murdered in the San José hotel because he had apparently gone off the deep end over the gambling business? That the Chinatown casino license was to be granted to one of the other families in town?

The capo replied calmly, "Bernardino, my friend, we control the drug traffic in the city, we do business in the Bronx and Brooklyn. And we do well. There, everything that smells of drugs is ours. You should respect our business just like we don't get into gambling and prostitution, which are yours. The senator deserves to have his throat slit, since he has screwed our clans a big movie business, no less than five billion dollars to be divided between the two families. It is a murder that happened to the Mafia commission, to the Big Boss, to you, and we respect you very much. For us you are the Godfather of the Mafia.

Bernardino answered very seriously, "My respects to you too. We will respect your drugs and you must respect our gambling and prostitution. The family that does not comply with this agreement will have breached this blood pact, our "Cosa Nostra"."

They both stood up from the table and shook hands firmly under the watchful eyes of their bodyguards, who were standing next to the capos' table. Both capos left the restaurant in hope.

> "Sometimes you have to play the role of an idiot
> to fool the jerk who thinks he's playing you."
>
> Marlon Brando

The Capo Bernardino informed his clan of that meeting at the restaurant. El Padrino distrusted Zannini. Deep down, all mafiosi distrusted their colleagues in the underworld. It was something common to all of them in the Mafia. The five families in New York City shared all the illegal businesses, from drug trafficking to gambling, prostitution, bribing politicians, judges, prosecutors and lawyers. They also extorted money from the city's most renowned businessmen. They ran the city as if they owned it.

At the top of these families was the Godfather, who was the capo dei capi or Boss of Bosses, the Don, who was Bernardino Mancini, boss of the Lamborda family, one of the most important families alongside the Lucini family. What happened was that when there was a lot of money at stake, the businesses of one and the other were confused, there was no more respect, there was a lot of blood, ambition, power and money prevailed over the deals between families.

In the end, it was the more powerful man, or so each Mafia boss thought, who managed the other members of the Mafia. And here disputes between organized crime families were the order of the day. The whole Mafia was called "Cosa Nostra", and they worked together as an untouchable group.

Would the FBI and DEA agents already be aware of the activities of each family as a result of the information given by Warrent? Would they have already started investigating all the mobsters? The mafia didn't know what they had behind them and that they were the most powerful, or so the underworld thought.

Jolanta was waiting for Detectives Malone and Brigitte, from the mafia-related squad of the New York City Anti-Mafia and Anti-Corruption Prosecutor's Office. Hours passed and they did not leave their superior's dark glass office. The senator's wife began to despair at the fact that they were not leaving that room, which exuded mystery and intense emotions.

Suddenly, Malone opened the door with a worried face. The news about the senator was not what the FBI police officers expected. Next, out came Brigitte heading towards Jolanta, she wanted to find out more about Senator Warrent. Both of them went to Jolanta at the same time, apologizing for the delay, and they asked her questions carefully,

"What do you have for us about your husband? The FBI will help you if you cooperate with the police. We can offer to include you in the state's witness protection plan for the safety of you and your daughter Olivia," Detective Brigitte said.

"And what does this witness protection plan consist of?" Jolanta asked doubtfully, looking at Brigitte attentively.

Malone, who was an experienced policeman with thirty years of service behind him, clarified, "You don't have to worry about anything, we will take care of everything, you will see. If you help us, we will provide a new identity for you and your daughter, of course, you will be protected and hidden, they won't find you."

"Who won't find me?" asked Jolanta with great lucidity.

Detective Malone, who saw the senator's wife slipping away from him like a poacher poaching game in a reserve, pulled in degrees of experience, "We need information. We don't know yet who is after your husband, but we have some well-founded suspicions. You would be of great help to us, and you could certainly help us solve the case. With your collaboration, everything will be easier."

Jolanta, who had learned with the senator to deal without remorse or sentimentality, laid her demands out for the officers, "I want a million dollars in an account that I will give you, a new identity for Olivia and me, a house in the Maldives surrounded by verdant gardens, the most exquisite pleasures that can fulfill my desires."

Malone and Brigitte threatened Jolanta that she could be committing the federal crime of obstruction of justice by not cooperating with the detectives, which could be punishable by imprisonment. The senator's wife, for her part, hinted that without her they would have serious difficulty solving the case. The detectives left the deal hanging, blushing, claiming they had to talk to their boss. They could not believe Jolanta's demands.

They were eager to obtain evidence about the murder of the Englishman, Howard in the Costa Rica hotel, of the murdered New York politician, linking him to the Senate vote and his group of trusted senators, as well as to her husband's shenanigans and the underworld. From what Jolanta said they could get evidence about the senator's alleged bribery and criminal activities with his group of senate colleagues and the underworld.

Here would be part of the evidence, since the Lamborda family could have bought a group of senators through Breska, in exchange for the creation by the latter of companies in tax havens for the diversion of money from the casino in Chinatown. But the gangsters still did not have the casino license, a priority assignment to the lawyer by the gangsters of the underworld. Would the Capo Bernardino, Breska and the Lamborda family be the masterminds of that operation?

Almost everything depended on the senator's location, Jolanta's statement to the FBI and that the volcano did not move too fast, which was unlikely. The mobsters were on the lookout for these events, like owls perched on a tree branch.

Liam had given himself away.

Breska stood pensively in the mobsters' house. He didn't know how to proceed with Captains Lucky and Maranzzano. He had snuck up there, excused himself to his fellow detectives, claiming that he had been called by his mobster clients to attend an urgent meeting. Bryan doubted the veracity of his claim but Antonio and Lucas were confident. The lawyer was very eager to talk to the two members of the Lamborda family. He had to resolve the concerns that he couldn't let go of.

Breska was generally a direct person, except when faced with mobsters who didn't value his life. Now he risked finding himself in a hopeless situation, he was not a man of bloodshed, but of solving problems amicably. Now he carried his worry in his heart.

He would use his diplomatic charm to captivate Lucky and Maranzzano. He would make use of his lawyerly verbiage on the stand. The Mafia captains were smoking cigarettes on the terrace of the house. They were not happy with the day's events and it showed on their faces. It was a hot night in Laguna. Both were sweating. They had to inform the capo as soon as possible of the development of events and the instructions were clear: if they did not find the senator very soon, a wave of horrendous crimes would be unleashed. Blood would begin to spill over the mountains of the island.

Breska addressed Lucky, "I am informed by the detectives that the tortoise is on the way down, I am confident that the senator will be delivered to us very soon. We are pretty sure we know where he is and what he is doing. The detectives are doing a great job."

Lucky looked at the lawyer very suspiciously and said in a challenging manner, "Breska, we have nothing yet, it's too late, you are going to be lynched by our colleagues since you are not delivering on your promise to find the senator. So really, what do we have so far, counselor?"

Breska thought fast, "We have a senator in a wooden house who is making the most of his human qualities to survive in these rocky mountains. He spoke with a girl, apparently his daughter Olivia. We are pretty clear that she is in New York. We know that someone was willing to go to the FBI and the DEA to denounce something or someone but we don't know what or who."

That she was in New York left was barely news, given that the senator had spoken to his daughter, who may have been accompanied by someone. The Mafia obviously also intended to find Olivia in New York.

Lucky responded sternly, "So you have nothing new for us. The senator should already be drowned with the fish in the sea. I am going to communicate what you inform me to the boss. Be aware of the consequences, counselor."

"Is that a threat, Lucky?" asked the lawyer boldly.

"Take it as you like, Breska, but there is no doubt that things are not going as we would like them to, and you are to blame here," the mafioso replied vehemently, "First thing tomorrow morning I'll be contacting you with instructions. The worst of it all is that that bastard Warrent is still alive and kicking, to our disgrace."

Breska, gloomy after his talk with Lucky, set off in his car from the mobsters' house as soon as possible. Now the detectives were waiting for him to take the final step. It had slipped the lawyer's mind that the car's wheel had not been fully repaired, they had just managed a temporary fix. There was a clicking sound in the repaired wheel. He was speeding along those cliffs and huge deserted mountains.

Liam was feeding his beautiful German Shepherds. He had returned to the subterranean tunnel with some food gathered from the house kitchen. He was also carrying dog food. The dogs jumped desperately until their heads hit the earthen ceiling of that horrifying and secret place. Their tongues were so long that they would need two or three buckets full of water to quench the thirst they showed, besides, in that place there were high temperatures and the dogs did not stop moving from one side of the den to the other. They even nipped at their owner. Liam knew it was a way of playing with him. In fact, the dogs were beginning to look malnourished, they were getting thinner, and you could almost see their ribs. Liam spent the hours of his life looking at emails, WhatsApp, mobile apps, internet and watching TV, he had all the time in the world for it. In practice, it was as if he was locked up in a federal prison.

He did not come to any positive conclusion about the real betrayal of those friendly senators. He had everything prepared and organized for that vote in the senate to get the film license and make that wonderful movie in the Hollywood studios, in the premises of the Mafia family. He would get the longed-for money with his friend Breska. His mind was driven towards the

Mafia, with these you could not make deals that would not be fulfilled, he knew what could happen to him, but he did not know to what extent. He could not even think about the dire consequences of that beautiful opera song, he did it fully relaxed to escape from the unpleasant conversation with his daughter Olivia. He was deteriorating physically and mentally due to his strange situation, far from any civilization. Quite the opposite of what he was used to. His mood had become bleak, life was no longer the same for this prestigious senator.

And between thoughts, in the twists and turns of his deranged head, he began to relate the failed outcome of the vote to the lawyer Breska, his friend, the one he would never have mistrusted. Already thoughts were going in all directions. What he did know for sure was that he was there, hidden and concealed, waiting for his unknown future.

He wept and felt self-pity to an aberrant degree, more tears fell from his eyes than from a newborn baby. All he had left was the comfort of his beautiful German Shepherds. Man's best friends, or so the wise say.

The news from the volcano was not positive. The lava was getting closer and closer to the forest of Liam's wooden house. It was already only three miles away.

It was October 21, 2021. The lava from the volcano's lava flows, which had destroyed homes and shops in Laguna, was drifting into the mountains, and was approaching the site of Warrent's wooden house. The spread of toxic gasses, dust and large smoke caused by the two lava flows in the Laguna neighborhood would soon reach the senator. The lava had caused the abandonment of at least two hundred people in the Laguna neighborhood and the destruction of many homes and dwellings of the palm tree population.

The senator, Breska, the mobsters, and the detectives were in serious danger of being disturbed by the crushing lava, which would soon reach their homes through the forest and mountains. Breska conveyed to his fellow detectives the concerned tone of the conversation with Lucky and Maranzzano. The lawyer urgently summoned everyone upon arriving from the mobsters' house. They were in the dining room waiting to listen carefully to the lawyer's words. The lawyer sat down on the sofa and put a cushion behind him.

Now calmer, he told Bryan, Lucas and Antonio that he was going to call a trusted mechanic in the area to fix the SUV's wheel, as it was banging on the rim and he didn't trust that it would stay on. He feared it could break at any moment and cause an accident.

So he called a trusted mechanic on his cell phone at the same time as he was talking to them. He arranged with the mechanic to come to the house in the woods to fix his car tire in a few hours. Once they heard the lawyer talking on his cell phone with the mechanic, Bryan said to the lawyer, "I suppose you have already spoken to Lucky and Maranzzano about finding the senator. What did they tell you, Breska?"

The consigliere, felt as if he were in a sea of doubts, and so he avoided of the chief detective's question, "I can only tell you one thing, guys, there can be no more delay in locating Warrent, we have been given an ultimatum, in which I include myself, as the person responsible for your recruitment: either we find the senator or they will kill us all. It's as simple as that. We're working for the mob, folks, don't forget, this is not just any client. It's live or die."

Lucas and Antonio saw the devil in the lawyer's face and, for the first time since they were in the forest, they took the initiative to locate the senator. Lucas said, "Let's hurry to the senator's house and have Breska wait for the mechanic to fix the SUV's wheel. Bryan and Antonio nodded emphatically. All the detectives took the 4x4. Bryan put his .38 revolver in the glove compartment. He drove up the mountains at breakneck speed and arrived at the senator's house with the lights off so as not to create suspicion. Surprisingly, they found the lights of the house turned off. Maybe Warrent had left. They got out of the car, very slowly, so as to make no noise. It was a walk similar to that of a worm on the branch of a tree. Only silence could be heard in that Laguna Forest. There were no seismic symptoms in those mountains now.

They agreed that Bryan would enter through the front door and Lucas and Antonio through the back door, all exercising extreme caution. Anything could happen, was Bryan's message to his colleagues. Bryan was heading towards the front door with his .38 revolver, gripped in his right hand. He raised his hand in a protective gesture. He took cover just as he passed the small entrance to the house, it was a kind of room next to the main door of the house, he stood for a few seconds and prepared to enter.

Lucas and Antonio were about to enter through the back door, they took out their skeleton key and tiny flashlights. Lucas turned the key and opened the door. There was no sound, total silence. They were fearful of this cop game. They followed the corridor, illuminated by that small light until they found a light switch, Lucas pressed it and two big lamps at the bottom of the apartment turned on. They both felt more relaxed now.

"The light was not cut off," said Lucas.

"So there must be someone here!" exclaimed Antonio with fear.

Suddenly, voices were heard in an adjoining room. It was Bryan cursing that there was no one in the house

"Come, come, come, boys!" he called urgently for the presence of his colleagues in the room. "Let's assume that the senator has left since this is the third time we haven't found anyone," said the chief detective emphatically.

Then he remembered the microphones and hidden recording cameras installed by them a few days ago. That could be the evidence they were looking for with such perseverance.

And what was Breska doing at this time?

"There is no combination of events which the intelligence of a man is not capable of explaining."

Sherlock Holmes

Chapter IX
Crossfire

"Persistence is often the best ally of a detective."

Lara Adrian

JOLANTA WAS DEALING WITH THE FBI. The amount of information they could extract from Senator Warrent's wife was impressive but the director of the bureau, Mr. Sloan, had not received authorization from his superiors to make the million-dollar payment she had demanded.

The FBI detectives did not have it all their own way, the mere fact that she was demanding anything without offering any guarantee of information was entirely out of their comfort zone. This unexpected situation was beyond their control. Before the FBI can seek funding for witness protection, law enforcement has to assess the threat or potential for danger. This assessment includes an analysis of the extent to which the person or persons making the threats appears to have the resources, intent and motivation to carry them out, and how credible and serious the threats appear to be. When threats are deemed credible and witnesses request police assistance, witness protection funds can be used, which helps law enforcement keep witnesses safe and ensure that witnesses appear in court and give testimony.

In criminal organization cases, they can also provide witnesses with a full new identity, particularly where law enforcement sees a serious risk of witness intimidation.

The FBI did not know how to proceed with Jolanta. There were some clear truths to her claims, but they were not necessarily useful to the investigation. They knew they were in a desperate situation. The senator's wife knew how to handle herself in these dealings having learned from Warrent over the fifteen years they'd been together. She had amassed much experience in how to negotiate successfully as well as a good idea of his suspicious activities.

Sloan, as head of the FBI investigation, began to take a stand with the senator's wife. He summoned her to the main office in New York at 10 am. Jolanta showed up at the appointed time, looking friendly. Sloan was late as his earlier meeting overran but he did not keep her waiting more than ten minutes. He asked her to wait while he read over documents taken from Malone and Brigitte's office. Sloan had a serious look on his face, as if he was worried.

He came in from the next office with some papers under his arm and said to Jolanta, "We need you to collaborate with us in the investigation of the case. Your information will provide us with conclusive evidence of your husband's involvement in certain criminal activities with undesirable people. If you cooperate with us, our detectives will do the same with you. I do not want to go into other legal matters that do not interest us."

Jolanta told him flatly, "If you pay me the agreed amount and give my daughter and me new identities, I will give you the information you need. Don't mess with me, detective."

Sloan was an old dog in these dealings, in the spirit of reaching an understanding that was good for both parties he told her, "We are in a position to offer you five hundred thousand dollars now, since we know of your honesty and you will not deceive us, or so we believe. We have done our homework on you. Once the review of your information on your husband has been completed, we will pay the rest of the money depending on the information you provide us. The new identity, the brand-new house and moving you and your daughter to the Maldives will be done after the trial. We must catch these damned people. During the judicial process you will be protected by our best federal agents. We want to ensure your presence at the trial as the main witness in the case. This is what I can offer you. We need each other to clear up the whole mess. What do you say, Jolanta?"

"What will become of Olivia?" Jolanta didn't trust the FBI. "She's a fourteen-year-old girl who is not guilty of anything. She is my everything."

Sloan reassured her, "The best thing for you is to collaborate with us. If you refuse to testify you will be in trouble with the law, as you know, since you know a lot about your husband. Remember, you'll help us solve the case for us and we could put that scum behind bars."

Jolanta was perplexed by his evasiveness to the question about her daughter, "If something happens to my daughter, detective, I will denounce the entire FBI, including you, I don't care what happens to me, but a fourteen-year-old girl is untouchable, do you understand?

Sloan drew on his extensive experience in this type of case, "The state will shatter these bastards, don't worry about your daughter, she will be in the best hands."

"Tomorrow I will send you my account number so you can make the payment. I hope I don't have any problems, detective, I'm going to start trusting you," the senator's wife finally agreed.

The murder of the Englishman Howard in the Riu Guanacaste hotel in San José, Costa Rica, was starting to give the FBI a real headache. They had been investigating it for some time and had not been able to find any convincing evidence.

Howard's father, Mr. Smith, owned a wonderful gift and jewelry store in Brooklyn. The Smith family had emigrated from Sicily to New York in the 1960s with the intention of getting away from the Sicilian Mafia, who had threatened to kill them over money matters. A descendant of the Corleone's family had lent them the sum of ten thousand lire to pay off debts on the coffee shop that the Smith family had in Corleone.

Smith was unable to pay back the Corleone's family and they had been forced to leave town. He survived an ambush at his home where men dressed in black opened fire on everyone there. Smith's wife and other son were both shot in the head and killed instantly.

Howard's father escaped from the Corleone family by hiding in a small bunker next to the master bedroom, where he stayed for several hours. He heard them open fire against his wife and son. He took the first available flight and left for New York without knowing anything more about the killers. He swore revenge.

Howard had never been involved with the Mafia. His work as a real estate agent made him leave the coffee shop business run by his father in Sicily. When he was very young, he emigrated to the United States to make a living. In New York he set up his real estate business, close to where his father had his gift and jewelry business. The business of selling houses was not going too well, he did not have enough income to live in a good neighborhood nor the necessary contacts to make a living.

Howard, beleaguered by debts from home sales, one day received a visit from a man who occasionally wandered into his business. This man was dressed in a plaid shirt, varsity jacket, bell-bottom pants, smart shoes. This guy was into gambling and giving loans to people in need, in short, he was a loan shark. Smith had warned his son not to deal with these types of people since his own father had instilled in him from childhood, a hatred and absolute enmity for these mobsters.

Howard, contrary to the advice of his father, started doing business with this man to the point of getting involved in buying land and gambling with this guy. He started going to the Palma Boys Social Club, where mobsters and locals from Queens and Brooklyn gathered. The Mafia lent money to people in these neighborhoods who had no resources, people in great need. In exchange for lending them the money, they demanded a high percentage of their businesses. In reality the Mafia exploited Italian immigrants residing in New York City. This way, Howard became involved in Mafia business. He was related to the Lamborda family, one of the most important in the city.

1970, NEW YORK CITY.

The New York press called it the "city of fear". The five most important families of the city, the "Bonano", "Luchese", "Gambino", "Genovese" and "Colombo" families controlled New York. They had the whole city living in fear.

The U.S. Government passed the Rico Act with the aim of dismantling the Mafia. Thanks to this act, a person could be convicted for acting on behalf of another. Since there was no way to link Mafia soldiers to their bosses before the act, its passage led to the conviction of both soldiers and bosses, since the latter were untouchable until then.

Thanks to the Rico Law, a criminal organization could be convicted, where all men could be convicted even if they had not technically stained their hands with blood. The Mafia business had thrived for a hundred years in New York City. The Mafia oath or Omertà meant that witnesses would not cooperate, nor of course testify against the Mafia itself. If they testified, they paid with death. The FBI intended to use the Rico Law to crack down on the mob and the terror it was causing in the city. The FBI was paying mob informants well to try to uncover the big fish.

JANUARY 1980, NEW YORK CITY.

The early 1980s were the best years of the Mafia. Mafiosi controlled gambling, building construction, labor unions, transportation, fishing, longshoremen, hotel employees, banks, judges, prosecutors, and lawyers, among others. They controlled practically everything.

The FBI had set up a special brigade for each of the the city's five families. The gangsters partied hard, consumed alcohol and drugs as a general rule, despite their denials.

The executive committee of the Mafia, called "the commission", controlled everything the Mafia families did. What was intended was that the capos avoided disputes among all the soldiers of the criminal organization; bad blood between the families was not good for business. It was intended that all the mafiosi would benefit. A mafioso's suit might cost about two thousand dollars and shoes around one thousand dollars. The Mafia's motto was "speak now or forever hold your peace".

In 1986, a trial was held against the Mafia. Prosecutor Giuliani, who later became mayor of the city, put an end to the New York Mafia of the 1980s thanks to the Rico Law and evidence from wiretaps installed by FBI detectives. In the trial that took place, all the bosses and gangsters were convicted by a jury of the people.

OCTOBER 2021. LA LAGUNA,
CANARY ISLANDS, SPAIN.

The detectives and the lawyer had already left for the wooden house after their discouraging visit to the senator's home. Breska was very concerned. They had not yet obtained the necessary evidence of Warrent's whereabouts. The mobsters would wait no longer. He immediately asked the detectives to listen to the microphones and review footage from the hidden cameras, installed by them a few days ago. Would the evidence be there? Bryan, Antonio and Lucas thought so since the lawyer requested their presence urgently in the dining room of the wooden house.

Bryan brought the recordings with him. Everyone hopeful that this time they would have something useful. The detective pressed the button on the recorder to listen to the contents of the recordings. Finally they could hear something. It was crisp and clear, with no interruptions. As the minutes of the recording went by, the detectives took notes on the recording. At the same time, their faces began to show signs of immeasurable joy, they could not believe what they were hearing from Senator Warrent.

The detectives laughed at the contents of the recording. Breska looked more serious than the others. The senator had given himself away in the stupidest way, singing opera. It was like a fairy tale, not at all real.

When the recording finished the laughter ended and there was silence in the room. They stared at each other and frowned.

"We can't celebrate yet. We still don't have him," said Breska.

Bryan tried to convey to his colleagues how the senator's location could be found, "We have to move to the senator's house as soon as possible, Warrent must be alone and it is time to hunt him down.

Lucas, who was self-absorbed, said, "I can't believe this man was such a jerk to rat himself out."

For his part, Antonio said, "This is a crucial moment, guys, we are almost there. We will be able to collect the money we are owed. We will put in our pockets another eighty-five thousand euros. And we will comply with the mafia."

Breska took the pulse of the meeting, "We're already late. I'm going to the car, grab your things, I'll be waiting for you at the door. Don't forget your shovels, picks and buckets. Don't even go to pee. If any of you feel like it, we'll stop by the mountains in the forest, come on, we mustn't waste time."

Apparently, the lawyer had forgotten to repair the wheel of the SUV due to the urgency of the situation. Breska did not contact Lucky and Maranzzano for the time being, lest the mobsters screw up the operation.

They drove deeper and deeper into the cliffs and ravines of the forest, straight for the senator's house. They were already close to the place, all overly excited. As usual, Breska turned off the SUV's lights as they drew closer to Warrent's hiding place.

Again, the lights were off in the house. Everyone sensed that he would be found in the hideout under the kitchen. Breska was relegated to the tree next to the house in case they needed his help. The lawyer had his Colt in the glove compartment. Bryan went in the front door, Antonio and Lucas from the back. Bryan went with his gun.

The Lucini family was starting to get deeper into gambling, prostitution, extortion and bribery, the businesses controlled by the Lamborda family. They had already forgotten the blood pact between the capos. This would not sit well with the Lamborda family. The Lucini family's business was drug trafficking according to the pact made at the De Gretia restaurant. The Lamborda family was unaware of certain dirty and shady business of the Lucini family related to gambling and prostitution.

The Lucini family, with the Capo Zannini at the head, Captains Vicenzo and Giuseppe and soldiers Joe, Frank and Rocco, the latter the hitman of the Mafia group, had started to step on the Lamborda family's toes in the gambling business months ago, indiscriminately interfering in their usual business.

Certain news had reached the Lamborda family of this attitude on the part of the other main family of the city. They did not want there to be a bloodbath, but something had to happen between the two families so that there would not be a war within the Mafia itself, this was very bad for business.

But the bloody spirit among the mobsters did not disappear, like the sun that gives us light every day. Moreover, both families were upset about Warrent's disappearance and whereabouts. Apparently, the senator had made deals with both families, he had played both sides. A meeting of the capos of both families was urgently needed. They met at the behest of the consigliere in a secret location far from the city, a sort of bunker where no one could locate them.

Zannini and Bernardino were face to face, seated at a round table and accompanied by their bodyguards.

The boss, Bernardino began to speak, "Thank you for coming. We are here because your men are not respecting my family. *"Amo la mía famiglia"*. They are screwing up our business and this is not acceptable. Our pact was you get the drugs, and we played the game. I have specific information that you are playing dirty games with our gambling business and that is unacceptable. The pact between us has been broken, *"il patto é stato rotto»*.

Zannini replied, "Don, thank you for being here. We don't get involved in your gambling business, I show you my respects,." He waved his hand to the Godfather. "If there is any idiot in our family who is doing something without my permission, he will be annihilated, there will be no excuses. Business comes first. *"Gli affari vengono prima di tutto."* I promise you I will gather my family to check who that asshole is."

At all times during the conversation between the capos, their bodyguards remained impassive and concentrated.

"Business is business, if touched, a lot of blood will be spilled. *"Verra versato molto sangue"*. I respect you too, but this one is won with loyalty and honor, not with cheating. I don't want cheating, Zannini, we don't like you dealing in drugs in the Bronx and Brooklyn, however, we accept them for the sake of our families. Silver or lead, *Argento o piombo*, do you understand?"

"I will assemble my men as a matter of urgency," Zannini exclaimed, "The lying lackey who is making deals behind my back will be eliminated. We know that more is achieved with a handshake and a gun than with just a handshake. *"Parola da Zannini.""*

Both capos stood up and gave each other a hearty handshake of loyalty and left, accompanied by their impassive bodyguards. But Zannini was already considering another Mafia strategy. Zannini was a malevolent man, he only cared about getting to power. He had a great ambition for money. In reality, he did not respect anything or anyone, he did not even love himself.

Things were starting to get ugly, *"Le cose cominciavano a peggiorare"*. As soon as the meeting with Bernardino was over, he contacted Captain Vicenzo Graviano, to whom he passed on a strategic message, "You have to infiltrate the Lamborda family, we must have as much information as possible about their men, they are our enemies in business. They want to take away the bread we eat. Be very careful, they can kill you. *"Con grande cura possono ucciderti»."*

"I got it, boss, "sono io capo capo""

"Travel is like sunset, if you wait you will miss it".

Fernando Arrabal

Chapter X
The Dungeon

"If you don't go, you'll never know."

Anonymous

THE NEWS FROM THE VOLCANO WAS BECOMING INCREASINGLY UNPLEASANT. Lava was about to break through the cliffs and ravines of the forest near Liam's wooden house. It would be there in a flash.

It was October 26, 2021. The spread of toxic gasses, dust and smoke caused by the two existing lava flows in the Laguna neighborhood was now just a few miles from Liam's house.

The senator, Breska, the mobsters, and the detectives would be devoured by the crushing lava, when it reached their homes through the forest and mountains as voraciously as a crocodile devours its prey.

Would lava and magma from the volcano reach Warrent's subterranean tunnel?

The Lucini family, some time ago, had begun to sell drugs in the Bronx and Brooklyn. Cocaine was supplied by the Sinaloa (Mexico) and Medellín (Colombia) cartels. In the mountains of the city of Culiacán, Mexico, drug labs were planned to produce both cocaine and heroin. They began trafficking in the 1980s and had maintained contacts with some members of the Lucini family from then until the present day.

The way the Mexican cartels conducted business was quite similar to the Italian-American "Cosa Nostra" Mafia. DEA special agents, in collaboration with those of the FBI, were already aware of this type of drug trafficking activities. The soldiers of the narco clan had express orders from the drug lords not to talk on the phone, and not to transmit clear messages, they were required to be extremely guarded and deliberately vague in their communications. They were never to say their name in telephone conversations since it could be incriminating.

The drug gangs were defended by the army, whose members were well paid by the capos. Drugs were hidden in churches and soccer fields in a manner similar to that of narco Pablo Escobar and his gangsters in Colombia.

DEA special agents in collaboration with the FBI, intended to obtain evidence about the drug gangs in Mexico and Colombia. There were already secret conversations in the U.S. Government about Mexican and Colombian drug trafficking and its relationship with the New York Mafia.

What the DEA was trying to do was to get the soldiers of the drug traffickers to talk about their bosses, in order to obtain information about their criminal activities. The idea was to obtain information from one criminal to locate another criminal, within the same drug trafficking organization, to eventually reach the bosses. The work by the FBI in collaboration with the DEA could prove crucial in proving the relationship of the Mexican drug gangs with the New York "Cosa Nostra" Mafia, and here the Lucini family could be truly implicated. The senator had also been investigated by both the DEA and the FBI. According to them it appeared that Warrent was playing dirty with the FBI, the DEA and the Lucini family. The senator's wife could prove pivotal to the development of the investigation.

As agreed at the FBI headquarters in New York, Jolanta gave Sloan her account number so that he could wire her the sum of five-hundred thousand dollars. The chief detective was fully convinced that the deal would prove fruitful. The senator's wife had a lot of information about Warrent's activities. Living together for approximately fifteen years, she knew enough about her husband's life, his dealings with the Mafia, his relationships with the FBI, the DEA, ATF and undoubtedly with his colleagues in the Senate and other New York politicians.

Jolanta was very hurt by her husband's actions. She did not recognize him, she did not understand why he had left their New York home in such a hurry, abandoning her and their daughter. She gave no clue as to his whereabouts until that phone call, in which she reported his location on the island of La Palma, his change of name and new identity. Something big must have happened to him to carry out such nefarious acts. And the Mafia was after him.

The money arrived in Jolanta's account. As promised, she now had five hundred thousand dollars at her disposal. The witness protection plan for Senator Warrent's wife and daughter was being put into effect.

The FBI was already officially beginning to act on the potential key witness in the case. Malone and Brigitte got down to business. They wanted to put an end to the "Cosa Nostra" Mafia. The investigation would be arduous and extremely difficult.

Jolanta took a deep breath. She was already beginning to think seriously about a new life with her daughter Olivia, away from those deadly gangsters. But first she had to work with the FBI, that was the deal. There was still a long way to go and she was aware of that. The senator's wife was an intelligent, beautiful, tall, green-eyed, blond-haired woman. She was a sincere, honest, well-educated college professor, who had been raised as a Catholic in Manhattan. She came from a humble American family. She wanted the best for her young daughter, that she would not be involved in this shady and dirty business.

Malone and Brigitte were left to work out the plan of attack against the Mafia. Vicenzo Graviano, captain of the Lucini family, had express orders from the boss to infiltrate the Lamborda family. It was an essential strategy to get first-hand knowledge of the business dealings of his greatest enemies in the city. He had a special surprise in mind to carry out the capo's orders.

Breska was resting under the tree by Senator Warrent's house. He was waiting for his detectives, who were inside searching for Warrent. He was more relaxed after listening to the conversations on the video and audio camera recordings. He could not quite believe the physical change in his friend the senator, he looked nothing like the Warrent he had met in Los Angeles. He found himself pensive, pondering how his trusted senator could have gotten to this place and what dirty games he might have been up to. He felt like grabbing his Colt gun from the glove compartment with the intention of heading for the house.

Bryan opened the front door. He was armed with his revolver. Lucas and Antonio, for their part, were behind the house, right next to a huge ravine, with the objective of entering the house through the back door, hoping to finally locate the elusive senator.

Bryan went straight to the dining room. He turned on the lights of that splendid room. There was not a soul in that place. How was this possible, the chief detective asked himself over and over again.

Both the fireplace and the sofas were lonely, the cushions and tables in the living room looked as if they had not been used for a long time. What would his life be like there, Bryan wondered. In all his long professional career he had never seen a case like this. He went to the kitchen, but still found nothing relevant. The silence of the night penetrated deep inside him, as deep as the sting of a bee in the body of a human.

He used technology, he went into the application of his cell phone to listen again to the audio and video recording captured by the cameras installed there. Again, he watched the senator singing an opera: "I'm just stuck in a dungeon under the wooden house where I live, dragged by life...". The detective could not locate the dungeon under the kitchen of the wooden house, but he knew it was just a few meters away from him.

Lucas and Antonio entered through the back door with their false key. They turned on the lights in that dark room. Nothing had moved from the last time they were there. They went to the kitchen, both remembering the recording of the cameras placed a few days ago. The hiding place must be there, right in front of their worried eyes. They heard no one, just some bustle of someone moving things around. They were reassured to think it might be their boss. They finally reached the kitchen and again found no hiding place. All the appliances were in their proper place. They opened the fridge, found hardly any food, only four or five bottles of water, some soft drinks, canned dog food and some rotten vegetables. There were also some smelly, inedible bananas.

Suddenly there was a loud yell in the next room, "Antonio, Lucas, Where are you?"

They immediately recognized his voice, it was Bryan. He had found the hideout, it was not in the kitchen, rather it was in a kind of storage room, right next to it. The looks of Antonio and Lucas were very penetrating. The head detective sent a WhatsApp to Breska, he told him that they had found the dugout. Breska took off towards it with giant strides. He met up with his colleagues in a split second.

Everyone gathered at the entrance to the storage room, overtaken by the emotion of the moment, it was an extremely small room. Only two people at the most could fit in it. It was very difficult to access the place. The tunnel was located just below the parquet floor and was covered with a round metal plate and was almost invisible unless you knew what you were looking for.

Breska and Bryan began to carefully descend down the hanging ladders of the cell. They were very tense, but at the same time hopeful. After descending fifteen feet, they found themselves in a tunnel. At the same time, Lucas and Antonio finished descending the ladders. Everyone was already down.

They spotted a long, dark tunnel. They were carrying lamps for light. Bryan took out his .38 revolver, and the lawyer his Colt. Lucas and Antonio carried some very sharp knives, which they took from the kitchen. Suddenly, they heard the barking of dogs in the distance. The detectives and the lawyer tensed, suddenly stopped in their movements through the tunnel. They leaned their backs against the earthen walls.

Bryan made an unmistakable gesture to silence his colleagues. Everyone was alerted and nodded their heads in agreement. Deep in the tunnel they saw something. Then boom, there was a deafening noise, as if it were an earthquake.

Above the heads of the detectives and the lawyer, the earth began to shake abruptly, and they felt something on the ceiling just above their heads. It was like the end of the world. Lava from the volcano finally made its presence felt in Warrent's house. They began to feel certain fissures and the opening of holes, as pyroclasts, small rocks formed by the agglomeration of materials, began to fall on the earth. Other small stones were formed, the hyaloclastites, which are also agglomerations but of more glassy materials that resemble obsidian, although they are less shiny.

Low viscosity lavas, called pahoehoe, were beginning to fall into the tunnel. The dogs began to bark more loudly. The team could barely stand. The faces of the detectives and the lawyer were pale. They were all terrified, convinced they were about to die.

Bang..., bang..., shots were heard coming from the end of the tunnel. Bryan and Antonio were both hit. They fell to the ground badly wounded, bleeding heavily from the chest. They hardly moved from the ground after the fall. Both had been shot by the senator who was a very good shot. His dogs did not stop barking. They were jumping up and down in desperation. Breska opened fire aiming at the end of the tunnel, where he thought Warrent would be. He could barely see anything and was not well balanced. He responded firmly to the senator's armed attack. He sensed it was him, though he was not entirely certain.

Lucas was hiding in some kind of shed. There was no time to talk, far from it. It was fire at will from the senator, who kept firing his gun. Three, four, five... Breska and Lucas were defending themselves as best they could. Bryan and Antonio were still lying on the ground, bleeding profusely.

Pebbles continued to fall in the tunnel. A certain amount of lava was beginning to seep through the earth where they were. Suddenly the senator's firing stopped. Breska advanced through the rocks, now more determined, towards where his friend was. He had a few bullets left in his pistol. There was a sepulchral silence. He continued to walk, making his way back and forth, given the movements of the earth.

There he found his friend, lying on the ground, bleeding from a blow to the head. He was neither breathing nor moving.

He looked dead. His dogs were lying on the ground, apparently dead, lava had enveloped their bodies. The senator had an open wound on his head and part of his face, it was deep and bleeding. Breska reluctantly took his pulse. His heart was beating slowly, a sign of life.

A voice was heard at the other end of the tunnel, "Breska, are you there?" Lucas asked in a trembling voice.

"Yes, come over here, Warrent is barely moving. He is lying on the ground badly wounded. The dogs are dead. There is no danger now."

"I can't, Breska, there are stones falling and I think the earth is on fire," said the detective fearfully.

"Come on, man, don't be afraid, we'll be out of here in a flash, but we've got to get Warrent. You have to help me. We also have to get Bryan and Antonio off the ground, they are seriously injured," said the lawyer courageously.

Breska and Lucas took the senator between them, and supporting him with their bodies they tried to climb up the ladder of the tunnel, leaving their companions Bryan and Antonio badly wounded on the ground. They should return immediately for them so that they would not bleed to death.

Pebbles and chunks of lava continued to fall, passing right next to their heads, again and again, they dodged them with small movements. The senator was hit by hot rocks and lava. They reached the surface of the house with Warrent's bloody body. They placed him on the sofa and quickly returned to their colleagues. Droplets of lava were falling in that tunnel. Some of them had fallen on the bodies of the detectives. They lifted Bryan's body and tried to carry him up the ladder. They felt less and less strength in their aching, wounded bodies, that were chafed with bits of pahoehoe. With a mammoth effort, they placed the body next to the senator's bleeding form and they went back for their remaining one, their badly wounded colleague Antonio. His eyes and head were barely visible, they were covered by pebbles and some pieces of burnt lava.

They wanted to place him next to Bryan and Warrent, but they could not incorporate him given the large number of pieces of burnt stones on his body. He was immobile. He was rushed to the stairs. Neither the lawyer nor the other detective could manage anymore but they knew they had to keep going. They carried him up the ladder, slowly, with the occasional stop, exhausted, until they reached the top.

He was left on the other couch. It felt as if the volcanic eruption was subsiding. Or so it seemed to them. The lawyer contacted Lucky Russo. Breska was surprisingly slightly injured.

"Have we got this bastard yet? Is he dead or alive, Counselor?"

The cold and distant tone was usual for a Mafia member following orders. Lucky and the other clan members only cared about finding the man they had been hunting for a long time. It was as if they were in another life away from an erupting volcano, even that detracted from their minds to fulfill the mafia oath. Fascinating indeed, but would the lava and chunks of volcanic earth have passed through the mobsters' house? Would lava have made an appearance there?

Breska responded despite his weakened state, "We have Warrent alive, just about. The tortoise is in the lair but you need to come very quickly because he is dying. Bring medical help, they are all dying."

"Good job, lawyer, in an hour and a half we'll be there, as long as our helicopter manages the journey. I hope you are well," said the mafioso with some compassion.

Within an hour the mobsters showed up at Warrent's house bringing two trusted doctors, other Mafia allies on the island.

Breska was surprised, "Hasn't the lava reached your house? It reached us here. We are devastated and wounded; we could have died."

"It didn't reach us. " Maranzzano answered.

"Look, there is no time to lose, the senator is dying, none of the three of them will last, look at the wounds they have, please."

The doctors intervened quickly. They gave them all cardiopulmonary resuscitations before taking them by helicopter to the General Hospital of La Palma. Breska stayed in the house, his minor wounds fixed by the doctors, waiting for news.

The goddess of fortune, called "Tique" in Greek mythology, made a surprise appearance at the mobsters' house that day. No trace of the immense lava reached them. The lava mantle drifted into the sea and did not reach the house of the members of the mafia clan.

Vicenzo had already thought about how to convincingly strike a blow at the Lamborda family. The task would be to infiltrate the Lamborda family, in the very heart of the mafia clan, so that he could gain access to all the relevant data of the group, its working methods, its contacts, associates, allies and people who collaborate closely with the criminal organization, including politicians and judges.

Zannini's order began by going to the center of the clan. They had received information about the condition of the wheel of Breska's SUV. For that, he would need to travel to Laguna, in the Canary Islands. They had been duly informed of the areas that had not been devastated by the volcano. He would be accompanied, Rocco Torrio, the family's hitman.

The Captain, Giuseppe Ganci, and soldiers Joe Mesina and Frank Riccobono stayed in New York to finish some work in the Bronx and Brooklyn. The members of the Lucini clan were waiting for a drug shipment to be transported from the port of Algeciras to Miami, Florida. The Colombian-flagged vessel "Nautilus" was to reach the Florida coast with fifteen tons of cocaine to be distributed in the Bronx and Brooklyn in collaboration with Mexican and Colombian drug traffickers.

Allies of the Lucini mafia group were ready in Miami for the cocaine landing. A Mexican customs agent spotted the ship on his viewfinder in the port control tower. The drugs were due to arrive in New York City where the mobsters were impatiently awaiting the shipment for distribution and delivery. A Mafia contact in the port of Miami, through Senator Warrent, had everything planned to unload the drugs in New York City. The senator was involved in all the dirty and illegal business of drug trafficking with the Lucini family, he had long been playing both sides of the Mafia clans.

Breska didn't know the real Warrent, nor did the senator know the real lawyer. They were like two wise heads playing tennis with the mobsters. The senator sold out to the highest bidder in business. He was the typical person who never said no to a business proposition, least of all from the mob. It made him feel powerful. He used politics for his personal gain, not for the welfare of the citizens he represented. Because of this, Warrent had enemies, any one of whom could play a dirty trick on him. He had made many shady deals and it was all coming back to him. For a couple of years, he had allies in drug trafficking, he was also an associate of the Lucini mafia group.

He did, however, enjoy the full confidence of a group of senators in the city of New York, his deal with them was based on the fact that he paid them to vote as he instructed in the New York Senate. He received his orders from the Mafia and would sell votes to the highest bidders. Depending on the Mafia's requests, the senator was in charge of bribing his trusted senators to obtain licenses, land and concessions in the city for the Mafia. Once the Mafia contacted him, everything should go according to the mafiosi's wishes, the mafiosi were more than generous to the senator. However, he always had to remember that if something did not go according to the request, or if there was a betrayal of a member of the Mafia clan, the person implicated would immediately be liquidated. This was the Mafia.

Vicenzo and Rocco landed at La Palma airport in a private jet from New York City. Three associates of the Mafia on the island were waiting for them in a fantastic Jaguar. They got into the car and drove to a house in the forest of La Laguna where the lava and magma from the volcano were not expected to reach. The rented house was owned by another Englishman on the island. Then, once near the vast, dark forest, a helicopter was waiting to take them to a wooden house shaped like a caravan.

Vicenzo had contacted a company on the island. It was a mechanic shop that did repairs on all types of vehicles. He had bribed the chief mechanic well. The plan was to intimidate the consigliere of the Lamborda family who was giving so many headaches to the Lucini family. Vicenzo and Rocco had promised the Zannini boss that they would give him such a scare that he would never forget it. How would this mafia plan be executed? The Lucini clan was on the move.

Malone and Brigitte contacted Jolanta. The senator's wife immediately appeared at the FBI's main office in New York City with her daughter Olivia. She was carrying with her relevant information about her husband that she had found on his personal computer. She was able to access all the files that the senator did not delete before his escape.

Brigitte asked, "What do we have, Jolanta? We have trusted you from the beginning and you cannot fail us. We have to defeat this mob."

"My husband is in contact with some undercover FBI and DEA agents. In exchange for receiving accurate information about the "Cosa Nostra" gangsters, your FBI colleagues, along with those of the DEA, pay Warrent huge amounts of money, thousands of dollars, even hundreds of thousands. The objective is for them to discover and understand the relationship of the bosses of the Lamborda and Lucini families with their soldiers, captains, associates and allies of the Mafia groups. In exchange for these sums of money, my husband gives them information on drug distribution and how the casinos are controlled. He has been collaborating with the FBI and the DEA for some time now. Warrent collaborates with the FBI, the DEA and the "Cosa Nostra" families," she said confidently.

"Which undercover FBI and DEA agents does he deal with? Do you know the names of the mobsters your husband collaborates with? Who distributes the drugs and who controls the gambling casinos?" asked Detective Malone.

Jolanta, who was a cultured and intelligent person, wanted to give the information to the FBI in dribs and drabs, there would be plenty of time to pass on what she considered appropriate. She answered the detective very coldly, "I only know that they are two women and a man, I don't know their names. I will have them soon. The gangsters he negotiates with are the Capos Bernardino and Zannini. I also know that he does drug trafficking business with the Sinaloa cartel, and the Medellin cartel, to transfer drugs from Mexico and Colombia to the U.S. in exchange for money from the Lucini family," Jolanta paused again, took another deep breath and said less eloquently, "This is what I can offer you, detectives."

Malone was still in shock, he said with a frown, "We already have almost all the information you have told us, Jolanta, this is nothing new. We expect you to give us more in the next few days, for everyone's sake. We cannot wait," he said with a wave of his right hand. "The overthrow of the Mafia is at stake. A lot is at stake for all of us, you know what I mean, Jolanta."

"I don't know, detective!" exclaimed the senator's wife.

Malone cut to the chase, "If you don't bring us new information, any of us could end up in a ravine and you could be prosecuted for concealment of evidence."

Jolanta, who did not scare easily, said, "Detective Malone, I hope everything goes well, I will do my best to make it happen."

"I hope so," said Malone more calmly.

Jolanta left the FBI office flush with victory. She had kept a huge amount of information up her sleeve.

Captain Giuseppe Ganci, soldiers Joe Mesina and Frank Riccobono were waiting on the coast of Miami for the cocaine shipment coming from the port of Algeciras. They had been sent to oversee its arrival and transport up north by their Mafia bosses. The drugs would be unloaded from the ship "Nautilus" into the port of Miami, then trucked by associates in the Bronx and Brooklyn to the gangsters, along with their Mexican and Colombian associates. The drug money would be split between the mobsters and the Mexican and Colombian narcos, with Warrent, of course, taking his cut. The role of the associates in the Bronx and Brooklyn area consisted of distributing the drugs in various apartments that served as drug laboratories, from where, in turn, their mules would drop them off at various locations where they would be sold, directly to the end consumer.

Vicenzo and Rocco had prepared the plan to perfection. They had to get as much information as possible from the Lamborda family and here the lawyer Breska was in their sights. Breska needed to fix the wheel of his SUV. It was making little jerky zigzag movements every time he put it in gear. The consigliere made a call to a mechanic's shop as he settled onto the couch.

He had chosen mechanics with a high level of competence in vehicle repairs on the island. The man agreed to stop by the wooden house in a couple of hours. Breska waited impatiently for some news from the hospital. The doctors who assisted the lawyer had treated the wounds caused by the magma and the gunshots. He was not in a bad condition considering all he'd been through. He had some superficial wounds and slight burns, but no fractures or wounds of importance.

The house had been ruined by the lava from the volcano. It was urgent to get out of there as soon as possible. Warrent, Antonio and Bryan arrived at the hospital more dead than alive. The doorbell rang. Breska got up from the sofa, very slowly, to open the door.

"A heart formed in intrigue and accustomed to crime cannot long conceal the poison that feeds it, and though the explosion of its malice is sometimes delayed, its progress will be uncovered."

Juan José Castelli

Chapter XI
War on the Cosa Nostra

"There must be no worse feeling than
knowing you're dead and still breathing."

Pablo Poveda

WARRENT AND THE DETECTIVES ARRIVED AT THE HOSPITAL
GENERAL OF LA PALMA. The senator was seriously wounded, he
had suffered a serious blow in the tunnel. One of the bullets from
his friend's gun caused a severe cranial wound, and his body was
also filled with several wounds caused by burning hot lava.

He had an open wound on his head and part of his face was
bleeding profusely. His medical condition was very critical. Once
he arrived at the hospital emergency room, he was taken on a
stretcher straight to the operating room.

Likewise, Detectives Bryan and Antonio were taken to
another operating room. There, the senator and the detectives
were attended to by the emergency physicians and nurses, in
addition to the surgeon on call.

In the hospital emergency waiting room were Pimponassa,
Gamberra, Gianluca, Maranzzano and Lucky Russo. They had

received express orders from the capo not to miss any detail of the senator. The Mafia had controlled the medical personnel surrounding Warrent. Their associated doctors were to keep a close eye on his progress. Bernardino gave express instructions to transfer him from the hospital to New York City in the event he survived his deep wounds. Pimponassa and Gamberra controlled the access of unknown persons to the hospital waiting room from their position in the waiting room. They were wearing Panama hats and navy-blue trench coats. Maranzzano and Lucky, similarly dressed, were sitting in chairs in an adjoining room next to the nurses and doctors on duty,

where they carried out the senator's protection control.

In addition, next door, without being visible to the gangsters, two pairs of Spanish national police sniffed around the hospital waiting room. They were waiting for developments on the senator's medical situation. They had been called by one of the doctors on duty because of the gunshot wounds. They were also required to identify the persons being treated.

After about two hours, a doctor on duty, Dr. Felipe Sanchez, a known Mafia member on the island, appeared and addressed Maranzzano and Lucky with a very pale look on his face, he said to them in a low voice, "Warrent has suffered a severe impact to his head and part of his face, which was caused by a bullet penetrating a section of his brain. He has undergone a surgical operation consisting of a cut in the scalp. Then a small bone has been removed from the skull, this was done so that the surgeon could operate on his brain, placing it back and holding it in place with small screw plates. The operation was a success. He has bruises on his face and serious wounds on his body. He has survived the gunshot, is currently non-verbal and his eyes are closed, although his heart has not been injured. He will need a recovery period of at least six months. Now he needs to rest. The gangsters listened to the doctor with some sympathy.

"How long will he be in the hospital, doctor?"

"For now I cannot tell you exactly, it will depend on his recovery. What I can tell you is that he cannot be disturbed and needs to rest," Dr. Sanchez replied.

The mobsters could not believe that he had survived both the gunshots and the lava from the volcano. It was truly unbelievable.

"Can we see him, doctor?" asked the gangsters.

"Only two minutes and you can't talk to him."

The mobsters asked about Detectives Bryan and Antonio, they wanted to know their health status.

"How are Bryan and Antonio?"

"They died, they could not survive their wounds."

The mobsters appeared somewhat saddened by the death of the two. Finally, Lucky said carefully, "Let's go in to see Warrent."

The doctor allowed him to enter the room. In a room next to the emergency room was the senator completely intubated and with a bunch of devices connected to his body, also with many bandages covering the wounds. It was almost as if they were looking at a mummy. The gangsters were already aware of his cosmetic surgery.

The mechanic warned by Breska had difficulty crossing the forest to reach the wooden house given the mounds of sand and large amounts of burnt lava left by the volcano in the area.

The lawyer turned the doorknob of the house with the intention of opening the door. In his thoughts were the senator and his fellow detectives. Once he fixed the wheel of the SUV, he would go straight to the hospital. He heard a creak as he opened the gate, the hinges were a little rusty. Finally, he was able to open the entrance.

Facing him, and looking haggard, the mechanic he was waiting for appeared. He was a tall man, with dark hair, his jeans were covered in and he had aged hands. He was about sixty years old. He was chewing gum relentlessly. He was carrying a toolbox.

Sweating, he addressed the lawyer, "Are you Mr. Breska?"

"Yes, it's me, I was waiting for you," Breska immediately realized that it was the mechanic he had been waiting for. The lawyer was a very observant man and he was quick to see which person he was dealing with. "Come in, come in, I'll explain and let's get down to business, I'm in a hurry."

Breska began to give him details of what was wrong with the wheel while the mechanic amused himself by taking a closer look at things around the house.

"Where is the car?" asked the mechanic with interest.

"Parked at the door," the lawyer answered immediately.

"Let me see it. I have to see what's wrong with that wheel."

Breska and the mechanic went to look at the wheel of his car. The mechanic bent down to take a closer look. Breska waited for him, standing by the car door while he watched the mechanic.

"I'm going to need an extension wrench, the one I brought won't fit," said the mechanic in a doubtful tone.

"Don't worry, I'll go into the house and bring it to you," said Breska.

While the lawyer went to the house to get the wrench, the mechanic, who was allied with the Lucini Mafia, proceeded to hide a microphone under the driver's seat, as instructed by Vicenzo and Rocco.

As he finished, the lawyer appeared with the wrench", "Here you go," said Breska with some relief.

"Thank you, sir, this is yours. It won't take long. It is a matter of removing the bolts, changing the wheel and little else. It's pretty standard and I brought the right piece from my workshop.

I don't understand how it has lasted so long," said the mechanic, somewhat alarmed. The mechanic finished the job. Then he said, "It's two hundred euros for everything," satisfied with his good work.

Breska paid him cash for the repair. The mechanic said goodbye to Breska with a smile on his face. He immediately called Vicenzo and told him that the work had been done satisfactorily. Vicenzo confirmed that he had sent him an envelope containing five thousand euros and that they would return the favor with any help he needed from them. The mechanic nodded happily.

Breska quickly left for the hospital, where his friend the senator and his fellow detectives had been admitted. He had no news of them. He was worried about their health, especially that of his friend the senator. He feared that the senator might die, or even that he was already dead.

The Lucini family already had everything under control. They had infiltrated the heart of the Lamborda family, or so they firmly believed.

The consigliere arrived at the hospital exhausted. He approached a room next to the waiting room, where he found Pimponassa, Gamberra and Gianluca. Pimponassa motioned with his right hand that the way was clear. Maranzzano and Lucky were protecting the senator, keeping a close eye on the corridor, where doctors and nurses were passing by. Lucky made a polite gesture to the consigliere, who approached the door of the senator's room.

The consigliere, before he opened the door, asked Lucky, "How is Warrent? How are the others?"

Lucky walked up to him and answered, "He is in very serious condition, but he will survive, he could recover with time, that's what Dr. Sanchez told us."

Breska relaxed somewhat. He took a deep breath, "And how are the others?"

Lucky calmly delivered the fateful news, "They are dead, counselor."

Breska, who was a man of great fortitude both mentally and physically, began to lose heart and said, "They were good guys. Bryan and Antonio did a great job. Without their help we would not have been able to locate Warrent. The important thing is that the senator is alive but the death of colleagues is a tragic thing, really they felt like family."

"What do you mean, family, lawyer?" Lucky asked, very surprised, "The family is just us, counselor, let's be clear, don't get carried away by your feelings right now, there are no excuses here. You are here to mediate and give us good advice, you are the problem solver, feeling discouraged is not part of this business, as you well know."

The lawyer responded with silence. Breska was about to enter his friend's room to pay him a visit, he approached the door with no sign of the Spanish police.

The ship "Nautilus" would soon arrive at the port of Miami with the fifteen-ton cocaine shipment coming from the port of Algeciras. Warrent's contact and ally of the Lucini family had the port's customs agents under control so that the drug shipment could be unloaded by the gangsters Giuseppe, Joe and Frank, who were impatiently awaiting the arrival of the drugs. Once the drugs were unloaded, they would be transported in refrigerated trucks by their partners to be distributed through the apartments that served as laboratories in the Bronx and Brooklyn neighborhoods, to be later taken by their mules to the local clubs and discos in the area to be consumed by the customers.

The Mexican drug traffickers, together with their Colombian partners, had prepared the cocaine shipment from drug laboratories in the hills of Culiacán and the mountains of Medellin. The drugs were to be transported to Spain and the U.S. through the ports of Algeciras and Miami, respectively.

The percentage agreed by the "Cosa Nostra" was sixty percent for the Lucini family and the remaining forty percent for the Mexican and Colombian partners. The Lucini clan would be in charge of distributing the percentage to their partners in the Bronx and Brooklyn, which was around fifteen percent. Senator Warrent took an excellent commission of approximately three or four percent for controlling the non-interference of the Lamborda family in drug trafficking, in addition to other businesses. The price of the cocaine shipment on the market was around three to four billion euros. The drug was a big business for the Lucini clan, the senator, the drug dealers and their partners.

The FBI and DEA detectives in Miami had received information about the arrival of the ship in port with the cocaine shipment through a DEA infiltrator in the Lucini family. Ms. Irina worked for the FBI in collaboration with another beautiful blond lady dressed in white, who worked for the DEA.

The consigliere and the Capo Bernardino never became suspicious of the work of either of them in the club "Las Mariposas". Irina's work with the Lamborda family consisted in infiltrating the family to contact girls of dubious honorability to take them to the "Las Mariposas" club. Once there, they would interact with the mafiosi who did business in the club, getting to have privileged first-hand information to pass on.

Warrent became a regular at the club. As an inveterate womanizer, he got to know Irina, whom he liked very much. They struck up a romantic relationship over a period of time. They saw each other whenever Irina was at the club, which was quite often. The senator fell in love with her. Meanwhile, the beautiful blond woman dressed in white, who worked for the DEA, turned out to be Alexandra, who was working to get information about the Lucini family.

The FBI and DEA, through Irina and Alexandra, respectively, were getting a great deal of information, through Senator Warrent, on the Lamborda clan's business dealings and their relationship with the Lucini family, as well as Mexican and Colombian narcos and their associates in the Bronx and Brooklyn.

The other beautiful blond woman dressed in white was Alexandra's identical twin sister, Anastasia. The final blond woman with blue eyes had something of a model's body. She was also an informant of the Lucini family. Her name was Fiorela.

The FBI and DEA police were beginning to put together the puzzle of the illegal businesses of the two biggest families in New York City. The "Las Mariposas" club was the meeting place par excellence of the gangsters. Here, deals were closed and more than one celebration was unleashed, such as the one that took place when the order to assassinate Senator Warrent was issued.

It was located in the heart of Chinatown, down the road from the Lamborda group's laundry store. The senator had started going to the club some time ago, as the girls who worked there did pole dances with bare breasts, striptease and other erotic moves that enticed the mobsters and their associates. This place, a must for mobsters, began to be frequented by Senator Warrent a few years ago. He loved to watch the almost naked dances of the girls while enjoying a whiskey. He had a good time here and knew he could contact the mobsters to do his business outside of his usual place of business, the senate.

Things were no longer going well in the marriage with Jolanta, they barely had a married life, Warrent barely had time for his wife and daughter. His life was the senate, his trusted senator colleagues, his friends, who sometimes accompanied him, and the mafiosi of the Lamborda and Lucini clan, and then he would go to the club to have whiskey and drinks with the girls.

One of those days, while the senator was in a private room with a girl from the club, Irina came to him. She introduced herself as a girl who had recently arrived from the Czech Republic, and offered herself to him. She had it easy with the senator, since he never said no to a girl, much less to one as pretty and beautiful as Irina.

Irina followed the instructions of her FBI colleagues from the beginning, which were to get as much information as possible from Warrent about his business dealings with the Lamborda family, his connections with the Lucini clan, the gambling business and drug trafficking, and to find out the kingpins among all the members of both families. The agent was very smart, she knew how to deal with a man like the senator, who quickly grew obsessed with her and the idea of sexual relations with such an attractive woman. Warrent acted like a real idiot without giving the slightest thought to what could come out of that love affair. Irina got a lot of information out of Warrent and, what was worse, he didn't even realize that she was an FBI agent.

Breska was about to enter Warrent's hospital room. He was pensive and very concerned about his friend's health. He could not understand why it had come to this situation. With slow and silent steps, he entered the room of the General Hospital of La Palma. Suddenly, he could not take another step. The image of the face and body of the senator, his friend in deals, as he gritted his teeth, was unimaginable to him. He stood beside Warrent's bed. He was terrified by what he saw in that room. It was a completely intubated body with its head wrapped in neuromuscular bandages. His face was not visible. He could only see the tubes coming out of the oxygen machine, the serum and the needles inserted through his mouth. He was a truly monstrous being. His heart palpitations were measured by an electrocardiogram, his heart rate was normal in the opinion of the lawyer.

He touched his arm with great restraint, and addressed the senator, Warrent... Warrent... Warrent...” The senator did not answer. Again he spoke his name again, this time slightly louder, “Warrent, my friend...”. He moved Warrent's forearm slowly.

The senator still did not respond. Breska gave up, much to his regret. He met Lucky at the door,

“How is the senator, Counselor?”

“The senator will not last more than two days,” Breska replied firmly.

“We have to get Warrent out of here, no matter what,” said the mafioso emphatically. “I'll talk to the capo for instructions, Capisci?”

Upon contacting Bernardino, he ordered them to wait a few more days, to stand guard in the hospital room until they could see the senator's progress and transfer him to New York City.

Alexandra received a tip from Fiorela that the drugs transported on the ship “Nautilus” were to be unloaded at the dock of the port of Miami. The DEA agent infiltrating the Lucini family contacted her DEA colleagues in Miami for the dismantling and boarding of the ship. The gangsters were impatiently awaiting the arrival of the ship to unload the cocaine.

Fiorela was going to receive a fat sum of money for this information against the Lucini family. The Capo Bernardino had done his work through family allies in the area. Joe Mesina and Frank Riccobono were nervously awaiting the drug shipment at the port along with other helpers of their Colombian and Mexican narco partners. The Bronx and Brooklyn associates were waiting for the signal for the immediate transport of the drugs from the port to New York.

The FBI and DEA police were specially prepared to arrest the drug traffickers and mafiosi by deploying a brutal police operation, with helicopters flying over the area and numerous secret patrol cars. Everything was ready for the big police assault.

New York-based DEA Special Agents John Donovan and James Caliot, who had been pursuing Colombian drug kingpins Gilberto Fernandez and Orlando Pacheco and Mexican drug kingpins Hector Juarez and Beltrán Gallardo for some time, were waiting for the order to act with their FBI collaborators Sloan, Malone and Brigitte. Brandon Jones and Walter Harrison, the two from Brooklyn and the Bronx, in turn awaited the order from the narcos and mobsters to move the drugs with their trucks to New York City. The privileged information had been supplied by Fiorela, a DEA informant in the Lucini family, who was to receive a large amount of money from the Lamborda family, no less than thirty thousand dollars for her information. The FBI and DEA officers were impatiently awaiting the raid on the ship; it could be a great opportunity to uncover evidence about the Lamborda and Lucini mafia clans.

The FBI's main objective was the eradication of the two main New York Mafia families, Lamborda and Lucini, in order to get to the capos and the Don. The DEA, for its part, sought the arrest and elimination of the Mexican and Colombian narcos, as well as their associates in Brooklyn and the Bronx. But everything was connected in the Mafia, in short, everything was closely linked and at the evidentiary level it was not easy to dismantle. It was like a puzzle of ten thousand pieces that had to be put together correctly.

Irina, Alexandra, Anastasia and Fiorela were the perfect candidates for the dismantling of the Mafia together with Jolanta, Senator Warrent's wife. From the love affair with the latter, Irina was able to discover the senator's dealings and business with the consigliere, the lawyer's relationship with Bernardino and Zannini and the Mafia's drug trafficking business with Gilberto Fernandez, Orlando Pacheco, Hector Juarez, Beltrán Gallardo, Brandon Jones and Walter Harrison. Everything was starting to fall into place for the FBI and the DEA.

For her part, Alexandra was very savvy about how to get information out to her DEA colleagues. She made a good connection with her FBI partner, Irina. Anastasia, Alexandra's twin, in addition to confusing the mobsters with her physique, was dedicated to supplying secret information about the Lamborda family to her colleagues in the police. Fiorela was not far behind, trying to obtain information about relevant secrets of the Lucini family to pass on to her colleagues in police command.

The club "Las Mariposas" had become far less safe for the gangsters than they imagined. What had begun as pole dancing and stripping had become refined police work. The mobsters were so busy being turned on by the women on stage that all thoughts of Mafia work were forgotten. This was potentially lethal in a criminal organization like the "Cosa Nostra", where everything was solved with blood and crimes. And almost everything led to Senator Warrent.

The ship "Nautilus" arrived at the dock. Sloan, Malone and Brigitte were hiding in their patrol cars in an inconspicuous area. John and James were ensconced in luxury apartments rented by the DEA, directly across from the dock, armed to the teeth. They were accompanied by another group of policemen, who were ensconced in a warehouse, where they would apparently unload the fifteen tons of cocaine coming from the port of Algeciras.

The order for the intervention would not be given until the drugs were unloaded from the large ship. A large number of Colombian and Mexican nationals began to disembark from the vessel. It appeared that these were the traffickers. They were moving swiftly towards the warehouse for the unloading of the drugs. At the same time, Brandon and Walter were waiting with their refrigerated trucks for their Mexican and Colombian partners to load the drugs.

Out of sight, just across the dock, were Giuseppe, Joe and Frank, who were waiting for Zannini's order. They were armed to the teeth with assault rifles and M16 rifles, as well as small revolvers. They were calm and without any suspicions of what was to come.

The traffickers were arriving at the ship. Sloan, Malone and Brigitte were getting ready to act, they were waiting for the drugs to enter the warehouse. They were uncomfortable and impatient and they couldn't wait any longer. John and James, on the other hand, once they saw through their binoculars that the shipment was being moved from the ship, went to an area adjacent to the warehouse. There they waited in a crouched position for the arrival of the cargo.

The traffickers entered the warehouse with the heavy drug shipment. The idea was to load it immediately into Brandon and Walter's trucks to begin the journey to New York. Numerous refrigerated trucks with the labels of fictitious companies were waiting for them.

"Stop..., DEA, police!" said John.

"Stop, FBI police!" Sloan added firmly.

Boom..., boom..., boom... The dealers responded to the police by firing their guns directly at them. Sloan, Malone, Brigitte, John and James took cover, giving them no time to repel the gunfire coming from the dealers with their rifles and M16 rifles.

Giuseppe, Joe and Frank, for their part, opened fire almost instantly. The supporting police officers, who were standing ready on the roof of the building next to the warehouse where the drugs were to be unloaded, were tightly gripping their rifles with telescopic sights, returning fire.

In that thunderous silence inside the ship, only gunshots could be heard. Suddenly, and without any reason all the gunfire stopped.

Sloan spoke through a very powerful microphone, "Drop your weapons, on the ground, on the ground..., FBI police! Drop your weapons to the ground, raise your hands, that's an order!"

Nobody moved, there was a great silence, as when one enters a temple with stealthy steps. With an uncommon impulse, the traffickers appeared behind a door of the ship, with their hands up and without weapons. They slowly headed towards the policemen.

Giuseppe, Joe and Frank showed up unexpectedly from the other side of the ship, walking towards the place where Sloan, Malone and Brigitte were. They were also walking with their hands raised and without weapons, as if ready to surrender.

Sloan repeated again, "I said on the ground..., on the ground, everybody on the ground... with your hands behind your head, face down, where I can see them..."

They all lay on the floor with their hands behind their heads, face down, as if they were waiting to be shot. Immediately, Sloan, Malone, Brigitte, John and James arrived and handcuffed the dealers and gangsters one by one, reading them their rights.

Their faces betrayed the bitter taste of defeat. What would happen after the arrest? Would the evidence in front of them be enough? This was the least of it, it could start a big bloodbath between the Lamborda and Lucini families. This happened every eight or ten years in the Cosa Nostra.

Senator Warrent's IV bottle kept dripping. He was lying perfectly still in his hospital bed.

Dr. Sanchez approached Maranzzano and Lucky. In a subdued voice he said to them, "Warrent won't be here much longer, two or three days at the most. He isn't getting any better. The after-effects of the lava from the volcano have left his body immobile. The burns are fatal."

Lucky asked, "Doctor, you don't think he will recover?"

Dr. Felipe Sanchez exclaimed, "Only a miracle will make him survive!"

Lucky's face showed great astonishment. Now he would have to ask Bernardino's advice about the senator's life. The instructions were clear from the beginning: assassinate him, as the mob commission had approved. The mobster contacted his capo. He said he had to bring him back to New York alive but get as much information out of him as possible. They had to talk to him.

There was no more waiting, they had to get him out of the hospital any way they could. They would be rewarded for this little job. The consigliere, Lucky and Gianluca quickly made plans to get the senator out of the hospital. Breska stayed at the front door to watch for the Spanish national police. The consigliere gave the order with a characteristic gesture, that is, raising his right hand upwards as if he were scratching his armpit. From where he was, he could not be seen well by his Mafia colleagues. He approached the door of the room making signs with his hands, waving them forcefully.

"Now, now..." said the lawyer.

Lucky and Gianluca began to move the senator's bed back and forth, with rapid movements, making sure no one saw them. They disconnected all the devices plugged into the hospital bed. Neither the nurses nor the doctor were there, it was time. But at any moment someone could enter Warrent's room.

Breska was pretending to read a newspaper leaning against the door. His eyes were fixed on the people passing by, nurses and doctors in other rooms.

"Come on, come on, let's go..., now or never," said the lawyer.

Lucky was pushing the senator in the gurney, he was going to the elevator closest to the emergency exit, which was about thirty feet away. Gianluca, for his part, was holding tightly to the headboard of the bed in order to move it in the right direction so that Warrent's body would not move. They had covered the senator's body with a sheet, but even so, the bottles of serum and other medicines gave the mobsters' actions away.

Breska was waiting and concentrating. He gave the signal for the entrance to the elevator, Lucky and Gianluca were fortunate to catch it empty. They pushed the senator into the spacious elevator, trying to make as little noise as possible. They pressed the down button and the elevator descended slowly. It reached the basement and the doors opened. Surprisingly, they found no one.

They prepared to take him to an ambulance with opaque windows that was next to the consigliere's car. Two people disguised as nurses, allies of the Lamborda family, got out of the ambulance. They nimbly picked up Warrent and loaded him into the ambulance and headed for the La Palma airport.

Breska took his off-road vehicle, where Lucky and Gianluca got in, following the ambulance. Pimponassa, Gamberra and Maranzzano, for their part, were about to drive their 4x4 towards the wooden house to collect up everyone's belongings. A helicopter was waiting for them in a nearby area. They were all to carry out the kingpin's orders to take Warrent to New York, alive.

The ambulance came to a screeching halt behind the airport. Immediately behind them Breska slammed on the brakes, almost running into the Mafia-nurses who were removing Warrent from the ambulance.

During the trip, Breska and his Mafia colleagues spoke clearly about destroying the Lucini clan. Lucky and Gianluca, said that they would kill them all, that they had to be eliminated, that they were screwing up their work, and that they especially wanted to target the boss Zannini. They had to put a bullet in his brain.

At the boarding area, a private plane sent by the Lamborda family was waiting for them. Everything had been arranged by Jordan, the Mafia's customs agent. Would Warrent make it to New York City alive?

Sloan, Malone, Brigitte, John and James led the handcuffed gangsters and narcos to the patrol cars. The place chosen for the practice of the police proceedings on the arrest and reading of rights was the Miami Police Department. The formal charge was drug trafficking along with belonging to a criminal organization. The work of the striptease ladies in the club "Las Mariposas" had paid off. Irina and Alexandra had done an excellent job.

Gilberto and Orlando, the Colombian narcos, as well as Mexican narcos Hector and Beltrán, were not among those arrested. The narcos arrested at the police department offices were simply soldiers of the police department. Brandon and Walter were arrested along with Giuseppe Ganci, Joe Mesina and Frank Riccobono. The news of the dismantling of the ship "Nautilus" and the capture of the drugs, as well as the arrest of almost his entire clan, soon reached Zannini, who exploded with rage. He had run out of loyal and well-trained men, although the Mafia could always find new recruits. There were always people who wanted to grab a gun in exchange for a large sum of money or to lend favors to each other that had to be returned sooner or later.

The Lucini family, in fact, had been quite weakened. They only had Vicenzo and the hitman Rocco left on the books. The pair tracked the Lamborda clan following the investigations of the family's consigliere. They had recorded the lawyer's conversations with his mafia colleagues inside the SUV. And the kingpin's orders were clear: the urgent return of his men to New York.

Vicenzo and Rocco took a private plane to New York as soon as they received Zannini's instructions. The boss had called an urgent meeting on the outskirts of the city.

Sloan, Malone, Brigitte, John, and James began interrogating Brandon, Walter, Giuseppe, Joe, and Frank. The cells of the Miami police department were filled with mobsters and narcos. Sloan, Malone and Brigitte were in charge of Giuseppe, Joe and Frank. John and James, meanwhile, were gritting their teeth at the Colombian and Mexican traffickers, who were in the cells to see if they could corner their bosses, as well as Brandon and Walter.

Giuseppe, Joe, Frank, Walter and Brandon would invoke the Law of Silence, the much-respected Omertà in the underworld. Malone and Brigitte were trying to elicit honest and positive answers from the mobsters while Sloan watched through the translucent glass. Malone stood next to Brigitte in that locked room of the Miami PD, questioning the mobsters with a frown on his face,

"What were you doing at the port? Were you waiting for the cocaine shipment to take it to your bosses, the Bronx and Lucini family bosses? Do you know Hector, Beltrán, Gilberto and Orlando?" he asked the narcos as he laid out photos in front of them. "How much were they going to pay you this time? Fifteen tons of cocaine is a lot of money on the market, you'd be in over your heads, boys."

Giuseppe, Joe and Frank were silent, staring at the ceiling of the room. They looked serene and calm. Malone banged loudly on top of the table, almost touching Joe's right arm. The photos and papers on the table moved.

Bravely, he added, "You're fucking idiots, we've got you tied up by the balls, you'll get up to fifteen or twenty years in prison, assholes. You won't see the light until you're sixty years old. If you cooperate with the FBI and the DEA, your sentence will be reduced to ashes and we will get to Bernardino and Zannini, the capos of the underworld.

"Does "Cosa Nostra" mean anything to you, Mafia-boys?" asked Malone, "Do you know this guy?"

He showed them a picture of Senator Warrent.

Just as Frank was about to cave to police pressure and answer, the door was opened by a man wearing a Panama hat, a black tie and a navy blue trench coat. He called himself Malcom, a middle-aged Italian-American from Brooklyn.

He said, "I am the family's attorney, this conversation is over, gentlemen. I am taking my clients. I have paid the bail of two hundred thousand dollars. Not a word, boys. We're out of here. We'll see you in court."

Malcom, as the Lucini family's lawyer, had learned his lesson very well, he recited everything very fast and by heart, leaving no room for maneuver by the FBI. He was very good at his job. Malone was frozen in shock. Brigitte was horrified by the turn of events and Sloan, for his part, walked angrily away to the police computer while Malcom and his clients left the police headquarters looking extremely happy with themselves. They had beaten the FBI .

On the other side of the Miami police department, John and James were trying to get information out of the soldiers of the drug traffickers. Two of them, Colombian nationals, were overcome by desperation,

"We worked for Gilberto and Orlando, they put us in charge of transporting the drugs. They paid us twenty thousand dollars each. If you let us go free, we will collaborate with the DEA."

James said calmly, "If you sign a statement stating these facts, we will put you under protection and you will become protected witnesses for the Colombian government and the USA."

"We agree."

The soldiers of the narcos were detained by the DEA to await their fates.

Zannini continued with his plan against the Lamborda family. They had been screwed and they swore revenge. A bloodbath was beginning to run through New York City. But first he had to restructure his family, so weakened was he by the seizure of the ship and the drug seizure. In addition, his associates in the Bronx and Brooklyn, along with the narcos, were demanding revenge as well. Everything could blow up since he no longer had the shipment of drugs to sell. Many millions of dollars had been lost. And business came first in the mafia. If things didn't work out as they expected, there would be a bloody response. Zannini called a meeting with Vicenzo, Giuseppe, Joe, Frank, Rocco. They were in a farmhouse, inside a plot of extraordinary dimensions in Cold Spring, owned by the Lucini family, about an hour from the city. The boss had prepared the meeting thoroughly. His strategy had a job for all remaining members of his clan.

Once everyone was seated at the round table in the farmhouse, the capo spoke in a calm tone, "This is what we are going to do: Vicenzo and Giuseppe will accompany Rocco to the Lamborda mansion. I've contacted an ally from the Bronx, he is a friend of our partners there, an excellent assassin, he's one of ours. He will be handsomely paid for this job. He will pose as a post office official in order to deliver a registered letter there, he will wait for you at a crossroads just before the house. Joe and Frank will wait in a car on the same street. Dress in sports clothes, as if you were going to the gym. We have made our inquiries and we know they are all inside the villa. Our informant inside the family has told us that they have just arrived from La Palma. They have the senator hidden somewhere. They will be unprepared and will be focused on Warrent, they are not expecting us. We will give them where they deserve. Rocco will try to enter the mansion or wait with you and the Bronx hitman for the right moment to act. We have to take out Bernardino. Our hitman will take care of it.

Everyone nodded in agreement with the capo. He would remain hidden in the Cold Spring farmhouse surrounded by several mob thugs and bodyguards.

The Lucini clan was well prepared and armed to the teeth. They got up from the meeting and marched towards the Lamborda mansion. It was time for a great spilling of blood.

"Impossible is a word found only
in the dictionary of fools."

Napoleon Bonaparte

Chapter XII
Route through
Las Vegas and Panama

"I am not afraid of an army of lions led by a sheep;
I am afraid of an army of sheep led by a lion."

Alexander the Great

THE LAMBORDA FAMILY'S PRIVATE PLANE had arrived in New York City. Bernardino was very worried about Warrent's health. He ordered Pimponassa, Gamberra and Gianluca to move the senator to a secret room in Chinatown. The room was located under a Chinese grocery store, run by Chinese nationals whom Bernardino helped when they came to New York. They were waiting for the mobsters to arrive with several specialist doctors allied with the mob.

Maranzzano, Lucky and the capo, for their part, remained in the mansion waiting for news. They were protected by guards at the gate of the mansion. They knew they had to kill Warrent, but first they had to do a special job on the senator. They had to get as much information as possible out of him before he either died or they killed him.

Vicenzo, Giuseppe and Rocco found the guy from the Bronx. He was waiting for them at the meeting point indicated in the meeting, he was truly a bloodthirsty hitman, an excellent marksman and a strangulation specialist.

Joe and Frank were in the car, on the same street as their colleagues, just a few feet away, dressed in sportswear. The car's license plates were fake and the vehicle, a magnificent Lexus, had been stolen the day before from the garage of a Mexican millionaire.

Vincenzo and Giuseppe easily distracted the guards at the gate by throwing a rock over the wall with the intention of setting off the alarm. The Bronx hitman went to the front door of the mansion while the guards were busy dealing with the alarm. He rang the doorbell.

"Yes..., who is it?"

"Mailman, I have a registered letter for Georgina."

"One moment, please, I'll see if she's here." After a couple of minutes he returned, he said, "Please come on in."

The hitman prepared to enter the luxurious mansion of the Lamborda family. He walked steadily down the long path surrounded by exotic plants and natural grass until he reached the door, which was opened by a middle-aged woman, probably the maid, who told him in a friendly tone, "She'll be right with you, sir, just a moment."

A moment later, Georgina, the kingpin's wife, appeared.

"This is for you," said the hit man very calmly. The letter was from the city's IRS office.

"Where do I have to sign, sir?"

The Lucini family's contact in the IRS had done his job well.

"Sign and date here, please, ma'am," said the hit man.

Georgina picked up the letter, thanked him and closed the door. The letter carrier said a polite farewell. The guards were still busy with some problem related to resetting the alarm, because while the hitman was delivering the letter to the kingpin's wife, Vicenzo had called the service phone, pretending to be from the family and reporting a disconnection problem with the alarm. The guards were busy with it while the Bronx hitman took the opportunity to sneak into the house, through the back door into the kitchen.

Lucky appeared by surprise, coming from an interior corridor to look for something in the kitchen. The hitman and the mobster found themselves face to face. Lucky reached for his gun at the same time the hitman pulled out a large rope he was carrying inside his mail jacket.

The hitman pounced nimbly at Lucky, as if he were a cheetah in the jungle hunting for prey, he held his hands tightly around Lucky's neck, squeezing them tight until his eyes popped out of his head. He lifted him a few inches off the ground and then dropped him. The body of the mafioso lay dead on the kitchen floor. He did not even have time to draw his weapon. The hitman dragged the body into a small adjoining room without having spilled a drop of blood.

He was excited by his success, but a person like him recovered quickly. He was now ready to continue on his way to find the capo. With his hands a little shaky, and sweat on his forehead, he walked slowly and carefully, towards the inner rooms searching for the boss of the Lamborda family, the Don, the Godfather of the New York Mafia.

Boom, boom, boom...! three deadly shots ended the life of the Bronx hitman, the Mafia strangler. They were fired by Maranzzano from a small room, which was next to the secret room where Bernardino was. He took advantage of the overconfidence of the hitman, who was not expecting the mobster's hideout. Maranzzano had seen him walking stealthily towards the room.

The mobster stuffed the body as best he could into a huge bag and dumped it into an adjoining room. He quickly cleaned up the blood stains on the floor.

Meanwhile, outside, Vicenzo and Giuseppe had ended the lives of the guards of the mansion with knives, stabbing them repeatedly in the neck and face, even in the eyes. They were caught by surprise, and had no time to defend themselves. As they reached the mansion they realized that their hitman had disappeared. Vicenzo was about to enter through one of the front doors and Giuseppe through the back door. They had a clear path, there was no movement of personnel in the mansion.

Zannini was at ease in his Cold Spring farmhouse. He was protected by several bodyguards and hired thugs. He was enjoying a relaxing bath in the estate's spa area. Then he planned to take a gentle shower, and maybe spend some time in the hammock in the sauna or perhaps have a vigorous Turkish bath. He was calm, feeling sure that he had prepared everything in detail.

An armed and dangerous gang from Colombia and Mexico, was approaching the farmhouse. They had been sent by the narcos Gilberto, Orlando, Hector and Beltrán. They had an arsenal with them, it looked like they were going to go to war with an enemy gang. There were about thirty of them, and they would easily outnumber Zannini's bodyguards and thugs.

The narco mercenaries jumped over the walls of the farmhouse. They threw tear gas into the farmhouse, as well as toxic gasses to make the thugs faint. Those who were unfortunate enough to inhale the gasses began to cough, had difficulty breathing and suffered from temporary blindness. In the meantime, the bandits entered through the main gate of the farmhouse, firing their rifles and pistols wildly. Many died. Meanwhile, one of Zannini's bodyguards watched the scene from an upstairs window. He immediately went to the secret basement bunker, where he found Zannini.

They quickly jumped into the car and tried to drive up the steep slope leading to the other side of the hideout. Once the vehicle appeared at the back of the farmhouse, bandits pounced on the car, firing indiscriminately at it and at the bodyguard and Zannini, who was in the passenger seat. A bullet hit him in his chest, as several projectiles entered the Mercedes SUV. He was badly wounded. The bodyguard fired through his car window at the four mercenaries while driving the Mercedes with extreme difficulty. He managed to lose them by accelerating the SUV to the maximum, even running over some of them, who were left lying on the pavement. They managed to get out of the farmhouse, meanwhile, the shooting continued between the thugs of the rival gangs, leaving a Dantesque showcase of corpses scattered on the ground.

The survivors of that war between mafia gangs, many of them shot and wounded, and the soldiers of the narcos Gilberto, Orlando, Hector and Beltrán, completely ransacked Zannini's farmhouse, seizing valuable documents. Immediately after the battle, they informed the narcos of what had happened, who gave orders to their soldiers to leave the country as a matter of urgency. Zannini's bodyguard quickly took him to hospital. He was hovering between life and death.

A light push on the door was enough for Vicenzo to enter the Lamborda house. Giuseppe opened the back entrance with a moderate push, very slowly, and with a serious look on his face. They met up in a room next to the dining room, using WhatsApp to communicate whenever necessary as they searched for Lamborda's boss, the Godfather of the mafia.

They walked very slowly through the corridors of that great mansion, covering themselves from the probable enemy attack, calculating to the millimeter any strange movement. They were side by side, a little distanced from each other. They walked slowly as they searched for the capo. The corridors of the mansion were long and narrow. Rocco appeared out of nowhere, like a magician in the scene of a thriller. He was in the room in front of them, making a gesture of silence with his index finger placed in the middle of his mouth. He made another gesture that he would advance before his colleagues, he made slight gestures with his right hand, let's go... let's go..., he made several grimaces with his mouth. No strange noises or movements were heard.

They arrived at another room, there was no one there. They were all sweaty and tense. Giuseppe and Vicenzo checked the other rooms while Lucini's hitman left. They continued with their plan to uncover Bernardino's whereabouts: They were aware that there seemed to be no one in the mansion yet they continued searching, room by room of the mansion, finding no one.

Eventually Rocco found the secret room where Bernardino had been hiding. It was in a closed place, behind revolving doors, that opened and closed at the same time. There was no way to stop them moving continuously. He reached the end of the corridor and the capo was not there. The situation was one of absolute desolation.

They all left, crestfallen, and met up with Joe and Frank, who were waiting in the car, as instructed. Where had Maranzzano and Bernardino gone? The war within the "Cosa Nostra" seemed to be over.

NOVEMBER 2021, NEW YORK CITY.

Everything Jolanta had reported to the FBI about her husband's misdeeds was true but she had withheld a great deal of information., The evidence so far obtained by law enforcement officials about the illegal activities of the senator and his entourage was very similar to that given by Warrent's wife. Even so, it was still flimsy and was not enough to make arrests. The complex work on the part of the FBI to gather the evidence to incriminate the entire Mafia was proving to be difficult and time consuming. They had to demand more information from the senator's wife in order to have a chance of ending the American "Cosa Nostra".

Therefore, Jolanta was required, as part of her protection agreement, to tell the FBI everything she knew about the senator and his business deals.

Warrent enjoyed himself at the "Las Mariposas" club every evening. The days were long for Jolanta and Olivia in their Manhattan home as Warrent would leave home early in the morning and would not return home until late at night every day. This made it very difficult to combine family life with work. The senator was a kind and loving person and he loved his family very much. But his ambition for money, his desire for power and his association with the Mafia, made him lead a life that was risky. This, together with his vice for women and whiskey, led him astray and caused him to drift further and further away from his family, as well as his true friends to the point where Jolanta no longer recognized her husband, that great person she had married twelve years previously. Everything had become chaos, Warrent's life was a living hell. The files on Warrent's personal computer contained chilling data. Jolanta held back tears every time she read them.

There was a list of mobsters, of the people who made up the two biggest families in New York City, the Lambordas and the Lucinis. Of their allies in the city and abroad, of their associates in the Bronx and Brooklyn. There was also a file with the names of the Colombian and Mexican narcos with whom he collaborated, and in a file with misleading names were the commissions he charged for all of this. The name of "Breska", the lawyer of the "Cosa Nostra", appeared too. Finally, she found the names of girls and men in a separate file, called, "My Friends".

The senator had deleted some files in his sudden flight, but he had left the most relevant ones on his computer. Warrent and the Mafia lawyer were collecting indescribable sums of money from the underworld and its allies. Everything was perfectly organized.

Jolanta and her daughter were really in danger. She no longer asked about her husband's health or whereabouts, her hatred for the senator was all she had.

Malone called Jolanta's cell phone.

"Yes, Mr. Malone, how can I help?"

"I need to talk to you, it's urgent. I'll meet you at the Masseria Caffé & Bakery in one hour. Be there."

Malone showed up at the appointed time. Jolanta was sitting next to Olivia at a table next to the bathroom. The place was empty except for them. He spotted her from the doorway and approached her cautiously. He sat down on a two-seater sofa directly across from them. The waitress arrived, so he ordered coffee and a sugar bun. Jolanta and her daughter were having a soft drink. It was about midday.

"Have you not had breakfast, Mr. Malone?" asked the senator's wife with surprise.

"Not yet, I've had a crazy morning," said the agent nervously. Malone started with the questions, he didn't have much time, his colleagues were waiting for him in the FBI office.

As the waitress served him his coffee and bun, he asked, "Are you going to stop playing games with us now, Jolanta? We know you have valuable information about your husband but you're withholding. You are playing cat and mouse with the FBI and that is not right. I remind you that you are a protected government witness and you are required to cooperate with us, that was the agreement. Otherwise, we could go before Judge Thomas and inform him that you're playing games. You decide. You know what I mean."

Jolanta was not intimidated by the federal agent's words. She knew her rights perfectly well and how far she could go with her stance towards the police.

"How is my husband, Mr. Malone? Do you know where he is and how he is?"

"We know he's hiding somewhere, near New York, and we know he's in a very serious condition. We don't know any more at this time," said the agent.

"Malone, until you tell me where my husband is and how he is, I will not say another word to the FBI. You can tell Judge Thomas for me."

This was smart of her. Malone knew deep down that the senator's wife was right. They should inquire about Warrent's whereabouts and condition before speaking further with her.

The Chinese in the Chinatown grocery store were anxiously awaiting the arrival of the gangsters and the senator along with the medical specialists working for the mob. The mission of the Chinese was to ensure safe passage for the gangsters and their allies in that tumultuous neighborhood in return for the favor that Bernardino had once done for them. The gangsters were to move the senator to the secret hideout.

The bunker where the senator was to be hidden was an apartment located thirty meters below ground level. It had all the hygienic-sanitary conditions and comforts, to the point of containing a stretcher and the necessary surgical utensils for a possible emergency operation, an unreachable place for the police and the enemies of the underworld. How was it possible for the Mafia to build such a wonder in the middle of one of the busiest neighborhoods in New York? Only the Mafia could do it.

Pimponassa, Gamberra and Maranzzano, who had recently arrived by private plane from the Canary Islands, intended to transport the senator into the secret apartment. Gianluca was waiting for Bernardino's instructions.

The mafiosi of the Lamborda clan was devastated by Lucky's death, especially the capo, who considered him one of the bosses among the underbosses, with more than enough ability to rise within the organization. Now Bernardino had to restructure the entire family as well as extract as much information as possible from the senator. He gave the assignment to the family's hitman, who was an expert in inhumane treatment and torture. If anyone could make traitors and Mafia informants talk it was him.

Warrent was one of the possible traitors of the organization although this needed confirmation. The hitman was dedicated exclusively to this little job, while the other gangsters focused on the outcome of the war with the rival gang. They had seen for themselves how far their enemies in the underworld, the other big family in the city of New York, could hurt them. The war had caused deaths on both sides and this was obviously detrimental to the business, the bloodbaths were causing heavy losses for the gangsters in every way.

An FBI informant had phoned Maranzzano informing him of Zannini's condition. He was between life and death, something for the Lamborda family to celebrate, particularly since the attempt on his life had been carried out by one of the thugs of the Medellin or Sinaloa cartels. This brought a temporary victory for the Lamborda family as they regained full control of the city's gambling and other businesses.

Inter-faction warring was one of the main reasons why Bernardino had not gone into the drug trafficking business.

Gambling, prostitution, construction, extortion and bribery gave him better financial rewards and fewer deaths. Drug trafficking might pay better in the short term but in the long term it was almost guaranteed to lead to internal drug wars.

Gianluca had ordered his colleagues and allied doctors to leave the main room of the mafia's subterranean apartment lounge, he asked them in an adjoining room in case he needed their help. He wished to carry out the orders given by Bernardino regarding the senator.

Warrent was breathing very slowly through an oxygen tube. He was hooked up to all the various tubes and devices necessary to keep him alive. He was a walking corpse, but he was still alive.

Gianluca began to question Warrent, "How much are the Lucinis paying you... You son of a bitch pig. Why didn't that vote for a license to shoot the film go through?"

When Warrent remained silent the hitman turned to violence. He punched him on his badly wounded forehead, which began to bleed profusely. Next, he hit him in the testicles. Warrent gave a thunderous scream that was heard throughout the apartment. He seemed to make small movements with his mouth, as if he wanted tò speak, but due to the faintness of his voice and his extreme physical weakness nothing could be heard or understood.

Gianluca continued, "What, Warrent, you're not going to say a word? You lying, backstabbing, lying son of a bitch," he said as he spat in his face. He struck the senator's head twice, right on the craniocerebral wound inflicted by the consigliere's bullet. Warrent remained speechless as blood began to pour from his wound.

The hitman put his ear next to the senator's mouth, he seemed to say something, "Breska..., Breska... is the culprit," said the senator gasping for breath.

Gianluca was extremely surprised by what he had just heard. If this was true, his consigliere could be in question, although he didn't trust the senator one bit.

"Breska..., Breska... is the culprit," were the last words Warrent ever spoke. He died in bed in that apartment deep underground on Thursday 18 November 2021. Gianluca dissolved the body in sulfuric acid with the help of Maranzzano, who he had called to finish the job. Bernardino had ordered the assassination some time ago but only after they extracted information from the senator. Warrent's body was history. It was akin to a disappearance. Warrent was never heard from again. What would become of the mobsters? The FBI and DEA had been after them and the senator for some time, along with his wife and daughter.

The doctors at the New York-Presbyterian hospital went to attend to the Lucini family boss, who was badly wounded by the bullet embedded in his chest. Among those doctors was Dr. Fernandez, an ally of the Mafia family. However, Zannini died during the transfer from his bodyguard's car to the hospital emergency room.

Dr. Fernandez, together with other doctors on duty, tried to perform several cardiopulmonary resuscitation maneuvers on him after he suffered a cardiorespiratory arrest. Those resuscitation maneuvers proved useless. He suffered an internal hemorrhage due to that bullet, which penetrated him to the very depths. The head of the Lucini family died from a bullet fired by a bandit of his drug trafficking associates.

Instantly, the news reached the narcos Gilberto, Orlando, Hector and Beltrán, as well as their associates Brandon and Walter, who enforced the oath of revenge for the dismantling and capture of the drug ship "Nautilus" in the port of Miami by murdering Zannini. Fiorela phoned John and James to inform them of this tremendous news. Likewise, Anastasia informed

Irina of this event, who passed the information on to her sister Alexandra. In the Lamborda family, this brutal news was received as something historic within the Mafia. The main boss of the enemy family had been eliminated without firing a single bullet by the rival gang within the underworld. Thus, the war in the "Cosa Nostra" had ended in a final victory for the Lamborda family. And this had to be celebrated at the "Las Mariposas" club. The gangsters of the Lamborda family could not get over their astonishment. They were thrilled at this news.

Bernardino, who was very astute and intelligent, took advantage of this moment to restructure the criminal organization and secure control of gambling, construction, extortion and bribery of the top leaders of the city of New York, as well as to make possible alliances with the narcos in order to control the drug trafficking. The main objective would be, once the enemy gang was almost defeated, to concede drug trafficking to Colombian and Mexican narcos and associates in the Bronx and Brooklyn in exchange for a percentage of the profits, leaving them in full control of the drug trade.

Bernardino recalled the consigliere, his right-hand man, and legal expert.

Breska was shocked by the death of the rival capo, like all mafiosi, and although he had sworn the "Omertà" he was not a real mafioso. Bernardino wanted to take advantage of the lawyer's personal and mediating skills to take a giant step into the underworld.

The microphone installed by the La Palma mechanic under the driver's seat of the lawyer's car had recorded Breska's conversation with his Mafia colleagues where they vowed to shoot Zannini in the head. But this circumstance was no longer so relevant within the Mafia since the war between the clans had ended and the Lamborda family had emerged victorious.

The Lucini family had been drastically reduced, as now it was up to them to regenerate and restructure, although their Mafia enemies could not be trusted in the least. There was always some gangster who wanted to take the place of the murdered capo by moving up the ranks, and this happened frequently in the Mafia. The way to rise in the Mafia was through crime and violence, and in this sense they had already begun to prepare the offensive. Although it was peacetime after the war in the "Cosa Nostra", one should never give up on the rival enemy, and even less so in the Mafia.

In order to cover his back well within the Mafia, Bernardino met with the consigliere. For this purpose, a dinner was held at the "Las Mariposas" club following the death of Zannini. As a good Don, as Godfather of the Mafia, Bernardino did not want distractions at this event so he ordered his men to have fun earlier and then abstain during the important meeting.

While Pimponassa, Gamberra, Gianluca, and Maranzzano took advantage of the bottle of champagne and the girls at the invitation of the club, the Don met with the consigliere alone in a small private room next to the clan's secret room.

Bernardino told him with some enthusiasm, "This is what you're going to do, Breska. Warrent is dead. You're going to take a vacation in Las Vegas and Panama. Go with your family, with Emma, Evelin, Marc and Stalin, I know you haven't been with them for a while. This trip is both work and leisure. We've had some bad times, lawyer, but we've come out more or less unscathed. Gianluca will accompany you. The others will stay with me to prepare a shock plan. Our enemies are revolted by Zannini's death and I don't like that. You must ensure the patrimony of the family is safe. It is time to protect us, you have to use your knowledge of money laundering laws to launder our money safely. Tell me what you need, I trust everything to you, lawyer; my family, the money from the business, only you will know where to deposit it, far from the reach of the FBI and the DEA, from the other family, the narcos and their associates. Only you have the key to manage the family's money, you will hide it in stocks, companies, accounts in tax havens, whatever you think best. I trust you, lawyer, this was one of the main reasons you work for us. I trust you will do your best for the family. A car will pick you up tomorrow at 10 am. at your home. There will also be four escorts and five bodyguards. Prepare your family. There's no time to lose, Counselor. Capisci?"

The Don did not give the consigliere any chance to reply. The lawyer was moved by that message, especially by the news of his friend's death. He could accuse him, there had been a lot of business together and things that only he knew, not even the Mafia knew about it. He didn't know how far the family business was protected. And there were billions of dollars at stake.

As the best Mafia boss, he had had his speech to the consigliere scrupulously prepared for some time, and now was the best moment to execute his anti-FBI and DEA plan. The lawyer got the message.

He no longer had a problem transmitting these messages to his family. His wife and children already knew what it meant to work for the mob. Besides, Emma and her children loved Las Vegas and Panama, so he wouldn't have such a hard time convincing them. He had to tell his family what had happened with the senator, which he had tried to keep from them so as not to worry them. It could be time for business and a trip for relaxation and disconnection from everything around him.

The cars arrived at 10 am sharp at the Breskas' house to pick up the lawyer and his family. Gianluca and three other men were in one car, acting as bodyguards, according to the Don. Immediately another car arrived, an SUV at the disposal of Breska and his family. Once the escort opened the door and Gianluca got in, all the members of the family got in and headed for JFK airport.

The end of the war in the "Cosa Nostra" and the murders of Zannini and Lucky put the FBI and DEA agents on notice. Sloan, Malone and Brigitte, as FBI special agents, and John and James, as DEA agents, in collaboration with agents Irina and Alexandra, as well as informants Anastasia and Fiorela, and finally Warrent's wife, had gathered a series of evidence against the two families in the city, and also against the narcos and their associates in the Bronx and Brooklyn. The capture of the ship "Nautilus" by the FBI and the DEA had sparked the war between the city's mafia families and their partners in the drug trade.

In the arrest room of the Miami Police Department, some of the narco soldiers, contrary to the silent stance of the Lucini family mobsters and their detained associates, had given up their capos and, what was worse, were willing to sign an affidavit with the clear objective of collaborating with the police and thus being able to see their sentences reduced by half.

The soldiers of the narcos signed that affidavit before the police, and were then released on bail, awaiting trial. They had acknowledged that they worked for Gilberto and Orlando, both Colombian drug traffickers, and became protected witnesses in both the USA and Colombia. The same happened with the Mexican narcos, where their bandits admitted working for Héctor and Beltrán, charging about twenty thousand dollars each for the transportation of drugs. They had decided to wear microphones to monitor their bosses, and here too the Lucini family gangsters were trafficking drugs.

It had been Fiorela's tip-off to the police about the arrival of the merchandise at the port of Miami that provoked a confrontation between the narcos and the Lucini family gangsters and the bloody war between the two families in the city. In the club "Las Mariposas" many lucrative business deals were made by the Mafia, which did not go unnoticed by the FBI and the DEA. Irina had been able to use her body to stun the senator and his party buddies. Her relationship with Warrent worked for the entire FBI and DEA, since she had provided them with unbeatable information about the criminal activities of the Mafia and its allies. At no time did the late senator wonder about the brilliant FBI actress? It was hard to say.

What was clear was that the FBI had been getting information about the deals, the commissions, and most importantly, the people involved in the underworld and other evidence that could have been overlooked. Irina had information that could have sent shockwaves through the Mafia.

Irina was a woman of courage and bravery; she had been number two in her class at the FBI academy. She had done a sort of master's degree on the underworld, and was one of the most knowledgeable FBI officers in the fight against the Mafia. The FBI knew this. That's why they sent her and her colleagues on a trip to the Canary Islands, to follow the ins and outs of Warrent, the lawyer and all his entourage.

What evidence would the FBI agent who infiltrated the Lamborda family have obtained? Probably quite a lot. Would it be enough? Anything could happen in a trial.

Alexandra, for her part, was no slouch. This woman, as a DEA special agent, infiltrated the Lucini family, using her pole dancing skills to distract the Lucini gangsters and their drug associates in the Bronx and Brooklyn,. This woman could take care of getting all the necessary information about drug trafficking in the mafia and its various ramifications. In the eyes of the mobsters, she was nothing more than a two-bit prostitute, around whom they could say whatever they liked.

Finally, Anastasia, who sometimes pretended to be her twin Alexandra, led the gangsters by the nose, and the Italian Fiorela, who became informants for the Lamborda and Lucini families, respectively. Both entered the witness program after providing information about the Mafia's actions and even suffering at the hands of the gangsters. Both were handcuffed and kidnapped for not wanting to have sex with gangsters, and were tortured and savagely wounded by them, seriously endangering their lives and those around them. Both almost died but they had decided to collaborate with the FBI and the DEA. They swore revenge against these unscrupulous guys, who did not value life.

Only Jolanta remained. Where was her missing husband?

How long could Warrent's disappearance last? When would he show up?

The private plane of the Lamborda clan, carrying the consigliere's family, the hitman Gianluca and some of his escorts and bodyguards, landed at Harry Reid Airport in Las Vegas. Las Vegas, of course, was a great option when looking to hide Mafia money. It is a tourist city famous for its active nightlife, which is centered on its numerous twenty-four-hour casinos and other entertainment options.

Banker Murphy was awaiting the arrival of the consigliere. The banking laws of this tax haven were designed for banking secrecy and confidentiality of customer data. Here, banks could refuse to provide data on the balances and deposits of clients, taking refuge in the secrecy of these laws of Nevada.

In addition, the U.S. had not signed on to the standards of the OECD, the international trade organization that advocates international trade. The U.S. has its own laws on this issue, FACTA, which it imposes in its bilateral agreements with the countries with which it has financial relations. The strength of bank secrecy also determines how well money can be hidden in a country. In this context, anonymous accounts exempt the holder from tax liability if they hide it well from foreign authorities. The U.S. Treasury Department's Financial Crimes Enforcement Network may expect banks to report suspicious activity by their customers.

For this, the consigliere had traveled to Las Vegas and would then head to Panama. Breska bought off the two trusted senators of the late Warrent with the clear intention of pushing through the Senate vote on the Chinatown casino license and its Las Vegas subsidiary. The Chinatown Grand Casino license went forward with the favorable votes of Warrent's trusted senators, thus screwing up the expected vote on the movie production company in favor of the lawyer's other clients.

Why was the New York politician murdered and who was the perpetrator? The news was on the front page of the New York Post when the late Warrent was waiting for his plane to escape to the Canary Islands. The consigliere only cared about the fulfillment of his task in the Mafia, the one he had initially been entrusted with when he swore the Law of Silence in the underworld, which was to obtain the casino license above all else.

Breska paid two million dollars to the corrupt senators by setting up shell companies in tax havens, Las Vegas being one of them. Banker Murphy of Nevada State Bank was also paid off. He had been paid several million dollars by the mob's lawyer to keep his mouth shut and his bank accounts safe. He went to see him to catch up, discuss banking issues and see how the Las Vegas casino was doing. The escorts and bodyguards waited outside the office. The lawyer had the full powers of the capo on this venture. And he knew how to use them.

Murphy welcomed him graciously, "How are you, Counselor? Long time no see! I'm glad you're here. I am eager to know the reason for your visit. You look as if you are keeping very well, Counselor. Please convey my most sincere thanks to Don Bernardino, I have already confirmed the arrival of the five million dollars through the "Sabana Club" company. Tell me now how I can help you, lawyer."

The consigliere listened to the banker politely as he talked, prostrate on that lush sofa in his office.

"I need to open more accounts for the family, the income from the Las Vegas casino is increasing and we also need to launder the money coming from the Grand Casino in Chinatown, which is already up and running, earning millions of dollars. My family has joined me, I want to do something with them, Murphy, I'll make it up to you, you know."

Murphy was looking at him with some astonishment from his executive seat.

"Breska, we will put the profits from the Vegas casino and the Chinatown Grand Casino in the name of the usual companies. We will use "Sabana Club", which is in the name of a front man for the Mafia in Las Vegas, Mr. Tom Stuart, as you well know. We will also use "Nevada Transportation" for the other outstanding revenues. Anything else, counsel?"

"Tomorrow I will come with my wife and children. I must do something with them," said the consigliere slowly.

While Gianluca went to visit Tom Stuart at the casino in Las Vegas, the next morning, the entire Breska family showed up at Murphy's branch. He ordered the escorts and bodyguards to stay outside the bank's door. What was the lawyer's intention with this maneuver? Murphy was just finishing serving some Canadian tourists when he got up from his chair and greeted Emma Miller, Evelin, Marc and Stalin warmly.

"Bring chairs for everyone, please," he said to a bank employee. "You all look great, sit down!" He exclaimed with a beaming smile. "What brings you to Vegas?" he asked.

"My husband decided to bring us here, he's the culprit," said Emma with a chuckle.

Breska began to speak in his usual calm manner, "I want to open accounts for each of them. You must transfer half of the Lamborda family's money to these accounts, I will leave you a signed transfer order that you will execute at the moment I order you to do so. The price for this operation will be ten million dollars, which you will pay yourself from the casino account and for banking services, Capisci?"

The banker was hesitant, "What will happen with Don Bernardino? Has he approved these operations?"

"You know me, don't worry about that, Murphy, I have full powers, legal and moral. In any case, you know they would eliminate me if I did anything wrong," said the consigliere with some displeasure. The lawyer's family was no longer disturbed by these unpleasant expressions.

"I'll get to it, I've never had a problem with you, you're a great friend. You are the object of my sincerity and I respect you a lot. Besides, the people you work with move millions here. It will be done," said the banker.

The Las Vegas financial plan was underway. The consigliere informed Bernardino on the phone, and he was satisfied. However, the lawyer kept him in the dark about his family's accounts. The next morning, the Breska family and the gangsters intended to take the private plane to Panama, where they would to visit the law firm of the Breska's old university friends from Madrid.

The FBI and DEA were still following up on Warrent's strange disappearance. Only the mob knew the senator's true whereabouts. The news had reached the two great families of New York. The hitman Gianluca had executed Bernardino's plan to perfection. Warrent's poor state of health had left little opportunity for physical interrogation. The hitman had tried to make Warrent talk, but his near-fatal wounds had caused him to pass out almost immediately. The senator died before he could be forced to reveal too much.

"Breska... Breska... is the culprit."

The corrosive action of the acid acted quickly on the senator's body, and within forty-eight hours of the assassination he had almost entirely disappeared. Warrent had been eliminated in every way. His body was nowhere to be found. For the FBI, the DEA and his prosecution, without a body there could be no evidence against the mob. Sloan, Malone and Brigitte had their work cut out for them. They had a giant board in their office where they collated their evidence, including suspects involved in the various deaths pending investigation, and the criminal activities of the mob and their allies. But there were still many pieces to be fitted together, and they helpless that they had not yet completed the jigsaw.

The murder of Howard in the hotel in Costa Rica had not yet been solved either although there were suspicions that the Lamborda clan was involved here, too. Similarly, the murder of the New York politician remained a mystery: he had been a member of the Council, a friend of the trusted senators and traitors of the late Warrent, bought with money by the consigliere to obtain the license for the Grand Casino. Some pieces of the puzzle did not fit and this irritated the FBI greatly.

James and John continued their follow-up with the soldiers of the drug traffickers who had turned on their bosses to save themselves. In addition, they had to obtain evidence of the murder of boss Zannini, who had been killed by one of the gang's soldiers.

The private plane of the Lamborda clan, flew the Breska family and select members of the clan to Panama City, that well known tax haven. There they were met by several men dressed in navy blue suits, red ties, smart shoes, and Panama-style hats. They identified themselves as employees of the Panamanian law firm "Leandro & Fabio & Asociados, Bufete de Abogados" (Leandro & Fabio & Associates, Law Firm).

From the airport they were taken to the lawyers' offices where they were greeted by two friendly gentlemen. Breska spotted them as they pulled up and was eager to greet them.

A black Porsche SUV pulled up and Breska's wife and children got in and were driven to a luxurious apartment rented by the Lamborda family through their English contact in the area, just a few miles from the law firm. The effusive embrace between Breska and his university friends was long. They had been classmates at law school at the Complutense University of Madrid. When they graduated, Breska went to Los Angeles and his classmates did master's degrees in tax and fiscal law after which they were hired by a law firm in Panama, where they learned all the financial skills of offshore companies. They then founded their own law firm in Panama.

They three had kept in touch since leaving university and Breska was familiar with their methods of working on tax matters; he knew that Fabio and Leandro were real experts in offshore companies.

The three of them sat at a round, elongated meeting table made of sequoia wood reminiscing until the consigliere said with his usual calmness, "Friends and colleagues, I need your help and advice to deposit a serious amount of money. It really is a large amount of money. I am talking about several billions of dollars, owned by some very important clients of the Los Angeles law firm. To speak frankly, these clients are members of a criminal gang and they want the money to be hidden in off-shore companies. Obviously I don't need to remind you that I speak in confidence."

"We can create offshore companies, opening accounts with our trusted bankers. These companies are generally characterized by bearer shares, where the holder is the one who owns and holds the shares and, ultimately, the money. Our firm has hired more than thirty employees this year. They are the fiduciary directors, that is to say, the people who direct the destiny of the companies we create," Leandro explained, "It is these employees who sign on behalf of the companies, it is these names and not those of the real owner that will be on record."

Fabio, who was listening attentively to his partner, added, "They are the fiduciary directors. We just need you to sign some papers to allow us to create the shell companies. We will assign a nominee director, the figurehead in the financial sense, this guarantees the true owner of the company that their directives will be followed and no lawsuits or complaints will be filed against them or the company itself. They will also have general power of attorney, meaning the real owner cedes control to the trustee director making him a de facto director. Then the fiduciary director presents his resignation on an unsigned document, so that the real owner can remove the fictitious one whenever he wishes."

Breska was stunned by the diabolical knowledge of his colleagues, "Then we will be the owners of more than ten trillion dollars without America knowing that this money is hidden!"

"Correct. We have blank papers signed by our trustee directors on account opening. We charge five percent for our work."

"Right, let's get to work, you have convinced me that you're the men for this job. I will leave half of my clients' assets with you, since I have the other half in Las Vegas," said Breska cheerfully.

Leandro informed the director of the Banco General de Panama, Mr. Zenón, the most sought-after banker in the city, of the need to open checking accounts in the names of the clients. Breska gave the name of his wife and children for the creation of the companies and the destination of the five billion dollars, keeping something back for himself, of course.

The banker set out to do his job and Breska's second financial plan started to come to fruition. The fiduciary directors of the law firm Anthony, Carla and Fernando signed all the necessary documents for the processing of the order of the Breska family. After the meeting, they went to lunch at the Sorrento Italian restaurant, the consigliere's favorite.

Leandro and Fabio's idea was to create ten different companies to try to cover up the money, a real web of off-shore companies, a kind of financial holding where it would be almost impossible for the FBI and the DEA to discover the final destination of the money. In this way, they created two main companies, which they called "Virgin Residual" and "Dunas Paradise", in addition to eight other companies with misleading names.

"True wisdom lies in recognizing one's own ignorance."

Socrates

Chapter XIII
Business Comes First

"Not to be caught in a lie is the
same as telling the truth."

Aristotle Onassis

THE FBI AND DEA WERE OUT OF CONTROL AND DESPERATE. Warrent's disappearance had Sloan, Malone and Brigitte hard. The body was missing despite well-founded suspicions that he had been killed by the mob, they could prove nothing. Jolanta would not talk until the FBI agents told her the senator's true location. She wanted to know the state of her husband's health before divulging any more. FBI agents, Irina and Alexandra, were having no luck in their investigation into Warrent's fate. The federal agents considered entrusting Anastasia and Fiorela, their two best informants with the investigation. While the pair were not overjoyed to work with the Mafia their desire for revenge was strong so they agreed to try to help locate the senator. The narco informants could also be required to help. Irena knew well that Warrent had many Mafia contacts in both the Lamborda and Lucini families and she was beginning to see a thread that linked all activities to Breska, too.

Irena planned to prowl the mobsters' club in search of news for her FBI and DEA colleagues. She had plenty of suspicion but no evidence that could get them to trial. She also knew a lot about the senator's personality and character from her love affair within the club, but it was difficult for her to get to the sacred heart of the New York mob, that is, the capos, their captains, their soldiers and the consigliere.

She called for help from agents Alexandra, Sloan, Malone and Brigitte, as well as informants from the families within the Mafia, the informants of the Colombian and Mexican narcos. The FBA and DEA agents came up with a joint strategy: try to expose the mob and uncover Warrent's whereabouts. They went back to the case wall and organized all the marked photos of the people they were investigating while analyzing the job to be done by each officer. Almost everything revolved around the "Las Mariposas" club. This would be the nerve center of the operations of the FBI, the DEA and the police informants.

Sloan gave orders to Irina to use her charms inside the club again to uncover the gangsters. The head of the FBI's main office ordered Malone and Brigitte to follow Jolanta and her daughter closely. John and James were to follow the bandits who snitched on the narcos Gilberto, Orlando, Héctor and Beltrán in order to fully understand their movements and capture the real wiretaps of the microphones placed on their bodies. Alexandra had to follow the Lucini family. Anastasia and Fiorela had to use their feminine charms to disarm the gangsters inside the club. And so the mission was underway.

The Lucini clan needed a new capo. The waters were troubled within the family. The first reaction within the family was to avenge the death of their capo. They were thinking of going to war with the narcos for the capture of the ship "Nautilus", and for the murder of their capo, although they also knew that peace was vital to their business interests. Vicenzo, Giuseppe and Rocco were vying for the position of capo of the other big family in New York City. They all wanted to rise through the ranks and felt sure that they could do so if they committed further crimes within the underworld.

John and James commissioned Alexandra to get to know the entire Lucini clan in detail. They had to know the real ins and outs of the criminal organization. To do so, the DEA special agent got a job as a waitress in a magnificent restaurant frequently frequented by the family clan's mobsters. To do this, one morning at breakfast time she introduced herself as a college student who was studying law and needed a part-time position. Her irresistible charms, coupled with her oratory skills, quickly landed her the job. The restaurant manager, an Italian-American immigrant from Naples, was smitten with her large breasts. He thought that the customers would be delighted to spend their money if they were served by this beautiful woman from the East.

Vicenzo, Giuseppe, Joe, Frank and Rocco, together with their clan's bodyguards had arranged a dinner at the Paesano Restaurant in New York's Little Italy. It was around 8:30 pm. on November 28, 2021 and they had reserved a large table right next to the kitchen so that they could speak freely.

The Italian-American of the restaurant was well-known to the Lucini clan. He missed Zannini and at one point during dinner, he asked Rocco about the capo, "What happened to Zannini? I saw a picture of him in the New York Times. Such a great loss," exclaimed the restaurant owner dejectedly.

"If you hear anything related to his murder, Carlo, let us know immediately, you know, you will be rewarded."

Carlo nodded. Zannini had helped Carlo renovate the restaurant a few years ago with a loan of thirty thousand dollars, which the Italian-American more than paid back, but he remained very grateful to the capo for his help. With the Mafia, almost everything was favor for favor and money for money, plus usurious interest, threats and severe beatings if it was not paid back on time.

During dinner, the mafiosi were served by the waitress Alexandra, who was well disguised as a university student. They ate spaghetti Bolognese, macaroni in sauce, mussels in marinara sauce and drank a good Italian wine from Naples. At one point in the evening, when the effects of the wine began to take their toll on the table, Giuseppe addressed the Russian crudely, "Hey, will you give me a blowjob tonight? You're so fucking hot."

Rocco called out his colleague's behavior, "Stop this nonsense, Giuseppe, leave her alone, she is working. If you really need to fuck you know where to go. Stop bothering her."

Giuseppe shut his mouth and the meal resumed.

Alexandra had hooked up a tiny microphone under the mobsters' table and outside the restaurant, John and Sloan were waiting in a white van with the recording devices.

"Capo Zannini must be replaced soon, we must avenge his death, and catch the narcos off guard, they almost sunk us, their ambush was perfect."

Giuseppe, Joe, Frank and Vicenzo felt that it was time for peace and doing business with the narcos, as well as re-declaring cordiality with the other big family in New York. Vicenzo's even suggested a meeting with Gilberto, Orlando, Hector and Beltrán, feeling that old quarrels had to be brought up, in order to find a peaceful solution. Vicenzo was beginning to act like a real capo, using his intelligence and not violence. His other colleagues, Joe, Frank and Giuseppe, were only thinking of a deadly ambush against their narco partners, they had no other course of action in their minds.

Vicenzo told them, "The narcos need us and we need them. This is a fucking business and that's the way it has to be seen.

Let's stop pulling the trigger, let's stop killing people we do business with. The death of our capo has been very hard, but business must continue for the survival of our family."

The Lucini clan mobsters agreed by majority vote to meet with their narco partners and that they should send representatives to Culiacán and Medellin. The meeting was to be respected by all members of the families, without weapons or grudges.

The conversations of the dinner party had been duly recorded in the DEA's white van. John and James already had more relevant information about the Mafia and the expected meeting with the drug dealers. They just had to find out the place and time of the meeting.

Jolanta still had no news about her husband's whereabouts. She was beginning to worry about him. Olivia kept asking about her father and wanted to find out what he was up to despite the abandonment she and her mother had suffered when he ran away. Olivia wondered if they had done something to drive him away or if he had gotten himself into trouble. Warrent had always been a proud husband to his family, he loved his wife and daughter enormously so his disappearance didn't make sense. Neither Jolanta nor Olivia knew what had happened to him to hide.

The FBI were growing more certain that the Mafia had murdered him. It was much less likely that he had been terminally ill or had suffered a fatal accident. Sloan didn't know what story to tell the senator's wife to calm her down and persuade her to talk. As a shrewd cop and an expert in these police battles, he thought of pressing Jolanta, a protected government witness, before Judge Thomas, who was following the police investigation closely in cooperation with the New York District Attorney's office. Since Jolanta and her daughter had entered the witness protection program, they had a legal obligation to cooperate in the clarification of the facts under police investigation, and in this case, in addition, a pact had been made between the FBI and the DEA, consisting of transferring first-hand information about her husband to the police. And there was a significant amount of money to be paid to Jolanta by the FBI.

The problem lay in Jolanta's refusal to speak until she knew the whereabouts of her husband. The FBI, for its part, had no new evidence that could lead to Warrent's location. Sloan called in Malone and Brigitte to talk to Jolanta and get all the information she had on her husband. Malone met her again at a coffee shop on Manhattan's main avenue. It was 10:00 am. Brigitte waited outside in the police car while Malone went inside.

Before Malone could even sit down, Jolanta demanded, "Where is my husband, Malone? I'm not saying a word until you tell me where Warrent is."

Malone, for his part, had prepared a speech for Jolanta. He would threaten to haul her in front of Judge Thomas. "From now on our people will accompany you everywhere, even to the bathroom. Your daughter cannot go outside unaccompanied. You are the only people who can lead us to Warrent and the only people who can defend the evidence against him in federal court. You better speak up now or I will tell Judge Thomas. You will be liable for felony disobedience to authority and may serve a prison sentence for this stubbornness. Thomas will thank you, New York will thank you if you help us put an end to Mafia intimidation and activities.."

"Have you quite finished, Malone? Tell me where my husband is and I will tell you everything I know. You can tell Judge Thomas that for me. My life and my daughter's life are at stake."

The Panamanian off-shore companies, "Dunas Paradise" and "Virgin Residual", had been active since the assignment was made to the law firm in Panama. The banker Zenón charged fifteen million dollars to open the accounts for Breska's wife and children and to put the Mafia's money in safekeeping. In a separate account known only to Zenón and Breska was a huge amount of money available unknown to the Mafia or even to the lawyer's own family.

All the Mafia's assets were in the hands of the lawyer and the underworld's front men, let's say officially, although with essential nuances. Breska's colleagues, Anthony, Carla and Fernando, were the fiduciary owners of a large part of the Mafia's assets in the eyes of the U.S. authorities through various front companies. The other half of the Las Vegas casino money fortune was 'owned' by front man Stuart.

Breska had not only executed the financial plan perfectly but he had also moved some of the money without the knowledge of his Mafia bosses. Why? Only the lawyer could answer this. He understood perfectly well the potential tragic consequences that his deceit could mean. Breska had carried out the commission for the installation of the Grand Casino in Chinatown almost to perfection, and also for its branch in Las Vegas. The gambling business was always among the Lamborda family's priorities and, of course, this was the main assignment given to the lawyer when he was sworn in as Omertà. To achieve this, Breska had had to buy off the two senators who were friends of Warrent in order to prevent the vote in favor of the movie production company, against the direct best interest of his own clients.

The lawyer had to deal with the members of the Council, which was the body that controlled the municipal agents and determined the use of the city's land. The land on which the Grand Casino was finally installed was owned by the Lamborda family. In order for the family clan's land to be used as a casino with a gaming license, they had to obtain authorization from the Lottery Division of the Gaming Commission, where an advisory board would review the casino applications. This Advisory

Board would consist of about twenty members, elected by the Governor, from the Senate and the Lower House in New York City.

The Lamborda clan had expressly instructed the consigliere to obtain the casino license. Breska had to buy off a man named Brown, a long-term acquaintance and a member of the Council and clerk of the Gaming Commission to authorize the casino license for the sum of twenty million dollars. The road to obtaining the Grand Casino license for Chinatown was long, winding and tortuous, to the point that the Lucini family was also invested in the casino license. The late Capo Zannini had bought off Stewart, another member of the Gaming Commission, to the tune of twenty million dollars to obtain the Grand Casino license, an amount higher than the amount offered by the Lamborda clan through the consigliere, which was ten million dollars. This is what led to the death of the New York politician who was murdered by the Mafia. The votes of Brown and Stewart were the determining factors for the authorization of the casino. Stewart betrayed the Lamborda clan and that cost him his life. After Stewart's crime, the Mafiosi fixed the mess with the distribution of business in the underworld, gambling for the Lamborda family and drug trafficking for the Lucini family. In the Mafia, crime always pays.

Breska was saying goodbye to his university friends, the magnificent experts in offshore companies, Anthony, Carla and Fernando and then the Breska family, Gianluca, the thugs and bodyguards of the Mafia would be driven in a limousine to the airport in Panama City. The lawyer was in high spirits, as they were on their way home to New York.

The Mafia lawyer felt content with all he had achieved on this trip and didn't even think about what he had done with the

Mafia's money. Breska had covered his trail very well. The money was kept secret and confidential from third parties, including the Mafia itself.

John, James and Alexandra had worked hard to discover the place and time of the planned meetings of the narcos in Culiacán and Medellin. This was the conclusion the Lucini clan mobsters had reached at Carlo's restaurant. The DEA's Moscow special agent had done a sterling job at the location of the mobsters' convention by placing that microphone placed right under the Lucini clan's table.

Thanks to her efforts, John and James had an extremely valuable recording for the course of the mob investigation. The wiretaps received through the microphone were a real boon in the course of the follow-up against the gangsters. And, of course, the capture of the "Nautilus" was a win, too.

The bandits who informed on the Colombian and Mexican drug traffickers told the Miami police department that they were "used" through the payment of twenty thousand dollars to transport the drugs on the ship. They even signed an affidavit for police and official purposes in this regard. In addition, they undertook to wear wires in order to find out how and with whom their bosses trafficked. Quite an odyssey in drug trafficking. They had become protected witnesses for the Colombian and U.S. governments.

Pancho and Silvestre belonged to a group of bandits from the favelas of Medellín and Culiacán. They were considered to be small-time soldiers in the drug trade. Their need for survival in the favelas made them accept that deal with the narcos without really knowing the extent of the consequences of their testimony to the police. They were dead men for the Mafia.

The narcos Gilberto, Orlando, Hector and Beltrán kept remembering that one of them was the one who shot Capo

Zannini in his farmhouse on the outskirts of New York. In the Mafia, betrayal was paid for with death.

Special agents infiltrated by the FBI and the DEA, Irina and Alexandra, together with the informants of the two big New York families, Anastasia and Fiorela, continued to follow up on the plan for the illusory destruction of the Mafia. Alexandra, for her part, in her eagerness to uncover the Lucini family's illegal business dealings, set up an ambush on the narcos with her partners James and John. It would be on the trip to Medellin and Culiacán.

John and James planned to travel to Colombia and Mexico. They were impatient to know the location of the narcos' meetings. The departure of the feds' plane from New York City depended on the tip-off of the drug traffickers' snitching bandits. Pancho and Silvestre, for their part, hoped to infiltrate the convention with the excuse of collaborating with the feds and still holding up their end of the bargain. The DEA agents had assured them they would get a considerably reduced prison sentence in return for their cooperation.

Hector and Beltrán had told their Colombian narco colleagues, Gilberto and Orlando, that the meeting of the all-narco group would be at the Culiacán ranch owned by the Mexican, Hector Juarez. The ranch was located more than 3,000 feet above the city of Culiacán. The area of the farm was about ten hectares. It housed a large stable and even a private zoo with wild animals typical of the Amazon jungle, such as parrots, caimans, monkeys, anacondas and piranhas, very much in tune with the Hacienda Nápoles of the narco Pablo Escobar.

The narcos wanted to keep the convention site in the strictest secrecy, but they were unaware of the presence of informers in their midst. James sent a message to Pancho's cell phone reminding him that he expected to be informed of the meeting place and approximate time.

"It will be at Héctor Juárez's ranch and all my bosses will be there, we still don't know exactly when," Pancho answered via message. "We will wear your microphones to try to record the conversation. You should wait right next to the ranch, so we are in range. Everything will be ready on our side."

James texted him again, "Be very careful, you could be discovered at any moment."

Pancho knew this to be true.

"The meeting will be at 12.00 noon on the second of December," Silvestre's message read.

"We're ready, go get 'em boys, we'll have several squad cars and federal buddies just outside the ranch gate," John replied with unbridled glee.

Everything was ready. The wait at the secret hideout for the FBI and DEA police felt as if it could go on forever.

Vicenzo finished the meal at Carlo's restaurant feeling as if he were already the new boss of the Lucini family. Rocco, Giuseppe, Joe and Frank, together with the family's bodyguards and thugs left the Paesano restaurant.

Boom, boom, shots rang out. The thunderous noise came from a dark alley just off the street where the mobsters had been. By the back door of Carlo's restaurant lay the lifeless body of DEA Special Agent Alexandra. Blood was pouring from her head, which quickly reached almost to the other side of the sidewalk across the street.

The two shots were fired by Vicenzo's gun, who had discovered the agent in the restaurant's kitchen. The wannabe capo had hidden in a room next to the kitchen, where he saw how their waitress had sent a message reporting on the content of the meeting to her colleagues from a half-open door. Vicenzo had understood almost everything. He was very astute and perceptive and had been analyzing her attitude during the meal. To begin with he had assumed that she was yet another jobbing actress but before long he had realized there was more to her than that. He waited for her and killed her when she had finished her work shift. Vicenzo's colleagues missed his presence as they left the restaurant. He called them with a whistle from beside the corpse, and explained to everyone what he had done. By killing a DEA special agent he had assured his position as the capo of the Lucini family. Joe, Frank, Rocco and Giuseppe showed their respect by giving him a kiss on the cheek. He was officially the head of the family. Afterwards, the corpse was removed from the sidewalk by Rocco and Joe on the capo's strict orders.

"Put the body in the oven at nine hundred degrees," said the capo.

Rocco and Joe nodded, while Giuseppe looked on, dumbfounded. It was not common for the Mafia to murder women but it was clear that here there had been good reason.. The gangsters could now travel to Culiacán, the narcos were waiting for them for a possible revolt.

More than a week had passed and the location of the senator remained unknown. The FBI office in New York was like a pressure cooker. As it was, not a word would come out of Jolanta's mouth. Judge Thomas was waiting for instructions from the FBI and the prosecutor's office to proceed with an entry and search warrant at several homes linked to the Mafia.

DEA Special Agent Alexandra was not answering her cell phone. She had six or seven missed calls from her colleagues James and John, and other FBI colleagues, who were concerned as to her whereabouts. By this point, the FBI, the DEA and even the ATF had forgotten their quarrels and had inexorably joined forces in their fight to dismantle the Mafia. Only in this way could they truly fight the gangsters.

Malone and Brigitte went to visit Jolanta and Olivia at their Manhattan home, which was surrounded by FBI police officers for their safety as protected witnesses for the U.S. government. The front door of the house was opened by an FBI colleague.

"Come in. There she is, watching television with her daughter. We found her today very discouraged and sad, she doesn't even feel like eating. Her daughter is almost depressed. They keep seeing on the BBC that Warrent is missing, they fear the worst. It has been almost a month since his disappearance. They are both really suffering," said the FBI agent.

Malone sat down on the couch where mother and daughter were stretched out while Brigitte turned down the volume on the television. Malone addressed Jolanta, "Are you going to talk to us seriously about your husband, we don't want to play games with you anymore."

"I told you I wouldn't say anything until my husband shows up, what don't you understand?"

"I just don't know why you want to play with us this way," Malone said.

"I will speak only when you give me information about my husband. I have already told you this and I will say it again."

At last Brigitte intervened, shushing Malone and saying to Jolanta, "Judge Thomas requires you to help us and provide us with the promised information before he agrees to us paying you another cent."

Jolanta, who was beginning to feel uncomfortable, changed her tune in an instant, "Okay, Brigitte, I like you, you're a great cop. I hope what I tell you now will help you catch those awful people. I loathe them all." Jolanta recited calmly while Brigitte and Malone listened, "On my husband's computer there is a folder called, "My Friends", they are the prostitutes he has been with in that club..., what was the name of the club..." the senator's wife paused for a few seconds, ""Las Mariposas", I didn't remember it well, my husband is known there as the terror of the girls, he didn't miss a live one, you know what I want to tell you..., much to my regret... it seems that they had a well-organized business. In another folder are the commissions he collected from the Mafia in his shady business in the Senate and in another folder there are the figures of everything he has moved with his little friend, that lawyer, a real bastard, my husband, an arrogant, disgusting and lying pimp, I hope he rots, he has screwed up our lives. This girl doesn't even eat anymore," she said, referring to Olivia, who listened with a sad face to what her mother was saying.

Malone and Brigitte's faces showed controlled joy, they had gotten Jolanta to talk and she had really done it. The FBI might have the information they had been seeking to implicate Warrent, to uncover the Lamborda family's business dealings, their relationship with the other big family in New York, their drug trafficking dealings with the narcos and associates and the role played by the consigliere in all of it, a tentative triumph for the FBI.

Now Jolanta had spoken. Was she that desperate to find her husband or did she want to collect the other five hundred thousand dollars at all costs?

The plane carrying the Breska family, the hitman Gianluca and some of the Lamborda family's thugs and bodyguards landed at New York's JFK airport. The consigliere felt more relaxed and calmer than at the beginning of the trip since he was returning having successfully fulfilled his task. Now, if the FBI or the DEA were to investigate the accounts of the Mafia family, they would never be able to link the origin of the money with the ownership of the funds, since a corporate structure had been created with several front companies. It was like having the money under a mattress, but safer.

The lawyer was starting to feel confused deep down in his soul. Something strange was happening to him. He didn't really feel like a mafioso and this could be a problem in the underworld. Not even his own family knew the true destination of the money and who owned it. In the Mafia there are always things that should not be told, not even to one's own wife and children.

Bernardino was serene in his New York City home, thinking that his family's money was nicely hidden away. This was the message he had been given by his consigliere, to whom he had fully entrusted the family's estate and accounts. However, there were other things that really worried him. The murder of Capo Zannini had revolutionized relations between the two families, the narcos and their associates in the Bronx and Brooklyn.

Would the FBI and the DEA really have obtained any convincing evidence against the family, the capo kept asking himself, would there be true peace within the Mafia given the latest bloody events? All these questions were flying in his head until he came to the conclusion that if they had not murdered the capo of the rival family by committing this crime, then they would be more than justified in defending themselves against the other big family in New York. Despite this he really hoped that peace would be restored within the underworld for the good of the business. After all, business was really what mattered. Nothing was calm, everything was up in the air and he could not risk more murders. It was clear to him that Warrent's body would never be found, and therefore he could not be held responsible for this particular crime. The Lamborda family had learned of the death of a policewoman at the hands of the rival gang; she had been killed by Vicenzo, the new capo. The news spread like wildfire through criminal New York.

The late Capo Zannini was ruthless and savage in the commission of crimes. Of the new capo, Bernardino knew that he was talented and intelligent yet was known for his cruel streak. Bernardino phoned Vicenzo to congratulate him on his appointment as capo of the Lucini family.

"My most sincere congratulations to you and of course, and of course, my condolences on the death of Zannini. My whole family sends you heartfelt condolences. We must talk. There are many things to solve. Let's meet next Tuesday at 7:00 pm. in a neutral place. We will let you know where an hour before."

Vicenzo hesitated for a moment in answering, his lack of experience as the new capo of the family made him think seriously about his decision, he took a breath and said, "My sincere respects Don. I must go to Culiacán for the convention with our narco partners the day after tomorrow as we must resolve our differences. I will update you on what is agreed. As soon as I return from the meeting, I will put my men in place for our meeting."

"All right, wait for Maranzzano's call to confirm time and place," Bernardino answered coldly.

Vicenzo did not much like the rival gang leader's treatment of him. He was unaccustomed to the delicate cordiality that came with his new appointment and wondered if this was just Bernardino laying the groundwork for the relationship between the two bosses from the very beginning. Whatever the case, Bernardino had much more experience in these things than he did.

Generally, in the criminal underworld, news moves very fast and the actions of one gang are known, in detail, by the other gangs almost immediately.

The Culiacán summit was duly prepared for the occasion. The chosen location made the appearance of the DEA and FBI police unthinkable. Gilberto, Orlando, Héctor and Beltrán waited impatiently and anxiously for the members of the Lucini family with their new capo at the head.

Vicenzo, Frank and Rocco drove two magnificent SUVs up the steep slopes of the Mexican mountains, the ranch was located high above the city of Culiacán. They were duly escorted by members of the army, allies of the narcos, who drove several trucks, accompanied by another SUV full of thugs and bodyguards of the New York mobsters.

They were all fully armed for the convention, although once they arrived at the convention, the weapons would be left locked in a room until the end of the meeting. It was around noon on December 2, 2021, and the temperature was pleasant.

The narcos' servants and henchmen had prepared a special meal for their visiting associates. At a round table next to one of the ranch's pools, some of the gangsters and narcos were gathering. The SUVs parked just outside the ranch's gate. The patrol cars with their recording devices, as well as John and James' federal colleagues, were hidden behind a huge grove of trees, about a hundred meters from the ranch of Mexican narco Hector Juarez, ready to act at any moment. The murder of their DEA colleague at the hands of the mob was very recent and they were aware of the risk of death they were running.

Pancho and Silvestre, meanwhile, stood in a room reserved for the narco mercenaries, right next to the kitchen, where the ranch servants were located.

The feds had an excellent police operation, similar to the interception of the ship "Nautilus", however this time they were in a

foreign country and they were dealing with consummate professionals on their home turf.

The Colombians, Pancho and Silvestre, had placed the tiny police microphones on their chests under their jackets and were ready to listen in on their bosses, eager to be able to wipe out their power and money.

The automatic gate to the ranch began to open slowly, and along the wide path walked the gangsters Vicenzo, Frank and Rocco. Joe and Giuseppe had been left in charge of business with their partners in the Bronx and Brooklyn. They were heading up a steep flight of steps where their drug associates were waiting for them. Once the members of the Lucini family, led by the capo, reached the top step, the two gangs greeted each other coldly before sitting down at the round table. On the left side of the table sat the narcos Gilberto and Orlando. A little to the right of them sat Héctor and Beltrán. Just in front of them sat the members of the Lucini clan, with the capo sitting right in the middle of his men.

While the servants began to bring a delicious selection of local seafood, the narcos began to drink wine. Héctor Juárez, the host, acted as the godfather of welcome.

He got up from the table and began to speak, "Welcome to my ranch, compadres. I convey to you the painful feeling that the loss of your boss Zannini has meant for us. May God rest his soul, compadres. We are all here to settle our business. Now, Conchita, bring more wine..., you slut!" While scratching his thick belly, he addressed Vicenzo in a loud voice, "My gringo-friend, let's make peace today. We are known here for the big business we do. It is thanks to you that our cocaine is ready to be sold and flown out of the country, compadres. Zannini's death has been a hard blow for all of us, I promise you that I will hang and kill with my own hands the stupid compadre of ours who did it. He is an imbecile, an imbecile," he repeated before the impassive gaze of the capo and his men.

The new capo looked stunned, he had been considering intervening at any moment, but he gave free rein to the extroverted and jocular Mexican.

Eventually, Vicenzo said quietly, "We have come from so far away for the good of the business; we are here to reestablish our business with you. If one thing is true, it is, as we all know, that anyone can kill anyone else. The death of our capo was due to a possible mistake by one of you, but that is forgivable. What is unforgivable is betrayal and disloyalty," everyone looked expectantly at the new capo, who continued, "That's why we have to reassess our agreement and the cut we take on this drug we move to the US markets for you. If we respect our old percentages, if we commit ourselves not to spill more blood, not to interfere in other people's business and to respect each other, the business can go smoothly. Zannini was my friend, a great friend, who did not deserve to die, but this is what happens in our business when we do not respect money and we let ourselves be carried away by ambition."

Everyone admired Vicenzo, even the narcos themselves, when suddenly Hector and Gilberto stood up from their seats raising their wine glasses and said in unison, "Let's drink a toast, the business will be respected and the percentages will be the ones we had with Zannini, our gringo friend. We give you our word of honor that it will be so. Now, let that pretty girl dance for our partner."

Pancho and Silvestre made their presence known at the meeting. Gilberto addressed them with contempt, "We missed you, compadres. Where were you? These gringo friends wanted to meet you. Come here. I have been told that one of you killed our friend Zannini in New York, is that true, boys?"

"No, boss, how could we have? We were at the farmhouse, but we did no such thing, I swear, boss,"" said Pancho.

"What's the matter, little boy, what's the matter?" asked his boss in an intimidating tone.

The microphone stuck to Pancho's chest fell to the ground.

"Fuck. Compadre, I always thought of you as low but I never imagined that you had sold yourselves to the cops," said Gilberto.

"Check the other one. Now. I think we have traitors in our midst," said the narco, referring to Silvestre.

Orlando checked him and ripped off the microphone that was taped to his chest, and said "Take them away. Feed them to the alligators, these low-life informers:"

Five of the narcos' henchmen carried the bandits to the alligators' pond while they kicked and made obscene gestures at their bosses. They were hurled into the deep water where the alligators sated their appetite for human flesh. The feds, for their part, lost the signal and decided not to act for now. Vicenzo shamelessly enjoyed watching that Dantesque and monstrous scene, as if it were a horror movie. Would that dramatic episode of drug trafficking be recorded in the federal recording systems? That summit in Culiacán was a success for the good of the business.

> "No business can succeed to any degree
> without being properly organized."
>
> James Cash Penny

Chapter XIV
Betrayal and Revenge

"Loyalty is not a word, it's a lifestyle."

Anonymous

PEACE HAD SETTLED IN THE UNDERWORLD. The thriving drug trafficking business had all but left crime behind. Narcos Gilberto, Orlando, Héctor and Beltrán had settled the blood debt with the Lucini family by murdering the informers Pancho and Silvestre and throwing them into the alligator pond.

Zannini had been murdered without an express order from the narco leadership, although in the Mafia world it was understood that when shooting breaks out between rival gangs anything can happen. The order that day had been to massacre the Lucini family, their thugs and bodyguards, and they knew Zannini would be there, of course.

The Lucini clan had not yet penetrated deep into the heart of the Lamborda family or reached the consigliere. The installation of the microphone under the driver's seat of the lawyer's SUV, by the chief mechanic on the island of La Palma, had revealed the most primitive killer instincts to wipe out the Lucini family, but it came of no surprise to anyone that one Mafia family wanted to wipe out another Mafia family. Vicenzo, Frank and Rocco had returned from the Culiacán convention happy and full of energy. They had successfully negotiated no percentage change on cocaine deals and had prevented full scale war breaking out over the murder of Zannini. The deaths of the informers Pancho and Silvestre was good enough for them.

Vicenzo had agreed with Bernardino that they would meet on his return from Héctor Juárez's ranch; he was to make a call to Maranzzano to arrange the location of the meeting. Giuseppe acted as an intermediary for Vicenzo, making the call to arrange the meeting place for him. They were to meet on December 14, at 20.00 at the club "Las Mariposas". The chosen place would be the secret room inside the club, which was inaccessible to the FBI and DEA police.

There was an undeniable mood of revenge between the two families of the New York Mafia. Too much blood had been spilled between the gangsters for the clans to pretend that business was going well. Vicenzo hated and loathed Bernardino. His ultimate desire was to end his life and become the king of the underworld. Bernardino, for his part, endured a heavy and painful heart because of the death of Captain Lucky, as well as the continuous interference of the rival gang in his business. Vicenzo wanted to annihilate Bernardino and Bernardino, in turn, wanted to eliminate the new capo of the rival gang to take over the Mafia in the city. But of the two, it was Vicenzo who was the more vengeful. He had just suffered the murder of his predecessor and the botched trafficking job. In his world, pride and revenge were almost as important as money and power.

Before their long awaited meeting, the two capos spent the afternoon at a boxing match, thinking to throw both the FBI and the DEA off their scent. The heavyweight champion of the

world, a guy from Minnesota, was fighting an aspiring young-
ster from Manhattan who happened to be an acquaintance of
the Lamborda family. The mobsters had made a big bet on the
boy and had bought off the members of the American Boxing
Federation in order to ensure that he would be the winner of the
fight. They felt that the result of this fight would set the tone for
what awaited them at the "Las Mariposas" club.

Breska was feeling bad about his work with his exclusive client,
the Mafia. What had happened to his life to make him begin to
hate those guys from the underworld? He kept thinking back to
his fabulous life in Los Angeles, where he had enjoyed everything
life had to offer, including the best contacts in the city: judges,
prosecutors, lawyers, politicians, prestigious businessmen but
where a close friend had been shot dead for no apparent reason.
Now, seeing only blood and tears, he resigned himself to continue
living his Mafia life. Why didn't he go to the FBI when they
chased him after his Lamborghini? Would it have helped if he
had reported them? Would the police have listened to him? Why
did he have to meet his friend Warrent at the Diplomat Prime
restaurant in Hollywood?

The truth was that it was going to be difficult to get out of the
Mafia, maybe even impossible for once the Omertà was sworn
there was a requirement to maintain a sepulchral silence about
Mafia business at the cost of one's life.

The lawyer was thinking of an escape plan. Would this be
possible? Would they discover him and kill him? The consigliere's
mind and heart were already spinning counterclockwise to the
Mafia clock. Mafia tradition had never known the possibility
that their own lawyer would think of abandoning them and
stop working for them. Breska regretted having sworn the Law
of Silence that day in New York. He thought back to the taking
of the oath and how the kingpin had stuck the pin in his index

finger, warning him that the lifting of silence was punishable by death and how informers would be buried in ashes. Since then, his life had taken an inexplicable turn, he was living in a forced march between life and death, dedicated only to carrying out Bernardino's orders and to providing legal advice and cloaking the illegal and shady activities of the Mafia clan.

Breska no longer wanted to lead this dangerous life, he wanted to regain that wonderful one in Los Angeles, but he knew it might be too late. He thought of his family, and how they could suffer the same fate as him; if he was 'disappeared' then they would be too. He writhed in regret, but he could not turn back. Breska was going to find a way to abandon the Lamborda family, the most devastating criminal organization in the city of New York.

Justice Thomas was watching his favorite team's basketball game at Madison Square Gardens when his cell phone rang – it was the weekend so he was only attending to emergencies. The Knicks were beating the Lakers.

Malone said, "Judge, we need that warrant to enter and search Warrent's home, we have the evidence that can solve this case. According to his wife, everything we need is on his computer."

"I'm sure you have something, Malone, I hope it's important, since I don't like to be disturbed when I'm watching the Knicks, so this had better be good," the Judge said firmly.

"Trust us, it has cost us a lot to get Jolanta to talk, she finally trusts us. We will have a strong case against the Mafia, between her information and the information we receive from "Las Mariposas"."

"First thing Monday morning I will prepare and sign the warrant. Come see me first thing. I will have it there."

On Monday, Malone and Brigitte anxiously showed up at Judge Thomas' office. The Judge was remarkably calm and together given that his team had lost to the Lakers over the weekend.

Malone, who was familiar with the Judge's passion for basketball, said, "If the Knicks win the next game, your honor, they go on to the NBA playoffs. They have a great team."

"Don't suck up to me, Malone, it doesn't suit you. Here's your warrant, as agreed. There is a lot at stake so don't screw this up. And don't forget that you'll need another warrant for "Las Mariposas" once you have more information. I know right now you know little more than the fact that Vicenzo and Bernardino are meeting but when you have something, come and see me. Now I must take my leave, I have a lot of work to do."

"Thank you very much, Judge, I hope we'll be back soon for that second warrant."

Brigitte and Malone hurried out of the Judge's chambers and went to prepare to search Warrent's house with their FBI and DEA colleagues. They took the police car and sped to the FBI's main office in New York. The visit to Warrent's home had to be arranged.

Jolanta and Olivia could hardly leave their home on Cody Cross Avenue in Manhattan, not even to buy bread, the situation reminded them of the pandemic lockdown. Malone and Brigitte knocked on the door several times as Sloan looked on,

"FBI, open up."

For Malone, Brigitte and Sloan it was an interminable wait, as after several minutes no one came to open the gate. It was very strange since just a short while earlier they had spoken to their FBI colleagues who were protecting Jolanta and Olivia. Sloan again knocked loudly on the gate of the house.

"FBI. FBI. Open up," they shouted.

They turned and saw their FBI colleague, walking towards them with a tray of coffees and pastries. They were stunned and horrified.

"I just went to buy coffee and buns for everyone, we were hungry," said the policeman with a frown.

"You could have told us before, we were getting worried. We got the warrant but it is time limited. We can't wait. Coffee could have waited."

Malone, Brigitte and Sloan prepared to enter Warrent's home. They went straight to the senator's table, which was next to the double bed. There they found Warrent's long-awaited personal computer.

"That's it, here's the key," said Jolanta, who had accompanied the detectives upstairs. Olivia remained downstairs watching The Simpsons on TV. She shuddered as she saw the agents walk up the stairs.

They were accompanied by a tech expert whose job was to extract all the data from Warrent's personal computer. It took him less than twenty minutes. The senator's laptop was then removed and taken to the judicial deposit. Everything went smoothly. The FBI detectives said goodbye to Jolanta and Olivia and left, sure they finally had the evidence they needed for their case against the Mafia.

Days passed and Warrent was still missing, at least for the FBI and the DEA. The hitman Gianluca, with the help of Maranzzano, had dissolved his body in sulfuric acid in that hidden apartment in Chinatown with the help of his allies in the area. Warrent had been tortured and killed in a macabre and deadly game due to his shady dealings with the mob. The last words out of the senator's mouth before he died were, "Breska... Breska... is the culprit."

The Lamborda family had never questioned the actions of their trusted advisor, in fact, they never even considered it. Bernardino was sure that he and the lawyer were united by great ties of friendship and blood. They were confident that the bank transactions and deals he had required of Breska were duly carried out according to plan. Although the Mafia consigliere was not a true Mafia man, that is he had not grown up around the Mafia, nor did he have Italian-American ancestry, Bernardino took it for granted that the act of Omertà tied him absolutely to their world.

Breska had become a mobster without really wanting to, he had been intimidated by the mob, that is, the mob had demanded his cooperation. They had followed him for some time and it was clear that he was the lawyer they required. He was the right lawyer for the clan and as far as they knew, he was proving it daily.

As far as the FBI and DEA knew, Warrent had simply disappeared. They did not know he had been murdered by the Lamborda family. Unofficially, though, there were suspicions that his disappearance was linked to the underworld. They had no knowledge of the shoot out in the subterranean tunnel on La Palma where Bryan and Antonio died. Only Detective Lucas survived to collect the second payment for their contract with the Mafia, receiving no less than eighty-five thousand euros.

Breska, for his part, had returned fire in that tunnel when Warrent had shot at them. By Mafia logic, the torture and murder of Warrent were rational actions. For the FBI and the DEA, Warrent had disappeared on a technical and legal level, without a body there was no possibility of conviction for his murder.

It was December 13, and Warrent had been missing for nearly two months. Where could the senator's body be? And now what were the detectives going to tell Jolanta about his disappearance? Would Warrent's wife continue to talk to the FBI? That was the deal they made.

Everything was being prepared for the meeting of the capos at the "Las Mariposas" club.

Through the microphones of Pancho and Silvestre's the DEA agents had managed to hear some information from their van in the mountains of Culiacán. Before being thrown into the alligator pool, they had provided some evidence of the link between the Mexican and Colombian drug traffickers and the New York Mafia, in this case, the Lucini family. The Lucini clan had been worried since their new capo murdered the agent outside the restaurant, causing the FBI and the DEA to monitor them more closely.

The microphone installed by the DEA agent under the table at Carlo's Paesano Restaurant, before she was killed by Vicenzo, had left conversations recorded in that white DEA van too. There, they heard the family talking about avenging the death of Capo Zannini, and about the drug trafficking business with their narco partners. The judicial authorization for these recordings had been granted some time ago by Judge Thomas, who was in charge of the investigation with the FBI, the DEA and the New York anti-corruption prosecutor's office against the Mafia.

Fiorela had received a tip from attorney Malcom a few days before the meeting of the big bosses of the New York Mafia at the "Las Mariposas" club. The lawyer had also enjoyed the company of the girls at the club. He worked for the narcos Orlando, Gilberto, Hector and Beltrán. The lawyer, who had escaped from Zannini's gang, had been a "mole" in the clan. Now he was in witness protection and his life was in danger.

The news did not go unnoticed in the club "Las Mariposas". Irina, Anastasia and Fiorela had a secret and dangerous mission to accomplish: to dismantle the Mafia via their sensual and erotic dances in the club. Fiorela wanted to avenge the death of her partner and friend Alexandra while destroying the Mafia once and for all. The gangsters had taken advantage of their status as members of the underworld to run wild in the club with these beautiful women. They went so far as to threaten and torture them if they would not sleep with them in the club's private rooms and suites.

Fiorela knew she had to be as overtly sexual as possible in order to drive the mobsters so wild with desire that they would be incapable of even considering that she could be a DEA informer. One evening, the lawyer Malcom, found himself with the Italian Fiorela in the jacuzzi of the club's upstairs suite, drunk and high on cocaine. When the lawyer began to lose control of his senses due to the influence of the substances, she held his head under and demanded to know when his colleagues would come soon to the club. She claimed she wanted to show off her beautiful breasts and her tight dress, which she was going to wear for the occasion, to which Malcom replied that all the big bosses would be there the following Tuesday and that there she would be able to show off her body however she pleased. The Dom Pérignon Rosé Gold and the drugs that his clients were selling would cause a serious fracture in the life of this narco lawyer. There was no doubt about it, Malcom was a dead man.

It was 8:15 pm. on December 14. The cold winter had arrived in the New York neighborhood of Chinatown and the evening was as cold as ice. At "Las Mariposas" club, there were only three or four patrons. They were celebrating the rise of bitcoin on the stock market, stuffing hundred-dollar bills inside the thongs of the beautiful strippers while drinking champagne and whiskey. The Capo Bernardino, along with his counterpart Vicenzo, had gone, at Maranzzano's behest, to the secret cabin of the club room along with the gangsters, thugs and bodyguards of each family clan. Joe, Frank, Rocco and Giuseppe were with the Lucini family. They were enjoying the girls from the club in a private room on the third floor. On the Lamborda family's side were Maranzzano, Gianluca, Pimponassa and Gamberra, who were sitting on the bar stools, raising their beers with laughter as they looked at the girls' tremendous asses. Not the Colombian and Mexican narcos, nor their associates from the Bronx and

Brooklyn, had been invited to the meeting, since they were not recognized as New York Mafia families. They were considered outside the "Cosa Nostra". The consigliere had stayed with his family at the New York house to await developments.

Not too far from the club was an apartment in which the FBI and DEA were staked out. Other agents were nearby in their cars. Everyone was waiting for a sign from the women inside the club. Sloan, Malone and Brigitte were inside the white FBI van with recording devices attached. John and James were in a DEA van, also recording that majestic mob meeting.

Irina, Anastasia and Fiorela were chatting with mobsters from both families. Their utter hatred was well disguised. Irina had placed a microphone behind a painting of Florence's Ponte Vecchio in the club's secret room, which was unlikely to be discovered by the Mafiosi. Anastasia and Fiorela had dressed like real luxury prostitutes with plunging necklines to impress and distract the Mafiosi.

Fifteen minutes had passed since the scheduled time for the meeting and the bosses had still not shown up.

The FBI and the DEA began to think that the tip-off had been a hoax by the gangsters and that perhaps they were on to them. Suddenly, two SUVs pulled up outside the club. Bernardino and the consigliere got out of a metallic gray one, which then sped off. The lawyer Malcom and Vicenzo got out of the other, which also left.

Once they made their way to the back door of the club, they greeted each other coldly as they passed into the secret room. Malcom and Breska locked themselves in a tiny room right next to the secret meeting room. Bernardino and Vicenzo, for their part, slipped inside the hidden room. Four thugs stood at the door of both rooms standing guard.

Bernardino and Vicenzo took their seats, both had been dispossessed of their weapons at the door of the club. They sat opposite each other, both aware of the recent bad blood between their families.

Vicenzo began to speak, "Buonasera. I thank you for organizing this meeting. I admire you very much, Godfather, I respect you. You and I both know that business has been hard. A lot of blood has been spilled. Zannini was assassinated by two damn cronies of our narco partners and we still haven't recovered from the blow. I'm trying to forget about the drug ship where you paid big money to a girl to get the feds on top of us. I won't pretend that didn't hurt us. We lost a lot of money, Don. So did the murder of our Bronx hit man by Maranzzano. I'll try to forgive the Chinatown Grand Casino license, your consigliere paid twenty million dollars to Warrent's friends, you were in business with. I will try to forget this too. I carry on my back our suffering on the Spanish island when the volcano erupted. You know we could have avoided so much pain if you had just given us the senator's location. And what do we do now? My men are waiting for my word; they are ready to spill more blood. You know the feds are on our heels, things are very ugly. My father told me that you could go far with a kind word, so in his memory let's allow words to prevail over bullets and save those for our mutual benefit. This is my commitment to you..."

Before he could finish his carefully prepared speech, Bernardino spoke, "Buonasera, I congratulate you on your new position and thank you for coming to this meeting. I admire and respect you too. I agree, things cannot go on like this. We must stop this for good. Blood has never been good for business and now things have gotten out of hand, we have let our damn egos get in the way. We have let our people, our health and the health of our families down. We have forgotten about our children, wives, friends and have prioritized our ambition for power and money. Warrent is history, he deserved what he got for doing business with whoever suited him best. Gianluca did his job well. I swear before the eternal God that we did not participate in the seizure of the drug ship and I promise before you that if I find the one of mine who did then I will kill him myself. I will try to forget the murder of Captain Lucky at the hands of your Bronx hitman, who got what he deserved. I will try to forgive your insults in our gambling business and the persecution of our consigliere. I'll forget that you didn't share information from the senator about the FBI and DEA. They are on our heels too. We are screwed, really screwed, you have to pull your contacts in the FBI to fix it. It was a bad idea to kill a cop. Very bad. I don't seek revenge, but I never forget. The world is ours with everything in it. Let's shake hands and settle our differences now. We'll leave the drug business to you, we've never touched it, but on the condition that you give us a percentage in exchange for lending you our contacts. If you respect our gambling business, I forgive Stewart, but I do not forget, you have my word of honor that there will be no more blood. Each must now focus on his business and hold mutual respect for our families, friends, allies. If someone must be eliminated we will authorize it between the two of us. I give you my hand in sign of eternal friendship. I swear to God that it will be so. Transmit this message to your partners. Business comes first and we will forget our differences up to here. Capisci?"

Vicenzo made a gesture to get up from the meeting while at the same time extending his right hand towards Bernardino. He said to him in Italian, *"Giuro davanti a Dio il nostro eterno onore e amicizia. Il sangue e storia per le nostre famiglie."* (I swear before God our eternal honor and friendship. Blood is history for our families.)

Bernardino got up from the table giving his right hand to Vicenzo and said, *"Giuro davanti a Dio il nostro eterno onore e amicizia. Il sangue e storia per le nostre famiglie".*

They finished the act by opening the door of that hidden room, saying goodbye politely. The capos' spirits were rusty from the blood spilled some time before, but revenge and mutual hatred were not reflected in their faces. What did those fellow professionals, Malcom and Breska, do in that hidden room? They all left the club.

The FBI and DEA police officers had listened carefully to that meeting between the two biggest bosses of the New York Mafia. They had heard and recorded the entire conversation and had decided not to intervene. They were already prepared to take them to Judge Thomas. If everything went according to plan, the FBI and the DEA had dealt the hardest blow to the Mafia. This was not an everyday occurrence.

The front man of the Lamborda family in Las Vegas, Mr. Stuart, had stopped by the bank office where the banker Murphy worked. He went to pay him a visit on the back of information that had just come to him from the company "Transportes Nevada". It appeared that some income was missing and he wanted to know what had happened. Murphy feared the worst. Stuart had his gun with him. Bernardino had warned him that something strange was going on with the money in those accounts and had issued orders to get to the bottom of it. Murphy greeted him as he walked in the door.

"Hello, Mr. Stuart, how are you? How can I help you?"

"Well," Stuart got straight to the point, "What's going on with my accounts, Murphy? I understand that income from the two casinos is not arriving. You can imagine who sent me to check up on this.

"I cannot give you that information, Mr. Stuart, it is confidential."

"What did you say? Confidential? Did you say confidential? Either you give me the information or you will face the consequences, Bernardino is waiting for my call." He casually opened his jacket to reveal his gun.

Murphy could not stand the pressure; beads of sweat began to form and his pulse quickened. Finally, he said crestfallen, "Part of that money goes to an account of Breska's. There are certain transfers of money from the Lamborda family accounts to the account of the lawyer and his relatives."

"Does Bernardino know about this?"

"I don't know, but it seems to me that they have spoken with Breska if this is a problem. I can't do more, maybe it's something common in the way they work with their clients."

"Well, I just needed to know that Bernardino's money is being transferred to the lawyer's account. Thank you for your time," Stuart said.

The front man immediately told Bernardino the result of his visit to the banker. The capo was stunned and perplexed.

The Christmas lights were up on Canal Street in Manhattan's Chinatown. People were happily strolling along, enjoying the atmosphere. Christmas had arrived in this post-pandemic year and there was a great desire to celebrate. Not far from there, in the main office of the FBI in New York, Sloan, Malone and Brigitte, together with their colleagues from the DEA, John and James, were compiling all the evidence obtained in the course of the investigation against the Mafia. They had the feeling that Judge Thomas, as the investigator of the investigation together with the Anti-Mafia Squad and the city's Anti-Corruption Prosecutor's Office, would be very happy, indeed. The atmosphere in the Feds' offices was noticeably different, more upbeat thanks to the solid work of the agents and their informants. Finally, they would be able to take down the Mafia.

The two biggest families in New York City, the Lambordas and the Lucinis, were indeed threatened by the possibility of long prison sentences, even life imprisonment. Warrent's body was still missing after two and a half months but now the FBI at least had confirmation that the senator had been murdered by the Lamborda family. They had had that confirmed when listening in on the capos' last meeting.

Judge Thomas was waiting for the battery of evidence from the feds so that he could decree the opening of the trial against the Mafia. Amongst the evidence collected was, of course, the most important piece of evidence against the Mafia: the files contained in Warrent's personal computer.

At the FBI office they continued to work night and day as they geared up for the trial. In the room set up for the FBI's sound and audio playback were Malone and Brigitte. In an adjoining room were John and James trying to decipher the audio and video recordings they had obtained from their work. Malone pressed the play button and put on his headphones. His face displayed his satisfaction as he listened to the first conversation. It was the recording obtained in the secret room of the club "Las Mariposas", from the microphone that Irina managed to install. He heard the entire conversation.

Malone felt a great personal liberation when listening to that recording. He thought that they would never have such high-quality evidence against the Mafia and he did not hide his emotional exaltation when he took notes. When he finished listening through the playback of the recording devices, he was eager to get out of that room and report back to his colleagues.

At the same time, John put on his headphones to listen to the conversations recorded in his white van, taking note of it all,

"We missed you, compadres. Where were you? These gringo friends wanted to meet you. Come here. I have been told that one of you killed our friend Zannini in New York, is that true, boys?" He heard Gilberto speaking. The recording continued,

"No, boss, how could we have? We were at the farmhouse, but we did no such thing, I swear, boss,'" said Pancho.

It was the recording obtained at Hector Juarez's ranch in Culiacán. Now James moved on to listen to the recording of the restaurant Paesano obtained by the Alexandra.

"Capo Zannini must be replaced, we must think of revenge for his death, we must catch the narcos off guard, they almost sunk us, their ambush was perfect," added Rocco.

"The narcos need us and we need them. This is a fucking business and that's the way it has to be seen. Let's stop pulling the trigger, let's stop killing people we do business with, the death of our capo has been very hard, but the business must continue for the sustenance of our family," said Vicenzo.

Malone, John and James opened the door to their offices at almost the same moment. They gathered the team and Malone addressed them all with a face of happiness never seen before, "Guys, we got them, we have won the battle against the Mafia, at last."

John then spoke with enormous joy, "We also have something, the Culiacán thing will be useful for the murder of the bandits Pancho and Silvestre."

The detectives were rewarded with a thunderous ovation from all the FBI agents and staff.

The Mafia's days were numbered.

> "Everything happens for a reason, but deep in our
> hearts we wish it could have been different."
>
> Anonymous

Chapter XV
Traveling to Paradise

"People don't meet by chance; they are all
destined to cross paths for some reason."

Anonymous

THE MOVING COMPANY HAD ARRIVED AT THE HOME of the lawyer and his family at the appointed time. The Mafia consigliere had taken advantage of the few hours of the day when he knew he was less watched than normal. Bernardino and the other members of the clan had gone to the city on business. At the Breska family home there were only a few escorts and guards, in addition to the estate's security personnel. Breska had summoned them to his home claiming he needed help moving furniture in his office. He had heard that some of the Lamborda family escorts and bodyguards were dissatisfied with the treatment they received and that they were considering moving to work for the Lucini family who were ready to offer more money to any defectors. Breska decided to take advantage of this situation and pay some of them off in exchange for their silence and help. They loaded the family's belongings into the moving company's van. Breska and his family were headed for the Bahamas by way of Miami. They headed to JFK airport where a friend of the lawyer was waiting for them. The family checked in at JFK and ensured that all their luggage was stowed. They were bound for Miami where they would board a private jet. Emma, Marc, Stalin and Evelin had been persuaded by the lawyer that they needed to move to a hidden place far away from the Mafia. The lawyer told them that his clients were "on their heels". His wife and children were already accustomed to this accelerated and changing life, and all of them told him that they were fine with the idea of living in the Bahamas. They had learned to live wildly and with the sword of Damocles hanging over their heads but of course, they missed their old luxurious life in Los Angeles.

The special customs agent, Mr. Jordan was told by the lawyer to go through passenger and luggage control with the excuse of organizing a business trip for his Mafia clients.

American Airlines flight number 3551 arrived at Miami airport around 7:00 pm. on December 20, 2021. The Breska family quickly boarded their private plane to paradise. At around 8:20 pm, on the same day, the Breska family landed in the Bahamas. The Mafia lawyer had bought a mansion on the island about two months earlier. The Breska family now had a new home, they had outsmarted the Mafia.

They left the modest airport in a gray Range Rover and drove to their new home. All were happy and content, they had successfully escaped the largest criminal organization in the city of New York. Passport control and security at the airport had been like a military parade for the Breska family. Everything was planned and organized by the mob's lawyer. The lawyer drove that new SUV down a long and battered avenue full of giant palm trees on both sides of the road, as if they were enjoying a beautiful trip along Route 66 in the U.S. As they drove they sang along to "Paradise" by Coldplay. The car stereo was almost at full volume. The lawyer turned the song louder to match the volume of Emma and the children. Out of nowhere a black Hummer rammed into the front of the Breska family's Range Rover. The impact was so brutal that it caused the car to flip four or five times until it stopped, upside-down on the asphalt with the wheels still spinning.

The lawyer had been driving excessively fast and had not noticed the Hummer join them on the otherwise empty road. Breska, Emma, Marc, Stalin and Evelin were trapped in the Range Rover. There was no movement from within the car. Maranzzano and Gianluca, inside their large black vehicle, had barely suffered from the collision.

The Hummer was driven by Gianluca, who had express orders from Bernardino to kill Breska and his family. Gianluca and Maranzzano slowly and carefully approached the Range Rover. Once there, they checked that no members of the Breska family were alive. Emma, in the passenger seat, had a deep head wound and was bleeding profusely. She did not move an inch and showed no signs of life. She would not survive. Evelin's chest had been pierced, which had caused her to hemorrhage and die on the spot.

At this time no vehicle appeared in the vicinity of the place, as the gangsters had prepared their unprecedented trap carefully. Marc and Stalin had been trapped between the iron bars. They were still breathing. They threw furious looks at Gianluca, who shot each of them twice in their chest and heart, ending their lives. Breska had suffered numerous wounds, including one especially severe wound to his head, which had been the ultimate blow. He, too, was thought dead.

A couple of young tourists showed up at the scene of the accident in their Mercedes Benz convertible. The gangsters, who had not expected to be disturbed fled before the young tourists alerted the authorities. They had done what they had been sent to do. Meanwhile, one of the Englishmen called the ambulance, petrified by what they had just seen. Neither of them had time to take note of the license plate number of that black Hummer. The English couple was left waiting for the ambulance and the police after their call to the emergency services. Would the emergency services arrive on time at the scene of that fateful accident?

At FBI headquarters in New York they were more optimistic than ever. They thought they had dealt a hard and sure blow to the Mafia in the city. Now they needed to turn all their good work into a conviction for all the mobsters, and Judge Thomas was a key player in this. An FBI agent worked through the flash drives and the files obtained from Warrent's personal computer. Sloan, Malone and Brigitte were absolutely focused on getting their hands on these files so they could analyze everything. The computer expert started downloading files from the senator's computer. Jolanta had given them a real password.

First they looked at a folder marked "Breska Commissions" where they found numerous documents relating to the senator's dealings with the consigliere. They learned of commissions for the purchase of votes in the Senate Chamber to obtain the license for the film production company, and of immense favors involving money and bribes to members of both the Lamborda family and the Lucini family. The essence of all that rough business was that both the consigliere and the late senator were buying people both in the city and abroad, at the behest of both Mafia families.

In the second folder of that strange file, with the name of "My Friends", they found a list of names of friends, politicians, judges, lawyers and prosecutors who had been intimate with the girls of the club "Las Mariposas". Among them were Irina, Alexandra, Anastasia and Fiorela, who the senator had seen as nothing more than luxury prostitutes to whom he paid for sexual and informative services. He had thought that these charming and captivating girls were police agents and informants. There were also several personal, family and work files of the senator and his family, of secondary value. The conclusion was that there could be a countless number of people who were related to the Mafia in one way or another and who, in short, worked for the underworld directly or indirectly.

The files on Warrent's personal computer, along with the microphone recordings obtained by the FBI, DEA and informants in the course of the mob investigation, were the real backbone of the case against the gangsters.

Malone received a call from Justice Thomas, at 8:00 am Christmas Eve, "Come to my office first thing in the morning, I must see you. It is a matter of the utmost urgency." The Judge's voice was rough and firm, it was the one he used when he had a matter of real importance to convey to the prosecution and the police who were accompanying him in the course of an investigation.

Malone froze, he could not work out if he would receive good or bad news from the Judge. He told the Judge that he would be there on time the next morning.

Judge Thomas was sitting in his chambers in the New York City Courthouse, waiting for Malone as arranged. He was staring at a poster of his favorite NBA team, the New York Knicks. Malone knocked on the Judge's door. He had Brigitte with him.

Come in, Malone, I was waiting for you. I'm glad you brought Brigitte," said the Judge kindly

"You have me on tenterhooks, what is it about, Judge?"

"Have you already prepared my resolution to open the trial against the Mafia? Have you made up the arrest warrants for all of them, including the consigliere, the Lamborda family, the Lucini family, the drug dealers and their associates from the Bronx and Brooklyn? Don't miss anyone out, right, Malone? said the Judge.

"I didn't know we were so close to being ready, Judge. Well, we have to find Warrent to finish with Jolanta, but it's the best news we've had in year."

"Hasn't Sloan told you? Yesterday afternoon we emailed, and quite frankly, I'm very surprised they don't know anything. You don't need to worry about Warrent, everything will come to an end even if we don't have a body."

"Maybe our boss wanted to surprise us for all the hard work we've been doing."

"Well get to work! You have a lot of work ahead of you, it's time, guys, these criminals and our society deserve what's coming," the Judge finished.

"Congratulations on the Knicks, I told you they had a great team!"

"Stop messing around, Malone, you're wasting your time, get off your ass quick."

Malone and Brigitte left Judge Thomas' chambers and returned to their office. They had done it; they had got their case against the Mafia.

A couple were making out on a bench under the Brooklyn Bridge, next to the cold river. They stood up and walked, hand in hand down to the water's edge. As they approached, a black bag dropped, almost out of nowhere, and landed not far from where they were.

They looked around and nervously then went to check it out. They smelled it before they bent down to open the zipper. Seeing the contents made Jonathan feel immediately dizzy. He fell to the ground in a faint.

"Ugh, that smell, what on earth smells that disgusting?" Agatha asked as her boyfriend fell down beside her.

She called 911, as her boyfriend lay, inert on the ground in front of her. She, too, was nervous and feeling faint. Within fifteen minutes, several patrol cars and an ambulance were on the scene. It was an FBI agent, a colleague of Malone's who first got a good look at the contents of the bag. It was full of bones, perhaps Warrent's. Malone's colleague instantly called the coroner to check if they were from the senator's body. She demanded that he take the bones to the Forensic Institute for thorough analysis. Once there, she entered the bones into a computer for detection and testing against the senator's DNA. The bones, indeed, were Warrent's. There was no margin for error, the forensic scientist used real-time PCR, allowing him to detect the smallest amounts of DNA and thanks to the appropriate use of TaqMan probes, then compare it with the senator's fingerprints. There was no doubt, it was Warrent.

While Gianluca and Maranzzano had dissolved the body in sulfuric acid they had not subjected the senator's body to high enough temperatures to adequately destroy all the bones. Now, finally, the FBI had the proof they needed, even if they didn't have his entire body.

The forensic scientist communicated the results of the test to the FBI office in New York. Judge Thomas, who was preparing the formal indictment against the mobsters in his chambers, also received the forensic evidence from the crime lab the day after the bones of the corpse were found. He immediately ordered the cancellation of the senator's arrest warrants.

He finally had the missing piece of the complex puzzle that would allow him to convict members of New York's most famous Mafia families. The New York State Attorney General's Office brought a host of charges against the Mafia: Mafia organization, murder, bribery, extortion, money laundering, gambling fraud, fraud, forgery, document fraud, prostitution and drug trafficking". The defendants were all members of the two largest families in New York, including their associates and allies. The list was long. Lamborda Family: Bernardino Mancini, 'Capo,' Attorney Breska, Pimponassa, Gamberra, Gianluca and Maranzzano. Lucini family: Vicenzo, 'Capo', Giuseppe Ganci, Joe Mesina, Frank Riccobono and Rocco Torrio.

Colombian and Mexican Narcos: Gilberto, Orlando, Hector and Beltrán. Partners and associates from the Bronx and Brooklyn: Brandon Jones and Walter Harrison. Attorney Malcom. There was also a long list of associates and allies of the Mafia, including Jordan, Thomas Cook, Ryan, Alejandro Escudero, Dr. Felipe Sanchez, Stuart, Brown, Fabio, Leandro, Anthony, Carla, Fernando, Murphy and Zenón.

The list of witnesses was completed mainly by Irina, Anastasia, Fiorela, Jolanta and Olivia, as well as Malone, Brigitte, Sloan, John and James.

Once the accusation was formalized and the list of witnesses presented, the next step was the arrest of all those members of the Mafia and bring them in front of the judge and jury. The penalty they would face could be life imprisonment. Judge Thomas did not take long to issue all the arrest warrants, a whole macro trial against the Mafia was in the offing. The FBI and the DEA began to take the first steps to carry out the arrests.

The ambulance arrived at Doctors Hospital in Nassau. Breska and Emma were seriously injured. That tragic 'accident' had caused serious head injuries. The English tourists had clearly saved the life of Breska with their surprise appearance. While the Mafia lawyer was being operated on, his wife was taken to the mortuary having died in the ambulance. There was nothing the paramedics could do to save her, the blow was deep and profound, it caused an intense hemorrhage, causing her to bleed to death. Breska was taken straight to the operating room. The on-call surgeon, Dr. Grajera, wheeled the gurney into the operating room.

"Make way, it's an emergency," said the surgeon as the orderlies carried the stretcher in the direction of the operating rooms.

The operation took five difficult hours.

Malone paid Jolanta and Olivia a visit. His FBI colleague had expressed instructions to let him into Warrent's family home in Manhattan. He went straight to the living room, where he found them again watching television. They looked incredibly unhappy but they were ready to leave for their new home as soon as possible. Their destination, of course, was the Maldives. Malone approached the couch where the late senator's wife sat.

"I suppose you have heard on the news that some of Warrent's remains have turned up, there is no doubt that it is him. I am very sorry; I offer you my sincere condolences."

Cutting off the conversation, Jolanta addressed Malone in a firm tone, "You need to follow through with your end of our bargain. I want our plane tickets to the Maldives and the rest of the money. No more crying for me. Quite frankly that bastard finally got what he deserved. My daughter and I were well aware that something serious could happen to him and that he could die. We were prepared for this eventuality even though he was my husband and the father of this fourteen-year-old girl. It's a very hard thing to always keep in the back of your mind, Malone."

"I know and I sympathize with you, but for now you must stay here, at least until the trial, which will be very soon, then you can do whatever you want. We must protect you until the hearing, your testimony against the Mafia is vital."

"Well, my daughter and I are not in a position to stay here any longer. We run the risk of being killed here but they won't find us in the islands," said Jolanta.

"If I put myself in your place then I understand you, but this is not the time to leave. You must testify," said Malone.

"I hope to have the money in my account tomorrow, that was the agreement. I have told you everything I know and I have collaborated with you, so tomorrow make the payment and I will stay here with my daughter, although it is not what I want. Do it for my daughter, she is the one who is suffering the most from all this and she does not deserve it. She does nothing but cry all day long. She can't study and she certainly can't be with her friends. Our lives here are over, do you understand me, Malone?"

"Tomorrow the money will be in your account; you have my word. We will protect you as we have done so far," said Malone .

Jolanta nodded her head in agreement. Malone left the Warrent home with some optimism.

All were arrested with little resistance. The members of the two most important organized crime families in New York City were arrested on the afternoon of that Christmas Monday in the year 2021. Sloan, Malone, and Brigitte took it upon themselves to visit the Lamborda home, where they surprisingly found all the members together. They were taken out one by one and placed in patrol cars. None made any statements to the watching journalists. John and James, for their part, went to the Lucini house, where similarly, everyone came out willingly with their hands up, placing themselves at the disposal of the police.

Judge Thomas issued extradition warrants for the narcos who were in Medellin and Culiacán. Brandon and Walter were arrested by a law enforcement team from the New York field office.

The Lamborda family, the Lucini family and other allies and associates of the gangsters were brought before a jury on December 27, 2021.

A FEW MONTHS LATER...

John Maverick went out to pick up a letter from his mailbox at 9 pm. He was wearing only his bathrobe and pajamas. As he reached in to pick up the mail, two individuals of tall stature and great physical strength, dressed in elegant suits, long turquoise blue trench coats, and Panama hats, appeared next to him, bundled him into a car and whisked him away with them. During the ride, which lasted about three or four minutes, one of them carefully opened his raincoat and pulled out a gun leaving John extremely frightened.

"John, have you picked up your jury summons yet?" Maranzzano asked intimidatingly.

The young man, an economics student in his last year of college, was impassive and very frightened. He could not muster the ability to speak when faced with these men.

"This is it. What do you want from me?" he answered.

"We have your girlfriend in that window across the street, Do you see her, boy?"

His girlfriend, Angelica, had been tied hand and foot by Pimponassa and Gamberra and was hanging upside down on the second floor.

"But what do you want from me?" John asked in terror.

"If you want nothing to happen to your girl, vote not guilty and we'll be good to you. If you go to the police, you're dead. If you follow our instructions, we'll reward you. You'll get a big trip to the Fiji Islands and a hundred thousand dollars in your account, Capisci?"

John Maverick nodded his head without blinking. They turned him out of the car and told him to walk home. John went back to his house anxiously waiting for Angelica to return. When she finally did, the two held each other tight.

The surgeon was pessimistic about Breska's medical situation. However, despite the difficulty of the surgery, the lawyer survived that difficult operation and was put in room 321 of the Nassau hospital to recover. There he waited for the nurse to put him on the abundant post-operative medication and refill his IV bottles. He was completely intubated and was barely alive. The blow suffered to the head had been nearly fatal. The surgeon had performed laser surgery on several clots in the brain and was clear that his rehabilitation would be long and difficult if he ever came out of the coma. The recovery tunnel was very dark and long. It seemed as if life had stopped in time all at once. For mob lawyer Valentino Walker Breska, his thoughts were dizzyingly transported back to his golden, magical time of practice at his Los Angeles law firm before he was intimidatingly visited by the mob.

He remembered that crucial meal with his friend, Senator Warrent, and could find no explanation for what happened to him afterwards. He would remember the high beams of the mysterious car that took away his innumerable desires to satisfy Hollywood movie producer and actor clients. The Mafia had stripped him in one fell swoop of everything he fought for: his family, his job, his friends and the best contacts in town.

But Breska had violated the Law of Silence, the one he had sworn to uphold or face death. He risked everything when he kept part of the Mafia's money. That was the reason for that tragic accident: the revenge of the Mafia. No one could escape in the underworld. He had also betrayed his best friend to obtain the license of the biggest casino of the Mafia. Each and every one of the events that had occurred to him as a Mafia lawyer since that traumatic month of August 2021 raced through his mind: the risk of losing his life during the eruption of the volcano on the island of La Palma, the bullets flying around his head like a bird fluttering on the branch of a tree, that war without quarter between the Mafia clans, the eternal parties at the club, "Las Mariposas".

Suddenly, his mind went into shock, his heart stopped and he went into cardiorespiratory arrest. His face was very pale and white, his eyes opened and then closed for good. How long would this coma of the former Mafia lawyer last?

Detective Lucas was lying in a hammock slung between two palm trees and sipping a mojito on a beautiful beach on Corsica. He had gone there to enjoy the money obtained from the Mafia assignment. While relaxing in his hammock, he was shot directly in the head. He tumbled out of the hammock and was dead before he hit the ground. Yet another victim of the Mafia.

Attorney Malcom was found dead on the couch in his office in the Bronx. He had been shot twice in the heart.

The Mafia had served its revenge.

John Maverick had recorded the entire conversation with the gangsters on the ACR app on his cell phone. Just before walking out to his mailbox he had been talking to a professor at the university and had been recording the conversation for revision purposes. It turned out he hadn't turned off the app. When John realized this he immediately went to the FBI's office in New York.

"What brings you here, boy?" asked Malone.

"I am juror number four in the trial against the Mafia and I have been extorted and threatened. Listen to this."

John turned on his phone and they listened to the recording together. Malone and Brigitte were stunned. Malone got on the phone with Judge Thomas, the mob had been blown out of the water.

All of the Lamborda clan gangsters, the Lucini group gangsters, their narco associates, their associates in the Bronx and Brooklyn, and mob associates and allies were found guilty, given the avalanche of evidence from the FBI and DEA presented by the U.S. Attorney's office, as well as the hard-hitting testimony of informants and prosecution witnesses at trial.

For his part, the mob lawyer was stuck between life and death, unable to stand trial because of his serious health condition. He was visited by the FBI in the Bahamas to take his statement but given that he remained in a coma there was little for them to do.

That conviction was a huge blow for the Mafia, and the sentences were likely to be extremely harsh.

Neither the FBI nor the DEA were ever able to locate the mob money; the consigliere had kept that safely hidden away.

Jolanta and Olivia landed in the Maldives with an extra five hundred thousand dollars in their account, a beachside mansion and great hope for a new life. Jolanta invited her daughter for a jet ski ride. Life was beginning to smile on them.

Suddenly, Breska opened his eyes in that modest hospital bed. He looked around and didn't know where he was. He glimpsed his surroundings as his brain returned to normal. It was amazing how many lives that lawyer had.

After a long rehabilitation process, Breska was declared healthy again, he had hardly any long-term problems. Medically it was an amazing thing, inexplicable even for Dr. Grajera.

Breska, while feeling the reality of his new encounter with life, noticed a stranger standing in front of his bed. He was a very tall guy with startling green eyes.

As he walked around the bed, he whispered, "I am Dmitri Lasparov, I have come to take you to work with us," he said while winking at the doctor who was standing in the corner of the room. We will wait for you as long as you need, a beautiful light will illuminate the dark tunnel at the end of your rehabilitation. My colleagues from St. Petersburg have been following your actions for some time. We need you in our organization. The best must be with the best."

Dmitri raised his right arm and said to the lawyer, "Nasdrovia."

The Russian Mafia had come to see him. Breska, with a smile, said, "I agree."

Note from Author

I ALWAYS WANTED TO WRITE AND PUBLISH A BOOK ABOUT LAWYERS, THE MAFIA AND DETECTIVES. I thought I would never get around to it, given the vicissitudes that have befallen my life in the last three years.

The present book is the fruit of my inspiration from reading various compendiums on the Mafia, lawyers and detectives, their documentaries, videos, movies, etc. I owe thanks to Mario Puzo for his brilliant novel about the Mafia, which changed the literary world, to John Dickie, and most especially to John Grisham, a fellow lawyer and writer, whom I deeply admire for his legal thrillers.

Regarding the subject of private investigators, I have such wonderful memories of time spent with my brother José Modesto Sánchez Fernández, a detective by profession, who passed away in March 2020. He introduced me to the fascinating world of investigation and espionage. With him I was able to carry out some follow-up and investigative work on various cases including unfaithful husbands, renowned businessmen who seized their partners' money, fake injuries from traffic accidents and even people claiming fake sick leave.

It has been very profitable and satisfying for me to study, read and document Mafia affairs, both the people who are dedicated to it in real life and their friends and acquaintances, whom I keep anonymous.

I traveled to the U.S. in August 2008, to New York City, where I made the long-awaited honeymoon trip with my wife. We toured the Bronx, Brooklyn, Chinatown, Little Italy and Queens. Then we visited Miami and the Bahamian Island of Nassau. Having the opportunity to use these experiences in my novel has been magical for me.

This book is the result of all this, together with my status as a practicing lawyer and all that this entails in real life.

Acknowledgments

I WOULD LIKE TO EXPRESS MY SINCERE THANKS to all those who have made the writing and publication of this book possible.

First of all, to my wife and daughter, who have both contributed to make this adventure a reality. They even offered their opinions of the story I tell in this book.

Secondly, to the writers Alberto Cerezuela Rodríguez, Óscar Fábrega Calahorro and Jorge Barroso Castilla, for their wisdom, advice, help and experience in the publication of this book.

I'd like to thank the City Council of La Palma and La Laguna for sharing with me their feelings about the eruption of the volcano and how life there is now after this tragedy.

Finally, to all those friends and acquaintances who have shared their experiences with criminal organizations with me, those who are involved in mafia activities and who remain anonymous. They have taught me how the mafias, their groups, their members and bosses work today.

www.ingramcontent.com/pod-product-compliance
Lightning Source LLC
Chambersburg PA
CBHW020136120726
47903CB00007B/2276